Adrift in Retribution Bay

Aussie Heroes: Retribution Bay

Claire Boston

BANTILLY
PUBLISHING

First published by Bantilly Publishing in 2023

Adrift in Retribution Bay: Aussie Heroes: Retribution Bay

EPUB format: 9781922916037
Print: 9781922916044
Large Print: 9781922916051

Cover design by Mayhem Cover Creations
Edited by Ann Harth
Proofread by Teena Raffa-Mulligan

Dedication

This book is dedicated to all the people who post informative videos on YouTube. You make my research so much easier.

Chapter 1

The steady beep drifted into Arthur Hammond's consciousness. He pushed it away, clinging to the peace in the dark, but like an incessant mosquito buzzing around his head, the noise refused to go away. As his mind refocused, he recognised the sound. A hospital monitor, the steady beep mimicking his heart.

His eyes flashed open as memories assaulted him. The click of the improvised explosive device, the crackle of the explosion, the excruciating pain in his right leg. He shoved at the white, starchy sheets, his hands hampered by tubes running into his veins. Finally, he uncovered his leg.

Or rather his knee and stump.

It was unbandaged and the scars had lost some of their redness.

He battled through the fog of wakefulness as more images attacked. The weeks in hospital, the myriad doctors and therapists, visits from his teammates and the pity on their faces. The never-ending nerve pain that made him want to cut off the rest of his leg.

His father's order not to return to the army.

Filling his mouth with pills, not caring whether it

was too many, just wanting to stop the pain, any way he could.

He'd failed.

Even as he stared down at his missing lower leg, the pins and needles began again.

Despair smothered him and he gasped for breath. No escape. This was his life—crippled, unemployed, useless.

If only the pills had rescued him from it.

His gaze lifted to the blue curtains surrounding his cubicle. The fluorescent lighting glared above, highlighting everything in a stark, jaundiced spotlight. The hospital bed with its thin, white blanket, doing nothing to provide warmth, the table designed to slot over the bed with a plastic jug and cup on it, and finally, almost behind him, the beeping monitor and some kind of IV fluid they were pumping into him.

Outside, people spoke, discussing a patient who had come out of surgery. "He's stable, but we won't know the effect of the pills until he wakes."

"Poor bastard. Do you think he did it on purpose?"

"Only he knows."

Arthur jerked. They were talking about him. Pitying him. Hadn't he had enough pity?

Hurried footsteps on the linoleum floor; two, maybe three people. They stopped right outside his cubicle, the scratched, dark brown Blundstone boots covered in red dust showing below the curtain. He tensed and then a female voice said, "I'm looking for Arthur Hammond."

He glanced left and right for somewhere he could hide. Stupid. He wasn't moving anywhere. He'd avoided this meeting for as long as he could, and now there was no escape.

Sam had promised not to tell Amy and Brandon about the accident.

Liar.

"He hasn't woken yet. Who are you?"

"I'm his sister, Amy."

Arthur's throat closed over. What was she doing here? Surely she didn't want a bar of him. Not after he'd chosen to go on a mission rather than attend her wedding to his teammate.

The curtain opened. Behind his sister stood her husband, Brandon, and Arthur's other ex-teammate, Sam.

His eyes focused on the small woman at the front. His chest squeezed. So much like their mother. Same frizzy blonde hair, same height, same green eyes.

"You're awake," Amy stated.

A male nurse hurried in behind them, pushed his glasses up on his nose and smiled. "Nice to meet you, Arthur. I'm Michael and I'll be your nurse today. How are you feeling?" He checked the monitor.

What was Arthur supposed to say? "I'm alive."

"Yes, you are," Michael agreed. "Do you know where you are? Have you any blurry vision? Pain?"

Arthur ignored the first question and stared at his visitors. Sam and Brandon both crossed their arms and stood legs apart, decidedly unimpressed. The same look they gave senior officers when a mission had gone to shit through no fault of their own. "I can see fine. Leg hurts."

"Your vitals are good. How much does your leg hurt on a scale from one to ten?" Michael asked and Arthur drew his attention back to him.

"Six." He'd been through the questions a million times. Six was his base level every single day.

Michael screwed up his face in sympathy. "I'll check with a doctor to see if we can give you anything for the pain. We'll move you to a ward as soon as we can. I'll leave you with your visitors." He strode out.

Arthur clenched his jaw to stop from calling him

back so he wouldn't be alone with them.

Coward. He'd brought this on himself.

Amy moved cautiously towards the bed.

"Ames." Her nickname fell from his lips like he'd seen her yesterday instead of a decade ago.

She flung her arms around him and squeezed.

Shock pierced him more painfully than the tingles in his legs, and his arms encircled her, inhaling deeply, trying to get any breath back into his lungs. She even smelled like his mother, the same sweet floral scent.

Amy drew away and stared at him. "Are you all right?"

He nodded, though it wasn't true.

"Good. I'm glad." She took a deep breath. "What the hell were you thinking?" Her voice rose, and the abrupt change from caring to anger left him reeling. "How dare you swear Sam to silence? How dare you not tell me you were injured?" Her hands clenched. "And then to overdose…" Her voice broke. "Like Mum—"

She might as well have stabbed him in the heart. He hadn't allowed himself to think about their mother in years.

Had she been in this amount of pain after her car accident? Did she just want it to all go away too?

He fought back the tears. Emotions made him weak, vulnerable to attack.

He looked past her to Sam. The man who had visited him every damned day after the accident. Had reminded him of everything he had lost. Had made him feel like a charity case on some days, but gave him hope on others. Hope—a subtle poison that destroyed from within.

"When you're discharged, you're coming to Retribution Bay," Sam stated. "No arguments this time."

Brandon nodded but stayed silent, his gaze focused but non-judgemental.

The attention was too much. No one should be here. They were better off without him. He moved his gaze to the side and stared at the blue curtains.

"Oh no, you don't." Sam shifted so he was in Arthur's line of sight. "We did it your way the last time around. This time we're doing it our way. You're not alone. You've got support, you've got people who love you, and who want to help."

Damn him. All this talk made hope raise her poisonous head. Couldn't Sam see he was nothing now? He was worse than useless. He was a burden. A disappointment.

"Why do you hate me so much?" Amy's quiet question whipped his head around.

"What?" She was the one who must hate him.

"I know we grew apart as you got older and didn't want a pesky younger sister hanging around," she continued, as if he hadn't spoken. "But I can't think of a thing I did to make you treat me this way."

"It's got nothing to do with you."

She raised her eyebrows. "You barely spoke to me at Mum's funeral, you didn't come to my wedding, you'd rather kill yourself than accept my help."

Arthur glanced at Sam and Brandon, hoping they would offer some suggestions on what to say. Their impassive stares told him he was getting no help from them.

He'd never been great with words.

And even if he had been, there was no way to justify what he'd done. No way she'd understand. Looking back, he didn't really comprehend it himself. "It's complicated."

"You'll have plenty of time to explain at the Ridge," Brandon said.

Amy glanced at her husband and then back at Arthur. "Brandon and Sam both say you're a good man and I trust their judgement. But I won't stick around for you to break my heart a third time." She strode out.

Brandon glared at him. "Time's up, Sherlock. Get your shit together, because if you hurt Amy again, you'll be dealing with me." He followed his wife out of the cubicle and into the corridor. Brandon murmured, "Don't cry, Ames. It will be all right."

Arthur flinched. Why was she crying over him? He wasn't worth it. He looked at Sam and his question must have been written on his face.

"Ames is tough. She's been through a lot, and it took some convincing for her to agree to even speak to you the first time. It was enough to make her hope to reconnect and you've hurt her again."

"I didn't ask you to be here."

Sam smiled, bemused, with a hint of irritation. "No, but we were on a plane within an hour of discovering what happened. Now, what does that tell you?"

He didn't want to think about it. "You should all just leave me be."

"We can't do that, Sherlock. Like it or not, we care for you. You're like a brother to me and Brandon, and we don't give up on family."

Family. A curse word if ever he heard one. He'd spent a lifetime trying to live up to his father's expectations, to earn his love, and it had amounted to nothing.

Sam stepped closer. "This is how it's going to be. I'm going to talk to your doctors and find out exactly what you need. Then I'll arrange you that help. You can choose to stay at the Ridge with Brandon and Amy, or you can stay in town with me. If you stay with me, you'll be my deckhand, and if you stay with Brandon, you'll help on the station."

Arthur scowled. "Haven't you forgotten something?" He threw back the blankets to reveal his ugly stump.

"You don't need a leg to chop a salad or cook sausages," Sam said. "And you were always a damned strong swimmer. We'll make it work."

It was more of his positive vibe bullshit. The stuff Arthur wanted so desperately to believe, but couldn't. Hoping and failing would destroy him.

He'd never even been good enough when he'd been whole.

He had no chance of pleasing anyone now.

***

Gretchen Wintie suppressed her impatience with her ten-year-old son. "Jordan, we need to leave right now. I'm going to be late for work."

He wandered out in his yellow and brown school uniform, dragging his backpack and his feet. "Can't I go later? I hate hanging around by myself, waiting for my friends to arrive."

"No." She grabbed his hand and pulled him towards the front door, ignoring the stab of guilt. "We discussed this, and you're not old enough."

"But Cody walks to school every day."

"Cody walks with his sisters," she corrected. And unlike Jordan, they didn't have a psycho father threatening to make them disappear on their way home. Goosebumps prickled her skin as she locked the door and then scanned the neighbourhood, looking for anyone who shouldn't be there. Lindsay from the grocery store walked her dog, and Mitchell from Parks and Wildlife jogged past, raising a hand in greeting. She waved back.

Quiet. Normal.

"Then can't you drop me at his place instead?"

She could appreciate Jordan was intelligent enough to form reasonable arguments in his favour, but right now, it wasn't helping. She relied on Cody's parents far too much as it was. "Not today." She drove the short distance to school. "Miss Simpson tells me she appreciates your help in the morning."

He folded his arms across his chest and pouted. "This sucks."

He was right. Before the threat, the year twelve student across the road walked Jordan every morning. But she had finished school and was studying for exams now. Gretchen had been considering letting Jordan walk on his own before Kurt's threats. But she couldn't even tell Jordan that. He had no idea Kurt had been in town and it was better he stayed in the dark. He didn't know the terrible things his father was involved in, had been too young and innocent to recognise the smell of alcohol and marijuana which often permeated his father's skin. Jordan only remembered the three or four good times when Kurt had spent more than a few minutes with them and that had been because Kurt had used them as cover for one of his illegal activities.

Gretchen suspected the only reason Kurt had wanted a child was so he could control her. She'd begun to have doubts about their relationship, had become suspicious about exactly what kind of work he did for her parents. She'd been planning to leave until she'd got pregnant.

It wasn't until she'd had a falling out with her parents that Kurt had decided she wasn't worth his time either. Broke, scared and with a baby to care for, she couldn't afford to leave.

Then Kurt had started manipulating Jordan in order to control her.

It was enough of a wake-up call to realise she couldn't afford to stay.

Not if she wanted to prevent Jordan from growing up in the same manipulative environment as she had.

She'd found a wad of cash in Kurt's office and left, travelling from place to place, wherever she could find work and a babysitter. Kurt hadn't tried to find her. Neither had her parents. She'd thought she'd made a clean break from them all.

She'd been wrong.

Jordan flung the car door open as she pulled up in front of the school.

"Have a good day," she called.

"Later." He slammed the door and Gretchen sighed. Maybe she should tell Jordan about his father's threats, but she wasn't certain he would believe her. He rarely asked about his father these days, but she'd once overheard him tell Cody he was a cop. Perhaps he remembered talks of drugs and raids, and figured Kurt was one of the good guys, instead of the bad.

She hadn't had the heart to correct him.

She waited until Jordan went inside the brick building before continuing to the marina. The tour bus pulled into the street behind her and she accelerated. She was supposed to be already on the boat and have the gear ready, morning tea prepared.

Hopefully, Rob would understand. She'd have to make sure she had things sorted with Jordan before her new boss, Sam, returned from the city.

She grabbed her backpack and jogged across the carpark and through the gate to the pens. The *Oceanid* was tied in place, and she spotted both Rob and Sam on the back deck.

Damn. She hadn't known Sam was back.

She walked on board and headed for the cabin. "Morning! Sorry I'm late. I'll be right there." She waved and was two steps inside the cabin when she noticed the man. Large was the first word that came to mind.

Unhappy was the second. He scowled, not dissimilar to Jordan's expression as he'd jumped out of the car. The man sat ramrod straight at the table, chopping fruit for morning tea. His hair was a tight mass of brown curls cropped close to his skull, and his eyes were sharp and judging.

Her smile faded as she placed her backpack in a cupboard. "Hi, I'm Gretchen. You must be Arthur." Her friend, Penelope had mentioned Sam was bringing his army mate back to Retribution Bay with him.

A short nod.

"Thanks for starting morning tea. I'll come and help in a second."

"I don't need help." Though the words were defiant, the timbre of his voice was warm, almost soothing. An odd contrast.

Gretchen didn't comment as she went out on the deck to speak with Sam. "Do you need help out here?"

The passengers had disembarked from the bus and were heading down the jetty.

"We're all good. You met Sherlock?" Sam asked.

She frowned. "Isn't his name Arthur?"

Sam nodded. "Sherlock's his nickname. He's going to be coming out with us for a while."

"Great!" Maybe he'd smile when the customers were on board. "I'm sure an extra pair of hands will be useful. I'm sorry for being late. Jordan was slow starting this morning."

"Don't sweat it," Sam replied.

The customers arrived and Gretchen got to work passing out stinger suits, and masks and snorkels. It was two weeks until the end of the season and Gretchen still hadn't found work for the off-season. Her final practicum for her occupational therapy degree was next month, as was her final exam, but she still had to find someone to look after Jordan. And what were the chances she could actually get a job as an OT in Retribution Bay?

She sighed and tuned in to Sam as he did his spiel about what the day would entail. When he was done, he steered the boat out of the marina and into the gulf.

Gretchen made the rounds, chatting to the passengers on board. One man grabbed her arm as she walked past. "Is it dangerous?"

She smiled, used to the last-minute nerves from some. "Any interaction with wild animals has an element of danger," she said. "We can't choose how the humpbacks will react to us." The man paled. "However, we follow the guidelines which reduce the risk. We never swim near a mother and her calf or get into the water when the whales are feeling playful. We keep a set distance from them and the boat is always nearby."

"Don't be such a worry-wart, honey," the older woman beside him said. "They wouldn't be allowed to do it if the risk was high."

The man fiddled with his mask.

"You don't have to swim if you're uncomfortable," Gretchen assured him. "We'll stop soon for a snorkel and then when we find the whales, you can assess the situation yourself."

He nodded. "All right."

She went onto the bow as they neared the mooring and readied the hook to snag it. The satisfaction of looping the rope first go and pulling it over the deck, tying it in place, never faded. When she was done, she caught Arthur watching her through the window. She smiled and waved, but he simply stared at her.

Intense, bordering on creepy, if she hadn't known what he'd been through. Losing part of his leg as well as his job would be difficult to deal with, and it sounded as if he was dealing with depression and chronic pain as well. Amy had called a few days ago to ask if Gretchen could help him with therapy when he came up, and while she was happy to help, she couldn't do it in any official capacity until she passed her degree.

She headed into the cabin and stripped out of her polo shirt and shorts, before slipping on her own stinger suit and grabbing her gear out of her backpack. "Are you snorkelling?" she asked Arthur.

"No."

"We've got floatation devices if you need a hand."

"I can swim."

"You should jump in," Sam said, walking into the room.

"You want me to scare away your customers?" Arthur demanded.

"You're not that ugly," Sam joked.

Arthur grunted. "You know what I mean."

Sam glanced at Gretchen and she got the hint to get out of there. She slipped by him and joined the group waiting to get into the water. It was her turn to monitor the snorkellers and figure out who was a decent swimmer. They kept the stronger swimmers together so they didn't have anyone falling behind when they reached the whales.

The water was cool, but not crisp, and the visibility was about ten metres. She swam amongst the guests, pointing out things of interest as she spotted them: a stingray gliding along the bottom, a turtle feeding near a clump of coral, and the brightly coloured clown fish were always popular. The man who had expressed his concern about the danger swam confidently next to his wife. At least that was one less concern. In fact, no one struggled with swimming at all today.

It made her job easier.

At the signal from Sam on the boat, she shepherded the passengers back. Morning tea had been laid out on the table and people were already enjoying the fresh fruit and hot drinks by the time she got out. All except Arthur, who was still sitting in the cabin in the same place. Maybe he needed help to move. She towelled herself dry, wrapping it around her waist, and then climbed the ladder to the top deck to talk to Sam. "Jasmine found us anything yet?"

"Yeah, there's a pod heading into the gulf now." He pointed north and in the sky in the distance she spotted Jasmine's microlight plane.

They were alone up here, but still she moved closer so she didn't have to shout. "Does Arthur need help moving?"

Sam grimaced and shook his head. "No, he can use the prosthesis just fine. He has an aversion to people pitying him and thinks if he goes out there, he'll ruin everyone's day."

How sad.

"He's struggling, and he wasn't the best conversationalist to start with. Don't be offended by him."

"I won't." She couldn't help but want to make him feel better. She returned to the lower deck and went into the cabin to throw her polo shirt back on. Arthur stared out the window and didn't so much as glance at her. He had a bottle of water next to him. "Can I get you anything to eat?"

A hesitation, but no response.

"You should taste some of your hard work." Still nothing. "Unless you filled up while you were cutting the fruit."

That got his attention. "I didn't eat while I worked." His eyes widened as if she was accusing him of theft.

She'd offended him. She smiled. "Well, you're stronger than I am. I wouldn't have been able to resist. Do you want anything now?" She gestured outside to where the passengers had all filled their plates and were sitting around the boat eating.

His eyes flitted outside and then down to his leg, and back to her. "Yes," he replied. "Please."

She grinned. "Have you got a favourite?"

"Oranges."

Interesting. Most people went for the watermelon or strawberries. "Be right back."

She filled two plates with fruit and cake and then delivered his plate to him. "I'd love to sit and chat, but I've got to make the rounds. Do you want to join me?"

He slid the plate closer to him. "No."

She waited a beat for him to say something else, but when he didn't, she headed back outside.

"Thank you." The words were soft, maybe even forced, but they were there. Progress.

Gretchen didn't turn around, but she lifted a hand in acknowledgement. "Any time."

Maybe she could get through to the injured soldier somehow.

Chapter 2

Arthur was a rude, obnoxious idiot. His mother would be appalled at the way he'd spoken to Gretchen. Grief swept over him, and his gut clenched. He'd spent years not allowing himself to think of her but seeing Amy again had brought memories flooding back. So many of them good ones, and he squeezed his eyes shut to stop the tears.

When she'd died and Amy had disappeared, he'd had no one to turn to except his father. And the Major believed emotions made you weak.

Gretchen chatted to passengers as she passed around plates of food and offered them drinks. She hadn't offered him food because she pitied him, but because it was what she did. It was her job. The realisation soothed some of his bitterness that had been building since he'd stepped onto the boat.

He was being baby-sat. Sam didn't trust him enough to leave him alone but had framed it as if he needed a hand on the boat. Bollocks. His crew worked in a synchronised rhythm which reminded him of his own army teammates. Sam had tried to convince him to go swimming, but he didn't need the shocked looks when people noticed his missing leg. He didn't want to be the subject of pity porn photos.

Another part of him was worried he'd make a fool of himself. What if he couldn't get back on the boat without help? That would be completely demoralising. Plus, his temporary prosthesis would rust if he swam with it.

Arthur bit into the sweet, juicy segment of orange and was taken back to his primary school days. Getting home from school, Amy in tow, and finding their mother waiting for them, afternoon tea already on the table. If they were lucky, they had melting moments with glazed cherries on top, however it was usually some kind of fruit, often oranges, and he'd stick the peel in his mouth and pretend it was his teeth. It always made Amy laugh.

He'd forgotten that.

Without thinking, he stuck the peel over his teeth and glanced out the door where a few passengers were still hovering around the table. A teenager looked at him and smiled. Arthur smiled back, forgetting about the peel, and the boy laughed, giving him the thumbs up.

Arthur hastily removed the peel, but it was too late. The boy's laughter had pierced his self-pity.

But if the kid had known about his leg…

The warmth left him. He had nothing to smile about.

The boat slowed and someone shouted, "Look!" Everyone rushed to the right of the boat, watching something in the water beyond where Arthur could see. Probably the whales.

In all his travels with the army, he'd never spent much time near the ocean, never seen whales in the wild. Some people were climbing the ladder to the top deck to get a better view. He wanted to see them too.

He checked to make sure no one was watching him and then shifted, craning his neck to spot them. Nope, wrong angle. If he wanted to see them, he had to get up and walk out on the deck.

He glanced down at his right leg. He'd worn long pants and his sneakers matched.

Then there was the whole issue of his sensitive nerve endings, the pins and needles. Every step was a reminder he hadn't practised as regularly as the therapist had told him to, not seeing the point of it. He felt as if he was walking with a peg leg.

Outside, Gretchen laughed at something a passenger said and then bent down to pick up goggles which had been abandoned on the floor. Long smooth legs, leading to very short navy blue shorts and a curvaceous butt.

Perfection.

His mouth went dry, and he smothered his body's reaction. She wouldn't look twice at him.

She spotted him watching her and smiled, walking over. "You coming out to have a look?"

He swallowed. "Not much space." The words felt odd on his tongue. He was never good at speaking, and he hadn't made much of an effort since the accident.

"There's always room for one more." She gestured him to stand. "Come on."

He shifted and his leg spasmed, sending pain throughout his body. He groaned.

She hurried over. "Are you all right?"

The concern on her face made him feel useless, helpless even. "I'm fine," he barked. "Leave me."

"You're not fine," she challenged, annoyance crossing her face. "I'm here to help when you're ready." She walked out.

He admired her a little for not placating him and shying away from the subject. It didn't stop his defiance though. He was supposed to be bullet proof, better than everyone, stronger, faster, smarter, not this disabled, bitter man wishing he could see the whales. He massaged his leg, trying to soothe the pain away. It was getting worse, not better. Maybe he should have listened to the therapists all along and only worn the prosthetic leg for a few hours a day while he got used to it, but he hated to see his limb just sitting there.

His stump itched, but he couldn't reach the spot with his pants and prosthesis on. He shifted again and scratched around the area, but it provided no relief.

Arthur gritted his teeth. Outside, the passengers were preparing to get into the water. After they were in, maybe he'd have time to strip and get to the itch. He counted down from one hundred, trying to ignore the prickly sensation as people took their time getting ready.

One of the crew members jumped into the water with a camera and the passengers followed. Finally.

His pant legs were too tight to pull up over his knee so he stripped them down below his knee and then worked to push off the prosthesis, being careful not to tip out the inevitable sweat. With the weight clunking to the floor, he stripped off the sock and liner and exposed his stump. The cool air was welcome and as he scratched, his eyes rolled back in his head. Sweet relief.

"Are you coming in?"

His eyes flew open at Gretchen's voice. She watched him from the door, seeing him at his most vulnerable. "Get out!" His hands covered his stump and heat burned his cheeks. He might as well have been caught masturbating for the horror he felt.

Gretchen's eyes widened, and she spun around. "Sorry. I didn't mean to interrupt."

Too late. His fingers fumbled with the liner. Damn thing wouldn't unroll. "Go away."

She stayed in the doorway, back facing him. "Do you want to go swimming?"

"No!" Why was it taking so damned long? He was more dexterous than this. Maybe he should just dive overboard and never surface. But that meant he still had to get to the edge of the boat.

"All right. I'll stay here in case any of the crew want to come in. Take your time."

His fingers stilled on the liner and he glanced up. Gretchen leaned against the door frame, facing away, guarding his vulnerability. His heart thumped uncomfortably in his chest. A protector. The tension lessened and he exhaled.

Beyond her, Sam approached. Gretchen put her hand out to stop him. "Wait a second."

"I just need to grab my towel."

She placed a hand against his chest and shifted from the door frame, stopping him. "Not yet. I'll get it for you when Arthur's finished."

Sam glanced through the window and Arthur ducked his head, shifting his body so his left leg moved in front of his residual limb and his hand covered his stump.

"What's he doing?"

"He's adjusting his prosthesis."

"So? I've seen his stump before."

"No, Sam." Her tone was firm. "He needs privacy."

Silence for a moment and Arthur looked up to see the confusion on Sam's face before he nodded. "I'll be back later." He strode away.

Arthur moved fast, replacing the liner liner, then the liner itself, the sock and finally the leg, before pulling up his pants again. Gretchen stood patiently, waiting. Bitterness welled at needing her protection. He was supposed to be the protector. He'd trained his whole life for that.

"I'm done."

She turned and entered the room, picking up Sam's towel. "I'm sorry for disturbing you."

He nodded.

"Let me know when you're ready to try swimming and maybe I can help." She shifted, and wrapped her arms around her waist. "I'm studying occupational therapy, and I've got another exam and practicum before I qualify, but I know a few things." She left the cabin.

Was she the person Sam and Amy had been thinking of when they'd said he'd have support up here?

He squirmed, liking the idea of spending more time with her, but hating the reason. Arthur let out a sigh, breathing away the residual bitterness.

While he didn't want help, he was beginning to think he might actually need it.

***

By the time Gretchen picked Jordan up from Cody's place, she was ready for a long soak in the shower, followed by a glass of wine. Unfortunately she had dinner to prepare before Jordan reverted into the Hunger Grouch, a transformation that wasn't pleasant to witness.

She handed him a biscuit to tide him over. "Have you got any homework?"

"I did it at Cody's."

"Great." Another thing she owed Holly. It couldn't be easy to get the two boys to sit down and concentrate on homework when they wanted to play. "Put your school bag away and have a shower while I make dinner."

"Can't I watch TV?"

"Not until you're in your PJs." They had this argument every night. She waited until he huffed out his dissatisfaction and headed for his room.

Someone knocked on the front door, and Gretchen frowned, going to answer it. A small lean woman stood there, her short, pale blue hair a little mussed from the day. "Hey, Georgie."

"I need all the dirt, and I need it now," Georgie Stokes demanded with a smile, moving inside.

"What dirt?" Georgie must have come straight from work as she still wore her khaki Parks and Wildlife uniform.

"On Arthur. Wasn't he on the boat today? Penelope said he was, but she didn't see him when he arrived yesterday, so she couldn't tell me anything."

Right. "I didn't speak to him much." Gretchen poured them both a glass of wine and pushed one across the kitchen bench to her friend.

"Why not? Is he a complete arse? He must be, right? He abandoned Ames."

While Gretchen appreciated Georgie's instant defence of their friend, she wasn't ready to climb on the hate Arthur train just yet. "He's... quiet."

"Serial killer quiet, or shy quiet?" Georgie sipped the wine and settled onto a stool.

"Shy quiet." She considered her words as she got the vegetables she needed for dinner out of the fridge. "I'd say he's still coming to terms with what's happened to him and lashing out at anything he sees as pity. He doesn't want to need help."

Georgie sighed. "Don't say things like that. It makes him empathetic, and I really want to hate him for being so awful to Amy."

Georgie never hated anyone. "There are two sides to every story."

"I know. Matt said that too."

Gretchen smiled as she cut the green beans. "When are you meeting Arthur?"

"Sam says we have to give him a week to settle. For some reason he thinks meeting the whole family at once might be too much."

The Stokes family was a lot to take in, particularly if you were dealing with your own personal demons. "If he grows horns and wings before then, I'll let you know."

Georgie laughed. "Thanks." She got a vegetable peeler out of the drawer and started peeling carrots, perching herself back on the stool. "How're things with you? Where's Jordan?"

Gretchen admired her ability to be comfortable wherever she went. "Jordan's in the shower. He's resentful he has to go to school so early at the moment."

"I wish I could help you, but I've got to start early too."

"I know. There's only a couple of weeks until the season ends and then I'll be home in the mornings."

"What are you going to do then?"

"I've got my last practicum in Karratha next month."

"Is Jordan going too?"

Gretchen shook her head. "He needs to be in school, but I haven't sorted out childcare yet." It was too much to ask Holly to have him for several weeks.

"I can probably rearrange my work hours for a week," Georgie said. "He can stay with me."

It was a lovely offer, but Georgie spent most of her nights out at the Ridge with Matt these days. "I'll sort something."

Georgie placed her hand over Gretchen's, stopping her from reaching for the corn. "Let me help. The prac is three weeks, right?"

Gretchen nodded, fighting the urge to say no outright. Relying on people left her vulnerable when they let her down.

"Maybe I can have him for a week, then he could stay at the Ridge for a week, and then with Cody's family."

It would spread the load, and Gretchen planned to come home on the weekends, so it would only be five nights each. Cautious hope filled her. "Let me talk to the others."

Georgie nodded, satisfied, and finished her wine. "I'd better get going."

Gretchen walked her to the door. "Are you heading out to the Ridge?"

She nodded.

"Tell Amy I'll find out what I can about Arthur." Gretchen was curious about the man anyway.

Georgie hugged her. "Thanks. I'll see you later."

Gretchen waited until she drove away and then smiled, closing the door.

Jordan wandered out in his superhero pyjamas. "Who was that?"

"Georgie dropped by to say hi."

He frowned. "Why didn't you get me?"

"Sorry, sweetheart. I didn't think. She wasn't here long." Georgie was one of Jordan's favourite people.

His bottom lip poked out.

"Why don't you watch some tele while I finish making dinner?"

He turned to do as she suggested, dragging his feet again. Gretchen sighed and returned to the kitchen. Her phone rang and her heart sank lower as she saw the caller ID. "Kurt."

"You're testing my patience, Gretchen."

Nausea swelled in her, and she checked to make sure Jordan was occupied in the living room before she spoke. "I haven't seen the Stokes in a couple of weeks. They had a family issue and were busy."

"Did you ask Georgie for information just now?"

Gretchen clutched her stomach and lowered herself on to a stool. "No." It had been over four weeks since Kurt had turned up in Retribution Bay unannounced demanding she spy on the Stokes family, but she'd thought he'd left. Had hoped his threat had been just to mess with her, because he'd only called once since then for an update. "She was upset about something. I didn't get a chance."

"You're not trying hard enough. Maybe you need some motivation. Do you know what happens to a child when a horse bolts?"

She clenched her hand. Jordan had pony club tomorrow. "No."

"Let's hope you don't find out." He hung up.

Gretchen gasped for breath as her heart raced. She closed her eyes to remember exactly what he'd asked her to do. That night at the brewery was a little hazy because she'd had a couple of drinks. Running into Kurt had sobered her fast enough.

He'd spoken about some company... Scorpionfish... no... Stonefish Enterprises, wanted to know what the Stokes knew about them. It wasn't something she could easily bring up in conversation. She'd googled the name and hadn't found a website, so she didn't know what they did.

Then he'd spoken about Lara and Matt being kidnapped.

She glanced to the door. That was something she could ask Georgie about, but what excuse could she use if Georgie asked her how she knew?

Finally he'd wanted to know the Stokes's plans and how much the police knew about the whole situation. She sighed. No way she could casually insert that into a conversation. Dot and Nhiari would give her the third degree.

As for the Stokes… there were so many of them. Three brothers and Georgie, and they all had partners now. Did Kurt mean just the siblings, or everyone?

Jordan laughed at something on the television, and the sound warmed her heart, calming her. She had to protect him.

She just needed to figure out how.

Chapter 3

Arthur followed Sam into his townhouse that evening and stared at the stairs up to his room. His leg ached and it felt too hard to tackle them now. He didn't bother suggesting they convert the downstairs study into his bedroom because he'd heard the therapist tell Sam he needed regular gentle exercise, including steps.

Sam was taking Arthur's recovery seriously. He was like a military-trained mother hen, all routine and precision, but with a slightly more caring undertone.

"You need any pills?" Sam asked, dumping his backpack on the kitchen bench.

Arthur clenched his teeth and nodded, waiting while Sam dished out his dose of painkillers.

Brandon and Sam had agreed he shouldn't have access to his own pain medication. While he resented the lack of autonomy, he didn't blame them. They didn't trust him.

He didn't trust himself.

He swallowed the pills and sank onto the stool, relieving the pressure on his stump. He rubbed the area, but it didn't help a lot through all the padding.

"What did you think?" Sam asked him.

"About what?"

"The boat and the tour."

Arthur was about to shrug and give a non-committal answer when he noticed the slight twitch in Sam's eye. Sam cared about his answer.

Why?

Sam always made things work. Surely he wasn't worried about his decision to leave the army and buy the tour boat.

The silence stretched. Shit, he had to fill it. "Runs smoothly. Crew are good. Customers seemed happy."

Way to list the obvious. He wasn't reporting back to a senior officer, he was talking to a friend. Before he could add something more meaningful, Sam smiled. "Thanks, mate."

Arthur pressed his lips together. He'd said nothing of value. Was that kind of response all they expected of him?

He considered it while Sam got something out for dinner. Had it always been that way?

He wasn't the best with words, always stuck to the facts first so he couldn't offend anyone, or say something wrong. Emotion was… difficult for him. His father had always berated him if he got emotional.

Someone knocked on the door and Sam was in the pantry, five different containers in his hands. He looked over his shoulder. "Can you get that?"

Arthur got to his feet, wincing as the prosthesis rubbed again. He shuffled to the door and opened it to find Sam's girlfriend, Penelope there, her long red hair tied back into a braid and still in her Parks and Wildlife uniform. She held up an insulated bag. "Hey, Arthur. I made a curry for dinner, and there's far too much for just me. I thought you and Sam might like some."

This petite woman had had Sam tied up in knots only a few weeks ago. Arthur had looked forward to his phone calls about her and Stonefish Enterprises. He'd felt useful for the first time since his accident, and he'd enjoyed hearing Sam unsure how to act around a woman for the first time ever.

He nodded at Penelope and held the door wider so she could come in.

"Oh, I don't want to disturb you."

"Come in." Sam would want to see her. She hesitated a moment and then entered. As he closed the door, he heard the joy in Sam's voice as he said, "Hey, Penny."

The longing was there as it always was. What would it be like to have someone so pleased to see you, even though they saw you yesterday?

He shuffled to the foot of the stairs.

"Where are you going?" Sam called.

"Shower." He'd give them privacy. He used the railing to help him shuffle up the steps, trying not to put too much weight on his prosthesis. The painkillers hadn't made a dent yet and aside from the rubbing, nerve pain shimmered up his leg, a constant reminder that one wrong step could take it from manageable to on-the-floor-in-agony pain.

He got out the clothes he would wear after the shower, as well as a fresh sock and liner and carried them into the bathroom.

Sam had installed a railing to help him, and he sat on the edge of the bath to remove his prosthetic limb.

What was he doing here?

Was he really so weak that he couldn't cope on his own? Was a breadcrumb of affection enough to have him move across the state in the hope of more?

Apparently yes.

Perhaps his father had been right about him all along.

He pushed the thought aside as the prosthesis came

free and he sighed. A moment of relief.

The therapist had said the pain would lessen the more exercise he did, and as his stump grew used to the prosthesis.

But he deserved the pain that came with it. He'd made such a stupid mistake.

He turned the cold water on, hopping under it with the help of the rail. The cold soothed his aching leg and he balanced there, eyes closed, as the water trickled over his body.

Was there any point to his life anymore? What was he supposed to do now his career, the only thing he'd ever wanted to do, was over?

He had his drawing.

Stupid idea. His doodles weren't good enough to provide him with an income. They weren't good enough to show anyone. His father had made that clear.

His fingers moved as if itching for a pencil.

He hadn't drawn since the explosion. Hadn't wanted to deal with the false praise the nurses would have given him for doing something other than staring at the wall all day.

Arthur switched off the water, the habit so ingrained in him that he did it without thinking. Water shouldn't be wasted even if he was lost in thought.

It took him some time to dress. His hand hesitated as he reached for the prosthesis. Maybe he could get away with just his crutches tonight. Let his stump rest.

But Sam would think him weak.

Gritting his teeth, he placed on the fresh liner liner, and all the other layers until he could stand, and then he washed the ones he'd worn that day.

Voices drifted up to him from the ground floor.

"You can't expect him to rejoin society in just one day," Penelope said. "He's going to need time, and you said he wasn't a people person to start with."

Arthur hesitated at the top of the stairs.

"The only time he left the cabin was to use the bathroom," Sam said. "Gretchen wouldn't even let me in when he had his leg off."

"Which means he still feels self-conscious about it. It's a lot to take in, Sam." A pause and the clatter of plates. "You might cope differently to him in the same circumstance, but it doesn't make his reaction any less valid."

"I just want to help him, and he won't let me."

"Give him time."

Arthur didn't hear the rest of her words. Apparently he wasn't even doing the cripple role correctly. Was he supposed to be grateful for Sam's help? He hadn't asked for it.

A sour taste in his mouth made him turn around and head back to his bedroom, shutting the door behind him.

He was a burden to his friends. Maybe he should leave. He could hitch-hike to the airport and fly back to Perth. Then he didn't have to live up to anyone's expectations.

The darkness closed in around him, pulling him down. He opened a drawer, pulling out his bag and a notepad fell out. The soft thud on the floor made him stop.

Arthur picked it up and, flicking it open, saw the sketches he'd done on his last mission, the last one of a child playing in the streets.

His body tensed and he moved to the next page, a blank one, the emptiness of it helping him to clear his mind of that day. He exhaled and took the pencils out of his bag, sitting on the bed with his notepad on his lap.

Drawing was a waste of time, a useless hobby.

Defiance made him make the first line, a light sketch

with no image in mind. He glanced up, spotting the chest of drawers across from him. The line could be the front of the furniture.

A tingle spread through him as he added another line, and then another, the quick strokes forming the outline in moments.

The darkness faded as the white of the page captured his focus and the drawers took life.

Three sharp raps on the door made Arthur jump. He slammed the notepad shut, tucking it behind him as Sam burst into the room.

"What are you doing?" Sam demanded.

"Nothing."

Suspicion crossed Sam's face. "You've been up here for almost an hour."

Arthur glanced towards the door. He'd lost track of time. "I figured you wanted time alone with Penelope." Sounded like a good excuse.

"What's behind your back?"

"Nothing."

"Bullshit. I saw you put something there."

"It's none of your business."

Sam moved forward. "Everything you do is my business."

"You're not my father."

"No, I'm nicer than him," Sam retorted. He exhaled heavily. "I'm worried about you."

Arthur looked him in the eye, saw the worry. What did Sam think he was doing here? "I'm fine."

"Then show me what's behind your back."

Panic filled him. "It's nothing, I swear." He'd managed to keep his drawing secret from all his teammates. Whenever they asked what he was doing, he'd told them he was writing notes, or strategic plans, or something like that.

"If it's nothing, it won't matter if you show me." Sam stared down at him. He wasn't going to let it go.

Arthur couldn't do it. Not another thing ripped away from him. This was the only thing he had left. "No."

"I won't let you kill yourself," Sam muttered, moving closer again, reaching for him.

"What?" The word shot out of him.

Maybe it was the confusion on his face, but Sam paused. "The noose you tucked behind your back."

Arthur shook his head. This was ridiculous. "What noose?" He pulled out the notebook, showed it to Sam, but when Sam reached for it, Arthur tucked it behind his back again.

Sam took a couple of steps away, the tension leaking from his posture. "It's a notebook."

Arthur nodded. "How the hell did you get noose from that?"

Sam didn't speak but the answer was on his face.

"You really think I'm going to try to commit suicide?" He clenched his hands.

A short nod.

Taking all those pills had been weak, but he'd never consciously thought about killing himself. "What would it matter if I died? I'm useless to everyone." He shouldn't provoke his friend further, but he wanted the answer.

"You're not useless. You helped me with Penelope, you saved my life on more than one occasion, and you're my friend."

He relaxed his hands. "I didn't do much with Penelope."

"You helped me understand her better. You gave me the information I needed so I could trust my instincts."

Arthur shrugged. "It was nothing."

"Not to me, it wasn't." Sam opened his mouth, closed it again, then sighed. "I know you don't like people to get close to you, but I'm here for you, whatever you need."

Arthur swallowed hard. It was too much to take in right now. "I'm not going to kill myself," he said. "I'll be down for dinner shortly."

Sam held his gaze for a long moment and then nodded. "Don't take long. It's getting cold." He walked out.

Arthur waited until he heard Sam on the stairs and then retrieved his notebook. The drawing was a little rough, definitely not his best work, but still he smiled. It was like greeting an old friend to hold a pencil in his hand. He hadn't realised how much he missed it. Maybe one day he'd have enough courage to show Sam.

But for now, he tucked the notebook in his backpack, placed the bag into the drawer and went down for dinner.

Chapter 4

It was two days before Arthur got up the nerve to bring his notebook with him on the boat. He'd been unable to block out the excited conversations of the passengers which only made him bitter and want to be out there with them. But no one wanted their expensive tour ruined by a cripple. So instead he'd tried to find something to keep him busy in the cabin, and there were so many things he wanted to sketch.

He'd assessed the situation closely. The crew rarely entered the cabin before they reached the snorkelling spot. They were too busy answering questions and ensuring the passengers had the correct equipment. That gave him half an hour to start sketching the goggles hanging up, or the cupboards, or whatever inanimate object caught his attention.

He kept an ear tuned to the engine, because when it slowed it meant the crew would be in to get their own gear ready and he had to hide the book.

As soon as the engine switched off, Sam clattered down the ladder. "Want to snorkel?" The hope on Sam's face made Arthur feel like a tool.

"No." It wasn't as simple as walking to the edge of

the boat and jumping in.

"Come on. You can't stay in here forever."

Sure he could. Sam had obviously forgotten how patient Arthur could be when staking out a target.

"I'm getting in."

"Go on then." Maybe Arthur would get a chance to sketch again before everyone reboarded.

Sam looked at him a long moment and guilt slivered into Arthur's gut. "Suit yourself." Sam walked out.

Arthur waited until he heard a splash, and then got his notebook out again.

By day four he'd run out of interesting subjects he could sketch from where he sat. He'd tried moving around the cabin, but there was only one spot he could sit which gave him warning of someone approaching and therefore gave him time to tuck his notebook away without them seeing it.

"Are you writing the great Australian novel?" Gretchen asked.

Arthur glanced up, slamming shut the notebook. "No," he snapped. He'd thought she'd gone up to the top deck, but she stood in the doorway, a cautious smile on her face.

Her smile faded. "Sorry, I didn't mean to interrupt."

She moved away before he could apologise for snapping. Damn it. He always took too long to consider his words, to make sure they couldn't be misconstrued, that inevitably the conversation would move on before he had a chance to speak.

Anxieties courtesy of his father.

He sighed as she climbed to the top deck and he heard her speaking with Sam. Hopefully she didn't mention the notebook.

After a week on the boat, the stress of keeping his

drawing a secret was wearing on him. At times it was easier not to draw because it was too difficult to focus on the page as well as what was going on around him. But now he had rediscovered his love of drawing, the forced inactivity was driving him crazy.

Instead he chopped fruit and sat in the cabin listening to everyone have fun outside.

His leg ached, the pins and needles back with a vengeance and his stump sensitive from wearing the prosthetic leg all the time. He only moved when he had to use the toilet, and even then, he had to time it so that he went out when the passengers were in the water. Not how he wanted to spend his days from now on.

He ignored Sam's repeated suggestions to go swimming, just like Sam ignored his requests to stay at home.

He wanted the opportunity to draw people and settings, but it was too much of a risk to reveal what he was doing.

Drawing was a useless hobby.

The only thing that had ever given him joy.

The one thing he'd kept secret from his father.

The one thing he could still do.

Voices at the stern of the boat made him glance up. The passengers were back.

He tucked the book away as Sam and Gretchen climbed on board, and spent the rest of the trip watching the passengers interact.

All happy and whole.

The love between family and friends was clear from the shared smiles, good-natured teasing and laughter.

Comfort. Ease. Two things he'd never had in the army. He rarely allowed himself to fully relax even when he was just with his teammates.

As the passengers disembarked to return to their accommodation, the rest of the crew cleaned equipment and did dishes. Gretchen entered the cabin carrying the last of the plates from afternoon tea. He hadn't had a chance to apologise about being abrupt a few days ago, but now he could. Arthur pressed himself to his feet and shuffled across to the sink. His steps were still hesitant, always waiting for the prosthesis to fall off. Gretchen glanced up, a question on her face. He took the tea towel from where it was hanging on a hook and dried the dishes.

"Thank you," she said.

He nodded. It was the least he could do. He swallowed, trying to figure out the right words. Was it even worth apologising over something that she'd probably forgotten about?

Don't be a coward.

His father's words made him straighten his stance. He cleared his throat. "Ah, about the other day…"

Gretchen glanced at him, a slight frown on her face.

"I didn't mean to snap."

She tilted her head as if she wasn't quite following him.

"When you asked me about the notebook." Her eyes widened as she realised what he was talking about. Obviously she hadn't given it another moment's thought.

"It's fine. I was being nosey."

He shook his head. "I don't share it with anyone."

She touched his arm and smiled. "Don't worry about it, but if you ever decide to share, I'd love to know what keeps you so focused."

He nodded, not sure there would ever be a day when he felt safe enough to share his doodles with someone. By the time they were finished cleaning, everyone was saying their goodbyes. Sam locked the cabin and Arthur followed Gretchen off the boat. His prosthetic foot caught on the slight lip on the edge.

Time slowed as he tripped. First, the pain as his prosthesis ripped off. Then he flailed, trying to stop his forward motion. Desperately hopping on his good foot, he crashed into Gretchen, the movement catching her by surprise and they both fell. The thump on the hard, cold, metal ground and more pain. Gretchen's warm body crashing on top of him. Glancing across as his prosthesis teetered on the edge of the boat before tipping over and falling into the water below.

Fuck.

Gretchen groaned and Arthur forgot about the leg. He'd hurt her. "Sorry, are you all right?"

He sat up, helping her to a seated position. She rubbed her elbow. "Fine. What about you?"

He shrugged. His stump throbbed and somewhere below him in the water was his leg. Sam offered Gretchen a hand up and then turned to Arthur, his gaze stopping on the missing limb. He looked around.

"It went under," Arthur told him. He'd have to go in after it.

"I'll get it." Gretchen stripped off her shirt, tossing it to the deck, and slid off her shorts. Arthur's breath caught in his throat, preventing him from speaking. She shimmied down a nearby ladder and into the marina.

Damn it. Rescuing him again. Way to make him feel helpless. He shuffled to the edge and looked down. She was under the jetty, but the leg was nowhere to be seen.

"Toss me some goggles," she called.

Sam brushed by him as he stepped back on to the boat to fetch them. Arthur just sat there like a cripple, unable to help. Anger, frustration and despair clashed together, all battling for dominance. A scream crept up his throat and the urge to release it was strong. He fought it down as Sam threw Gretchen a pair of goggles and she put them on and disappeared beneath the water. Arthur held his breath.

"Do you want to get up?" Sam stood above him, arm outstretched.

No, he wanted to be whole again. To not need anyone.

Gretchen surfaced with his leg. "Got it!" She thrust it upwards, and he grabbed the foot, pulling it towards him. "Thanks."

He emptied the excess water from it. It would need a thorough rinse as soon as possible. Sam handed him a towel and then one to Gretchen as she climbed out of the marina. Arthur shoved the prosthesis back on his stump, not wanting her to see it.

"Do you need a hand?" Gretchen asked.

"No," he barked. He needed a leg.

"Thanks for your help, Gretchen," Sam said. "I'll see you tomorrow."

Gretchen nodded and smiled. "Bye." Her phone rang. She fished it out of her bag and glanced at the screen. Her face paled. She looked at Sam, nerves clear, then waved and strode away.

What was that about? Was she in some kind of trouble?

"What is wrong with you?" Sam demanded, dragging Arthur's attention back to him. "Stop being a douche." His friend stared down at him, hands on his hips. "Gretchen was only trying to help."

Arthur focused on putting on his leg.

Sam was right, but he wasn't used to needing help and deep down he didn't understand why Sam hadn't given up on him yet, why none of them had. It made no sense that Amy and Brandon invited him to stay with them after the way he'd behaved. He'd failed all of them.

And he'd failed himself.

Did he deserve a better life?

***

Gretchen strode down the jetty, all thoughts of Sam and Arthur forgotten as she found the courage to answer her phone. "What do you want, Kurt?"

"Who's the cripple?"

She stumbled at her ex's casual question. "What?"

"You heard me. The cripple who's going out on your boat."

Someone was still watching her.

She pressed her lips together, but then figured it would be easy enough for him to find out. "His name is Arthur Hammond. He was Sam's teammate in the army."

"Hammond… why does that name sound familiar?"

"He's my friend Amy's brother."

"The chick who married Brandon Stokes?" His immediate interest gave her goosebumps.

She shouldn't have said anything. "Yes."

"Does the cripple have a girlfriend?"

"I don't know. I only met him last week."

"Find out. I want you to seduce the loser. The sap will be grateful for the attention from anyone, even you. He'll be able to give you information on the Stokes. I want it by the end of the week. You've taken too long as it is."

Gretchen cringed at the implication Arthur was so desperate he'd even look at her. At one time, Kurt's insult would have made her try to please him more, but now it irritated as much as it hurt. He had never loved her, had only been with her to get to her family's business.

"And if he's not interested?" She wouldn't do it, but it was worth asking the question.

"Put on that whole innocent act of yours. He'll fall for it. Diving in after his leg is a good start."

Her head whipped around, scanning the area. Another tour boat was coming into the marina, a man and his two boys were fishing off the rocks nearby and a couple were strolling hand in hand along the footpath.

Kurt chuckled, low and nasty. "You won't see me, babe, but I'm always watching. I'll call tomorrow." He hung up.

Gretchen lowered her phone. She stopped scanning the area, not wanting to give the bastard further satisfaction, and instead walked to her car, checking the back seat before getting in.

No nasty gifts.

Her hand shook as she turned the key. Nothing had happened at pony club last week and she'd been lulled into a false sense of security. She'd forgotten that was his style. Threats followed by a period of anxiety when nothing happened, and just as she'd started relaxing again, he'd follow through.

The purr of the car engine made her come back to the present. She drove away, expression blank while her thoughts raced.

He was watching her, probably Jordan as well, which meant his threat to make her son disappear was still very real. Her heart thumped double time as she drove to Cody's house to pick up her son.

Cody's mother, Holly, opened the door. "Gretchen! What are you doing here?"

Nausea rose in her stomach. "Picking up Jordan."

Holly shook her head. "He's not here. He told Cody he was going straight home today." She turned and called, "Cody, come here."

Heavy footsteps as the boy ran to the front door. "What?" He smiled at Gretchen.

"Where's Jordan?" Gretchen demanded.

Cody shrugged. "He wanted to walk home."

"No one turned up at school to talk to him?"

Gretchen asked. Had Kurt already delivered on his threat?

"Nah. Said he had stuff to do."

Gretchen raced back to her car, every horrific option running through her head. Kurt enjoyed inflicting pain, both physical and emotional. Just prior to her leaving, he'd started manipulating Jordan, playing emotional mind games similar to the ones her own parents had played on her.

"Call me when you get home," Holly yelled.

She broke the speed limit racing through the quiet streets to her house and parked out front, not waiting for the garage door to open as she flew up the steps and through the front door. "Jordan!"

She'd never been so pleased to hear the television blaring. She burst into the lounge room to find Jordan on the couch playing his favourite video game. "Hi, Mum."

The panic resided as she swept him up in her arms and hugged him.

"Mum! I'm in the middle of a fight."

Anger pushed aside the relief and she stepped back. "What the hell are you doing here?"

"Playing my game." He peered around her as she was blocking his view of the TV.

She snatched the gaming controller from his hand. "What are you doing at home and not at Cody's?"

He stared up at her, then leaned back as if realising how angry she was. The motion made her aware of her tense muscles, clenched hands, and she took a step back, exhaling.

"I didn't want to go. I'm old enough to stay here by myself. Nothing happened."

Gretchen took another moment to breathe and chose her words carefully. "When I went to Cody's place to pick you up and you weren't there, it scared me."

He looked down at his lap.

"I didn't know where you were, and I worried something had happened to you."

"Retribution Bay is safe."

She bit her lip. Gretchen didn't want him scared, just cautious. It was a relief he didn't remember the tension of their Melbourne days. She'd worked hard to keep the danger hidden from him. "It is, but there are also a lot of tourists in town. They don't always pay as much attention on the roads." Maybe she should get him a mobile phone. She'd always thought ten was too young, but there might be a basic handset which allowed them to call each other if necessary. She'd investigate and see if her budget stretched to it.

"I use the footpaths."

"What do you say if someone offers you a lift?"

He rolled his eyes. "I say no."

She nodded. "What if they say they're a friend of mine?"

"If I don't know them, then I don't go."

"And if they say they're a friend of your dad's?"

His eyes widened. "Dad? But he's in Melbourne. Is he coming to visit?" The interest, with a touch of hope in his voice, killed her. She'd thought he understood his father was out of their life for good.

"No."

Jordan shuffled his feet. "Has he called?"

Damn. She shouldn't have mentioned Kurt. Jordan hadn't asked about his father in at least a year. Hell, maybe it was time to tell him the truth. Kurt's threat was very real. She sat down on the couch. "What do you remember about him?" Jordan had been five when they'd left.

"He used to buy me chocolate all the time."

Bribing him. She nodded. "What else?"

"He took me to the zoo to see the orangutans."

Only because he was meeting a contact there and had smuggled drugs in the nappy bag. "Anything else? Can you remember other outings?"

A moment's pause. "There was my birthday party at Luna Park."

Another time Kurt had used them as a front for illegal activities. "You say you're old enough to walk home from school by yourself, so you're old enough to know the truth."

Worry crossed Jordan's face. "What happened?"

"We left because he and your grandparents were doing things they shouldn't, and it wasn't safe for us to stay."

Jordan frowned. "But he's a police officer."

She shook her head. "No, he isn't. He was involved with some bad men who broke the law."

"Like a bikie gang?"

"Yeah, kind of."

"Cool!" Jordan sat straighter. "Did he have a motorcycle and everything?"

Gretchen shook her head and placed a hand on his arm. "Not cool. They hurt a lot of people and that's never cool."

"I guess. Is he in gaol? Is that why he doesn't call?"

"No, he's not in gaol."

"Then why doesn't he ever ring?"

She let out a breath. "He called me today and asked me to do something not very nice."

"Why?"

Because he was a bastard. She hated to tell him the next bit, but she had to get through to him how important it was he wasn't alone, even if it made him grow up quicker. "He said if I didn't do this thing, he would make you disappear."

"Why? He's my dad."

She nodded. "He's not a nice person, sweetheart. He doesn't care who he hurts to get what he wants."

Jordan shot off the couch. "Liar! My dad loves me."

Gretchen reached for him and he stepped away from her. She lowered her hand. "*I* love you. I want to keep you safe. That's why you can't walk home by yourself."

He shook his head. "You're just saying that because you think I'm still a baby. I bet it's *you* keeping Dad away from me!" He ran out of the room and a moment later, his bedroom door slammed.

Gretchen sighed and ran a hand through her short hair, giving it a tug in frustration. She hated to burst his image of his father, but it would keep him safe.

She just had to get him to believe her.

Before it was too late.

Chapter 5

Arthur breathed a sigh of relief when he entered Sam's town house on the marina. Finally some privacy. He was tired of being around people, even if he hadn't interacted with them. Here he could relax, unwind, maybe even have a cold beer. His stump throbbed and pain ran up his entire leg. Nothing he did could stop it.

Sam tossed his backpack on the couch and headed straight to the kitchen. "Go shower," he called. "We're heading to the Ridge for dinner."

No. Nausea rose so fast he swayed. He wasn't ready for that. Amy had stayed in Perth for a few days after his overdose, but they'd not spoken much. He didn't know what to say to her, and she had been focused on his treatment and reasons for overdosing.

"Did you hear me?" Sam nudged him and handed him a beer.

"I've had enough of people today."

"You need practice with people," Sam retorted. "You can't stay sullen and moody all the time. You need some Lara time."

Arthur frowned. "Lara time?"

"Darcy's daughter," Sam said. "She's ten, and if she

can't get through to you, no one can."

Right. Sam wanted to subject some poor young girl to the cripple. "Which one is Darcy?"

"Brandon's younger brother who stayed at the station. Brandon's the oldest, then Darcy, then Charlie who died, then Ed who lives in Perth, and the youngest child is the only sister, Georgie."

"I'll stay here, thanks."

"Not an option," Sam replied. "I've already told Ames we're coming, and she needs us to buy groceries on the way out." Sam took a long swallow of his beer. "You don't want to disappoint your sister, do you?"

Manipulative bastard. He shoved Sam harder than necessary. "Not fair."

"Playing fair wasn't getting anywhere. It's time for a new tactic."

"Don't you want to see Penelope?" he asked.

"She's busy tonight."

Damn, Arthur had thought the mention of Sam's new partner would work. He cracked the beer and chugged it down, studying his friend. Nope. No budging a determined Sam, and Sam had that set look on his face. If he didn't go willingly, he'd likely find himself tackled and carried out to the car. He burped, handed Sam the empty bottle and went to get ready.

Not that he ever really would be.

By the time they reached the gate with a sign of an angry looking ram on it declaring Retribution Ridge, Arthur was regretting sculling the beer. It clashed with his pain meds, making waves in his stomach. "Pull over," he demanded.

"We're almost there," Sam said.

"Pull over." He retched and Sam swore, slamming on the brakes. Thrusting open the door, Arthur got his seatbelt off and the top half of his body out of the car before he threw up. Three waves of retching and a very strong yeasty smell followed. When it ended, Sam handed him a tissue.

"Nerves or the alcohol?"

"Both." He shut the door again and took a deep breath.

Sam passed him a mint. "The Stokes are the best family I know. You'll be fine."

He fought against the compassion, the weakness. He shouldn't need it, but Sam's words soothed him.

"Ready?"

Arthur took a moment before he nodded, and Sam drove the remaining distance to the farmhouse.

Quaint. Slightly ramshackle, slightly hodgepodge as if it had been expanded on a whim in the distant past. His father would look down his nose at such a lack of order. His mother would have adored it. He itched to get out his notebook and sketch it.

Large shady trees grew in the fenced off garden, a feat in this dry, dusty land. Someone must have tended them lovingly to get them to grow and keep them alive.

Across from the house were a couple of large sheds and what looked to be accommodation—maybe shearers' quarters, and behind all of that were camp sites full of caravans and tents. A small community in the middle of nowhere.

Trust Amy to find somewhere like this to put down her roots. It suited her sense of adventure.

As Sam pulled up outside the house, a blue heeler trotted down the steps to greet them. "That's Bennett." Sam said and the slam of his door made Arthur flinch.

Get it together. This was just dinner, not a mission where he risked his life.

His veins still thrummed with adrenaline.

Arthur cracked open the door, pushing it until it stayed in place and then lifted his prosthetic leg out.

Ensuring he had a good angle, he stood and waited until his prosthesis held before he shut the door. The dog moved around the car, wagging its tail, and Arthur patted his soft, dusty fur. At least someone was happy to see him.

Sam waited for him at the base of the steps.

Man up, Sherlock. With a soft exhale, Arthur joined him and together they climbed the steps to the wooden verandah. Sam rapped on the fly screen door before letting himself inside. "Anyone home?"

"Sam!" The girlish cry came from the other end of the house and a young girl ran into the kitchen wearing a yellow and brown school uniform, brown ponytail swinging, and launched herself at Sam. He caught her and swung her into the air, and she squealed in delight. "What are you doing here?"

"We came for dinner."

Lara peered behind Sam as he put her back on the ground.

"This is Arthur."

Her eyes widened and darted to his legs and then back to his face. She beamed at him. "You're Amy's brother! If she's my aunt, does that make you my uncle?" She hugged him, her grip strong. The action caught him by surprise and he stumbled back a step.

Lara grinned. "Sorry! I don't know my own strength. It's so great to finally meet you. I've been waiting ages. I have so many questions—"

"Hold your horses, La La," Sam interrupted. "Give him a second to adjust."

Lara slipped her small soft hand into Arthur's and tugged him forward. "Come in. Make yourself at home. Do you want a drink?" She gestured to a chair around the long wooden dining table and then went to the fridge.

Arthur looked at Sam. Was this kid for real?

"We'll both have water," Sam told her and grinned at Arthur, his cocky smile saying he was enjoying Arthur's discomfort.

Some friend.

The kitchen was a cosy affair, despite the table big enough to feed a couple of army teams. Two knitting projects lay bunched on the counter next to a bowl of fruit, a calendar marked with dates hung from one wall, and next to the door was a rack of hooks to hold jackets or hats.

A home.

The ache of longing blindsided him.

"Do you horse ride, Arthur?" Lara asked.

"No." Not anymore.

"That's all right. Faith can teach you." At that moment a woman walked into the kitchen. She wore a blouse and pencil skirt which suggested she'd just come from work in an office, her short brown hair neatly styled. She smiled at him.

"Faith, have you met Sherlock yet?"

It was kind of surreal having his army nickname coming out of a ten-year-old's mouth.

"Not yet, Lara," Faith said and held her hand out to him. "I'm Faith. Nice to meet you."

"Faith is going to marry my dad," Lara said. "Faith, you can teach him to ride, right?"

Heat rushed to Arthur's cheeks. Had they not told her about his missing leg? He cleared his throat. "No, I mean I can't. I lost my leg."

Lara tilted her head to the side. "Didn't you just lose it below the knee? I looked it up on the Internet and there are plenty of people with half a leg who horse ride. I checked so you didn't feel left out. It might be a little tricky at first, but all it takes is practice." She turned to Faith. "Can we go horse riding now?"

Faith shook her head. "We'll have dinner as soon as

your dad's back," she said. "But you can take Arthur out to meet the horses."

Lara beamed and strode towards him, grabbing his hand. "Come on."

Arthur's mouth opened and closed, but no words came out. This girl had just dismissed his lack of a leg as if it was inconsequential. She understood nothing. But not even he had sunk so low as to snap at her. Not with her beaming up at him, excitement and expectation on her face.

Sam chuckled as Lara dragged Arthur out of the house and down the stairs. Arthur stumbled, his gait stilted, and Lara glanced at his leg. "Sorry, should I slow down?"

He adjusted his stride and shook his head, following her across to the horse yard. The rich red dirt was an unfamiliar colour, and he wanted to examine it, find out whether different shades added together to make it so vibrant, but that would have to wait. Lara strode to where five horses grazed on hay. Lara ducked between the posts and climbed into the yard. Arthur hesitated, trying to figure out the best way to get his leg to move the way he wanted, before following her.

"That must be strange," Lara said.

"What?"

"Not having part of your leg," she replied. "Dad was helping me research it when we heard you were coming up, and it must suck having to think about doing everything again."

Something about the matter-of-fact way she said it made him smile for the first time in a very long time. "It does." He followed her over to where a dark brown horse was grazing, and she stroked the horse's neck. "This one is mine. Her name is Starlight."

"She's nice." The horse's hair was smooth and dusty, and his hand was covered in a film of red dirt by the time he finished patting her.

"The pony club is coming out on the weekend to do a trail ride and sleepover. You should come too."

"I don't know how to ride."

"It's easy. You just need to sit and steer. I overheard Faith telling Amy they didn't have enough parents interested in sleeping over with all the kids, so Dad and uncle Brandon have to help." She glanced at him. "But they work really hard, and it would be nice to have somebody else's help."

Arthur shook his head. The kid had a way about her.

"You will help, won't you?"

How could he refuse that hopeful grin? He didn't even stop to consider the potential problems. "All right."

"Yay!" She hugged him, taking him by surprise again. "You should come to pony club tomorrow night. It's for kids, but at least you'll get a chance to ride before the weekend. Or maybe we can ride after dinner." She waved at someone behind him. A dusty white ute pulled up to the house and three men climbed out. Brandon he recognised, and the other dark-haired man had to be his brother Darcy because they looked so similar. The indigenous man must be Matt, the farm hand Sam had told him about. They all wore checked shirts, jeans, brown boots and Akubra hats.

"Come on, dinner will be soon." She raced back over to the house without waiting for him.

Arthur followed more slowly, dusting the dirt off his hands before rubbing his chest. So this was what Sam meant by Lara time. He had to give his friend credit. He felt better than he had in a long time. She made him feel useful and wanted, two things he hadn't felt since before the accident.

He embraced the feeling, soaking it up like a dry river bed after the rain.

He felt good.

***

As he reached the stairs, a blue car parked next to Sam's four-wheel drive and a woman with pale blue hair hopped out. "Hey!" She hurried over, smiling at him. "You've got to be Arthur. I'm Georgie."

The only Stokes sister. His smile felt forced. "Nice to meet you."

"Likewise, as long as you don't hurt Amy again." She breezed past him and into the kitchen where she greeted the farmhand, Matt, with a hug and a smacking kiss.

Her words struck him in the chest like shrapnel.

She was right. He had hurt his sister, and now Amy's whole new family were inside the kitchen chatting. His hesitant footsteps as he climbed the steps had nothing to do with his prosthesis.

Slowly he opened the door as he assessed the situation. Lara spoke to Darcy and Brandon about her day, Georgie and Matt had their heads together murmuring to each other, Faith and Sam were setting the table, and Amy placed plates of chopped lettuce and tomatoes on the table. "Dinner's ready." She glanced at him and her smile became guarded. "Sit wherever you want, Arthur."

Talk ceased.

Shit. He almost turned and walked out, but Sam moved over to him and said, "You haven't met Darcy and Matt yet." He indicated the men.

Darcy stepped forward, hand outstretched and a smile on his face. "Welcome."

How could one word slay him? While Arthur's mind reeled at the simple acceptance, his body reacted automatically, shaking Darcy's hand. He cleared his throat. "Thanks for having me."

"Nice to meet you," Matt said.

Arthur nodded. "Likewise."

"Why don't you sit next to me, Arthur?" Faith patted the seat next to her.

He stumbled to the seat, his brain still processing the genuineness of the greeting. Surely they had to dislike him for the way he'd treated Amy.

Amy finished putting taco shells and tortillas on the table and then took a seat at the opposite end to him.

"Dig in!" Lara cried and helped herself to a taco shell.

Dinner reminded Arthur of his days as a young recruit, sitting around the mess hall tables with people talking across the table at each other. Noise and laughter, cameraderie. If he allowed himself to think back even further, it was reminiscent of before he joined the army, when the major was away on a mission and it was just his mum, Amy, and him sitting around the table talking about their day. There'd been a lot of laughter, arguments and noise then. When the major was back, dinner had been a silent affair, as if talking messed with digestion somehow.

Though Arthur said nothing, he enjoyed listening. The banter and love was so strong it was difficult to feel resentful about it. Not when this was the family Amy had finally found. She deserved happiness.

He put together a taco and as he crunched into the hard corn shell, it took him straight back to his youth. Tacos had been his mother's go-to meal for something quick and easy when she didn't feel like cooking and they were his favourite meal. She had made them chop the vegetables and grate the cheese while she cooked the beef, and then they'd all sat down to what was always a messy meal. He swallowed hard. How could he have forgotten?

"Everything all right?" Faith murmured next to him.

He sat holding the taco shell in front of him, staring at nothing. With a jerk, he nodded and took a second bite. Was it a coincidence, or had Amy remembered?

Amy chatted with Georgie at the other end of the table. She looked settled. The Stokes had been more family to her than he had been. How could he ever make it up to her?

"Faith, Arthur promised to help at the pony club sleepover." Lara's announcement silenced the table.

Arthur fought the urge to squirm as all eyes turned to him.

"Brave man." Matt raised his glass. "I remember what we were like as kids. It'll take some wrangling to keep them all together."

Faith made a shooing motion at him. "Ignore Matt. The kids are lovely and mostly well-behaved, but I'd appreciate another helper."

Sam and Brandon just smirked at him. Bastards. Had they set him up?

If they had, he couldn't help but admire their work. He hadn't suspected a thing. "I don't know how to ride."

"That's fine," Faith said. "The horses will follow each other and all I need is another pair of eyes to make sure they don't go in different directions."

"The kids?" he asked.

"Yeah, they might go off trail if they see something interesting."

Great. But he'd figure it out. How hard could it be?

He caught Amy watching him but couldn't read her expression. Was she impressed, annoyed, nonplussed? Before he could figure it out, Lara spoke again.

"Have you shown him the journal yet, Sam?"

"Not yet. I've been meaning to."

She had to be talking about Brandon's ancestor's journal. The ancestor who had been shipwrecked off the coast in the late eighteen hundreds and had discovered another wreck full of treasure. Lilian had buried her portion of the treasure for later if the family needed it.

"We should show him now." Lara pushed back her chair, but Darcy stopped her with a hand on her arm.

"Wait until we've finished dinner."

She pouted but sat back down.

Arthur loved her enthusiasm. She was so full of life, something that had been missing from his soulless hospital room for so many months. She was like a natural painkiller, helping his pain fade into the background.

After dinner, he stood to help with the dishes, but Lara grabbed his hand. "Come on. You have to read the journal."

He glanced over at Sam, who grinned and nodded, and so he followed Lara down a hallway full of family photos. He didn't have a chance to look as Lara tugged him forward. "This way." She pulled him into a lounge room where the couches sagged with age but looked as if you could settle in for a night and not want to move.

Had he ever let himself do that?

On the coffee table were photocopies of two journals. Lara pushed him onto a couch and handed him one. "This is Lilian's. She was my great, great, great whatever grandmother." She climbed next to him and sat on her shins, watching him with excitement.

Did she expect him to come up with a clue no one else had seen? "It might take me a while to read it."

"It's amazing. She sailed from England on a convict ship and she'd only just met and married her awful husband. Spoiler alert, he dies and one of the convicts takes his identity because they're in love." Lara clasped her hands together, her eyes shining.

Arthur vaguely remembered Sam talking about it when Arthur had been in hospital, but he hadn't been interested in the rest of the world. "Sounds exciting."

Lara nodded and tapped the document. "You should read the whole thing. The clues are at the end though, because they don't find the treasure until they get here."

Intrigue filled him. His favourite stories as a kid were mysteries. He'd read under the covers by torchlight until the early hours of the morning to find out what happened. At least he did when his father wasn't home. That kind of diversion from routine wasn't acceptable to the major—bedtime had to be strictly adhered to.

He began reading and was caught up in the tale of a woman who was moving to a strange land with a husband she barely knew and who made no efforts to form a bond with her. She was a trophy, as far as Arthur could tell.

He was so caught up in the story, he barely noticed Brandon place a mug of tea on the coffee table for him. He grunted a thanks and kept reading.

By the time he was finished, he was cheering for Lilian and her convict lover. He placed the manuscript on the table and glanced around. Lara wasn't next to him anymore and the lounge room was empty. He checked the time. Nine o'clock. Where was everyone?

His skin tightened as he got to his feet, placing the manuscript on the coffee table and wandering down the hallway.

His footsteps slowed as the wall of photos caught his attention. Each child had the same photos; birth, first day of school, graduation and then next to Brandon's was also a wedding photo of him and Amy. They both looked so incredibly happy.

Guilt stabbed him. He should have been here, should have walked his sister down the aisle or something. If he'd been here, he wouldn't have lost his leg. Was it punishment for being such a shit brother?

He never should have listened to his father. Should have trusted his team mates instead. Then none of this would have happened.

The wall was such a celebration of life and family. The major wouldn't have stood for such sentimentality or haphazardness. Their house had only standard photo frames, all white, with posed photos in them.

Why had his mother stayed with his father?

The question made him step back, away from the wall. He'd never considered it, had always thought the major was master of their domain and everyone had to follow his rule. As he grew older, he tried to take on the role whenever his father went away, but it was always difficult to get Amy and his mother to do what he said. And if he was honest with himself, he enjoyed the stuff they did when the major was gone—movie nights, trips to the water parks, picnics in the country. But then the major would come home, and Arthur would disappoint him by forgetting everything he'd been taught, and not being disciplined enough.

A scrape of a chair brought his attention back to the present. Taking a deep breath, he continued to the kitchen where Amy, Brandon and Sam were seated. Perhaps the others had already gone to bed. Sam had mentioned they were early risers at the Ridge.

Amy smiled at him. "Are you finished?"

He nodded.

"What did you think?" Sam asked.

"Fascinating story."

Brandon sipped his tea. "Anything that seems like a clue?"

"Just that line about food, water and shelter colliding."

Amy nodded. "We've looked everywhere, but the landscape would have changed over the past hundred and fifty years."

Excitement stirred at the thought of unlocking the clues and finding the treasure. It was something he needed his brain for. His leg didn't matter. "Have you got notes on where you've looked?"

Amy rolled her eyes. "The major was my father as well. Of course, I've got meticulous notes. I'll email them to you."

He jolted. Amy had always seemed more carefree as a kid. She hadn't let the major's strictness stop her from doing what she wanted, though she usually waited until he was away. "Thanks."

Brandon shook his head. "I sometimes forget you two are related to him. You're nothing like him."

Arthur stared at his friend, shock coursing through him. "You don't think so?" He'd tried his very best to be everything the major wanted him to be.

"Hell no. You're a marshmallow wearing kevlar, and Ames…" He took his wife's hand and kissed it… "is sunshine and warmth."

When had Brandon got all poetic? "Marshmallow?"

"We saw through your defences years ago," Sam told him with a grin.

Arthur lowered himself into a chair, trying not to smile. They'd been teasing him for years and he'd done his best to pretend like he didn't enjoy it, but he didn't have to pretend anymore. There was no one he could disappoint. "That's because I had to feed your egos."

He smothered his smile at the absolute shock on Brandon's and Sam's faces.

Brandon turned to Sam. "Is he trash talking us?"

"He's trying to," Sam replied. "Needs a bit more work until he's up to our level."

Arthur snorted but said nothing. Let them think what they wanted.

Sam slapped him on the back. "We should get going.

These oldies need to go to bed."

Arthur awkwardly got to his feet. This was ridiculous. It was time he got the hang of the leg. He'd been wallowing for far too long. "Thanks for dinner." He glanced at Brandon and then at Amy. They hadn't really spoken all night.

Coward.

The issue was he had no idea how to start the conversation with his sister. He followed Sam outside. No, he couldn't leave without saying something. "Amy…"

She studied him. "Yes?"

Crap, now what was he supposed to say? "Thank you."

She nodded and Brandon slid his arm around her waist, waiting for him to say more. The only problem was, he didn't have the words. "See you on the weekend."

He hurried down the steps, relieved Sam was already getting in the car. It wasn't until they reached the main road that Sam said, "It's a start."

Was he referring to the thanks or the fact Arthur had spoken more tonight than he had in the past few months?

"Lara's pretty special."

"So is Amy."

"I know." And eventually he'd figure out what to say to her.

Because if tonight had taught him anything, it was that he wanted his sister back in his life.

Chapter 6

Jordan still wasn't speaking to Gretchen the next morning. Discovering the truth about his father was a lot to take in. She tried not to let it bother her, but it was reminiscent of the way Kurt would shut her out and not talk to her when she'd done anything he disapproved of. His cold shoulder could last weeks.

It was not behaviour she wanted to cultivate in Jordan.

She got the muesli out of the cupboard and chopped an apple to go on top as Jordan dragged his feet from his bedroom into the kitchen. "Would you like toast or cereal?"

Jordan took the bread from the cupboard and put two slices in the toaster.

Right. "Would you like Vegemite?" She took the condiment out of the fridge and added peanut butter and strawberry jam to the table as well so he could have his pick. "Can I make you a Milo?"

She poured herself a cup of tea while she waited for an answer. He always had a Milo in the morning, but if he wouldn't answer her, she wasn't making him one.

"What have you got on at school today?"

The scrape of the butter knife over the toast put her teeth on edge. "Looks like it will be a nice day," she continued. "Should be good visibility on the boat. The passengers will be pleased."

Jordan stuffed the peanut butter slathered toast in his mouth and made a show of chewing.

"It's only about ten weeks until Christmas. You'll have to start your Christmas list."

His eyes widened, and he opened his mouth to speak before shutting it firmly.

Nearly had him. But if he wouldn't talk about what he wanted for Christmas, he was in this for the long haul. She finished her breakfast. "I love you, sweetheart, and I understand you're still upset. You can spend the day processing it, but then we're going to talk. It's much better to talk things through than stew on them."

He scowled, then pushed away from the table, his chair squealing on the linoleum floor, and stalked to his room.

Gretchen sighed. At least this time he didn't slam the door. She finished getting ready and then called, "Time to go to school."

Jordan surprised her by coming straight out, but the car trip to the school was icy and not even his favourite song on the radio thawed him.

Tonight after pony club, she would sit with him and talk. Surely he couldn't keep the silence up for much longer.

She froze, remembering Kurt's threat about a horse bolting. She'd given him no information. Would he hurt Jordan in response?

A car beeped behind her and she flinched, driving out of the school carpark.

Could she text him to say she had information that she'd give him tonight? No, he'd likely call demanding it straight away. And even if he didn't, when she didn't deliver, he would be angry enough to escalate things.

Gretchen would have to think of something.

She pushed the threat to the back of her mind when she arrived at the boat. Sam and Arthur were already on board, and Arthur was checking through the equipment, getting it ready for the day. Finally out of the cabin.

"Morning!" she called and put her backpack in the cabin before joining Arthur on the deck. "Need a hand?"

His smile was a little awkward, as if he couldn't remember how to. "I'm finished. Do you want to check?"

That smooth voice again, it sent shivers down her spine. "Sure."

She went through the list and found there was nothing left to do. "Perfect. I'd better watch out. You might put me out of a job."

He cracked a smile. Then he shuffled his feet. "I, ah, wanted to apologise about yesterday."

She frowned. "What for?"

"I was rude. I appreciate you fetching my leg." His cheeks heated as he looked her in the eye. "Thank you."

The intensity of his gaze, as if she was his only focus, was something else. "You're welcome. I know it can be tricky. You're doing well."

He said nothing else but nodded and returned to the cabin. Gretchen climbed upstairs to where Sam sat in the captain's chair. "All done. Arthur did most of it."

Sam grinned. "Did he say much?"

She shook her head.

"That's his style."

Gretchen hesitated and then lowered her voice. "He seems happier today."

"He met Lara yesterday and seems to have had a

shift in attitude."

Gretchen loved Lara, but she was surprised the girl could have that much influence in one meeting. "What did she say?"

"Invited him to go horse riding. Not sure what else she said when they went out to the horse yard, but Arthur seemed a little different when he got back."

Curiosity stirred in her. She knew from the practicums she'd done as an occupational therapist that some people were so focused on what they'd lost that they wouldn't listen to what they could become. How had Lara broken through?

"See if you can get him to go swimming today," Sam continued. "Even if it's just the snorkelling."

"Sure." Sam had asked him every day. Perhaps today would be the day he said yes. He wasn't putting out miserable vibes, which was nice.

That reminded her of Jordan and the threat. Maybe Sam could tell her something. "How's everyone at the Ridge?"

"They're great. They've got a few campers out there at the moment."

"Good. I was a little worried. Amy looked tired the last time I saw her."

Sam tilted his head slightly. "I think the situation with Arthur is stressing her out."

Gretchen nodded. Of course it would, but Amy had been tired before that.

The marina gate clanged open as the passengers arrived along with the rest of the crew and it was all hands on deck while they got everyone suited up and Sam took them out of the marina. Arthur sat on the top level next to Sam. He wore long pants still, so it had to be warm up there, but he seemed more relaxed than he had spending all day in the cabin.

When they reached the snorkelling spot, it was her

turn to stay on the boat and monitor the passengers in the water. When everyone was in, she spent her time making notes against the passengers' names. The deck was clear, and Sam and Arthur were on the top deck still. Gretchen remembered what Sam had asked her. She went to the base of the ladder. "Arthur, are you going to jump in today?"

Silence. Then finally he said, "Maybe tomorrow."

Satisfaction filled her at getting a response. He may not have made any promises, but at least he'd responded.

The rest of her day was filled with chatting to customers, helping them with their equipment, and preparing and cleaning up from the meals. It was simple work, and she enjoyed being outdoors, enjoyed helping people. It got a little rough as they were heading back in, and she handed out a few emesis bags, stumbling over the deck a little. Arthur still sat on the top deck, and he seemed content where he was. She'd even caught him talking to a passenger, though she hadn't heard the conversation. It was far better than he'd been last week. She'd been worried his accident yesterday as they'd disembarked might have set him back.

After the passengers left, Gretchen spent some time cleaning the seating around the boat and then stretched. She was done for the day.

"I'm off," she called to Sam, who was in the cabin with Arthur. "I've got to pick Jordan up from pony club."

Arthur sat a little straighter. "Is that the one Faith runs?"

"Yeah. Lara will be there." She checked her watch. "They've still got about half an hour, if you want to come."

Arthur hesitated.

"Go on, mate," Sam said. "I need to do a few things

here. I'll meet you back at the town house."

He was still for a long moment, thinking things through. Finally, he nodded. "All right. Thanks." He shifted to his feet, putting far more weight on his good leg than his prosthetic one. Lacking trust it would hold him. How regularly was he doing his exercises?

They walked to her car. For anyone else who was new in town, she'd ask how long they were staying, but it could be a loaded question. She wasn't certain he was here by choice.

"Is Jordan your son?"

She jumped, not expecting him to talk. "Yes. He's ten, like Lara."

"His dad can't pick him up?"

She shuddered. "I hope not." Damn, that was the wrong thing to say.

Sure enough, Arthur asked, "Why not?"

"He's not interested. He's not seen Jordan in five years, so if he turned up now, it wouldn't be a good thing." She'd told no one he was in town. The only person who had seen him was Penelope at Dot's birthday a few weeks ago, but Gretchen had told her he was a random guy asking her out.

"Do you have family up here?"

It would figure that he'd get chatty about the one subject she didn't want to talk about. "It's just Jordan and me. My parents live in Melbourne." Time to turn the tables. "Do you and Amy have any other siblings?"

"No." He turned to look out the window. "Are you friends with her?"

"Yeah. Georgie introduced us when Amy first moved to town."

"How long ago was that?"

"Around the beginning of the year." She hadn't known then about Amy's estranged relationship with her family, but she had recognised a kindred spirit wandering to find a place to belong. Amy had found her home here. Gretchen had thought Retribution Bay could be that for her and Jordan too, but Kurt might change that.

Speaking of which… She tried for casual as she asked, "Did she tell you about what happened to Matt?"

He glanced at her. "What do you know about it?"

Shit. What had Kurt said? "Not many details. Just that he was kidnapped and something about animal smuggling." She hoped the two events were related.

Arthur nodded. "It was bad."

Gretchen pulled into the pony club, which was just outside of town. The group of children sat in the centre of the ring, mounted on their horses, listening to Faith. Three barrels were set out in the arena in a triangular shape. Jordan had his horse close to Lara's, his hands relaxed on the reins, not the least bit prepared if his horse was to get startled. Fear gripped her. How could she warn him without sounding like a hysterical mother?

"Do the kids own their horses?" Arthur asked as they walked towards the seating surrounding the ring.

His question divided her focus. "No. There's three or four which belong to people in town and Faith received permission for the kids to ride them on Tuesdays. It's a good solution. The horses get fed and exercised, and the parents don't have to buy one." Thankfully. She couldn't afford a horse.

Lara spotted them and waved. Jordan made a point of turning his head away. Gretchen sighed. "Looks as if Jordan is still angry with me." Yelling at him to tighten his grip would not go down well. She gritted her teeth. She'd thought she'd escaped this life, the control Kurt had over her with mere words.

"Is he the boy next to Lara?"

"Yeah. How do you know?"

"He has the same blonde hair and your nose."

She frowned. "My nose?" What an odd thing to notice.

"It turns up a little at the end." His cheeks reddened, and he looked at the arena. "Are all the kids going out to the Ridge for the sleepover?"

"I think so. How do you know about it?"

He rubbed his knee. "Lara asked me to chaperone."

Gretchen grinned. "That's great. There was a remarked lack of volunteers when Faith asked the parents."

"I didn't say I agreed."

She glanced at the young girl who was high-fiving her best friend, Mischa. "You said no to Lara?"

A snort. "Does anyone say no to Lara?"

"I'm pretty sure Darcy's the only one who can." The group lined up across from the furthest barrel with Lara at the front. "You ever seen barrel racing?"

Arthur shook his head.

Faith blew a whistle and Lara's horse exploded into action. She thundered towards the first barrel, sticking to the left and circling the barrel before galloping towards the next barrel and circling it to the right and then circling the final barrel and racing to the finish line.

Fast.

It was the only word for it. Lara leaned low on her horse's neck and encouraged it all the way. When she reached the finish line, Gretchen let out a breath.

"Wow," Arthur breathed. "She's good."

"She could ride before she could walk," Gretchen said. "There are a few jealous kids amongst the group."

Jordan was up next. Gretchen took out her phone to time him, her finger trembling on the start button as she scanned the grounds for anyone not meant to be there. A couple of other parents watched, but aside from that they were empty.

Jordan's horse wasn't as explosive off the start and Jordan slowed him too much going around the barrels, but he made a decent time. Gretchen cheered as he crossed the finish line, but he didn't even look at her.

"Did you and your son have an argument?" Arthur asked.

"Yeah. He thinks he's old enough to stay by himself before and after school while I'm at work."

"What does he do now?"

"He goes to his best friend's house." She pointed Cody out. "His mum doesn't mind because they keep each other amused." Her phone beeped with a message. Absent-mindedly, she looked down. Her skin prickled. A photo with Arthur getting into her car and the words *good job*. She cleared the message and shoved her phone back into her pocket. The bastard was still watching her. She scanned the pony club again. Maybe it meant Jordan would be safe today.

"Something wrong?" Arthur asked.

Crap. Had he seen the message? "It's nothing." Two calls in two days was bad. She had to feed him something. "Look, it's Cody's turn." She pointed. Arthur studied her for a moment longer before turning his attention back to the barrel racing. She hadn't fooled him, but at least he didn't press the issue.

It wasn't long before pony club ended. The kids unsaddled their horses, brushing them, and feeding those that lived in the stables. Jordan rode his horse towards the stable, whereas Lara tied hers to the railing and ran towards Gretchen and Arthur.

"Arthur! You came!" Her delight was obvious as she hugged him.

Arthur's eyes widened as he looked down at the girl, and his hug was a little stiff. He seemed surprised at the greeting.

"Do you want to ride now?" Lara asked.

"I don't want to keep you."

Lara waved away his concern. "Nah, it's good. We have to stay to pack up and wait until all the parents arrive. There's plenty of time." She tugged on his hand, before seeming to remember Gretchen was there. "Hi, Gretchen. Do you want to ride too?"

"I'm fine, thanks." But she was a little concerned about how Arthur was going to mount. His right leg was the prosthetic one, but it might go badly. She walked with them to Lara's horse, trying to figure out how to broach the subject.

"You get on like this." Lara demonstrated, putting her left foot in the stirrup and swinging her right leg over the horse. She dismounted, and Arthur examined the stirrup.

"It's not going to work."

He needed a step up. The step platform some kids used caught her attention. "How about using that?" She pointed. At Arthur's scowl, she added, "The temporary prosthesis isn't a great fit. It will make it easier."

"How do you know?" Lara asked.

"I'm studying occupational therapy," she replied. "Therapists help people who have had injuries or can't do the things they used to do."

"That's so cool!" Lara led her horse over to the stand and Arthur trailed after her. Gretchen kept close enough to help if she was required, but not too close to crowd them. Kurt had mentioned something about Lara being kidnapped as well. What had that been about? The girl didn't seem to have any lasting effects. Could Gretchen ask Lara how she was?

"You did it!" Lara's excited cry drew Gretchen's attention back to them. Arthur perched stiffly on top of Starlight. "Now nudge her on the side with your heels."

Arthur did as requested and Starlight walked back into the arena. Lara seemed to have things under control, giving Arthur instructions, and Gretchen didn't want to spoil her mood by bringing up something that was probably traumatic. Instead, she went to help Jordan. He'd already removed the saddle and replaced the bridle with a halter. Now he was brushing the horse down and chatting to Cody.

"Hey, guys. That was some pretty fast riding there."

"I reckon I beat my fastest time," Jordan said.

Pleasure filled her at his joy and the fact he was talking to her. "Absolutely," she agreed. "We should have ice cream after dinner to celebrate."

"Yes!"

Cody glanced at her. "You should tell Mum I deserve ice cream too."

Gretchen chuckled. "I will."

"Who's the guy Lara's leading around?" Jordan asked. "Can't he ride?"

"He's Amy's brother. I don't think he's ever ridden before."

Natasha, one of the nastier girls at the club, said, "He needed the baby steps to mount." She laughed and a couple of the girls nearby laughed too.

No. That wasn't acceptable. "Do you know why he needed the steps?" Gretchen asked.

"Because he's a baby?"

Oh, the girl was a piece of work. "No, because he lost part of his leg in an explosion while in the army."

The girl gasped.

"He's still coming to grips with his prosthesis," Gretchen continued. "It's nasty to judge people when you don't know the complete story."

She bit her lip. "Sorry."

"You should be." Gretchen didn't have time for small-minded judgemental little so and sos. She moved back to Jordan.

"Mum, is that true?" Jordan asked. "Does he have a peg leg like a pirate?" He peered around her, staring at Arthur.

Gretchen smothered a smile. "No, he's got a prosthesis, and it's not polite to stare."

"What's a prosthesis?" Cody asked.

"It's an artificial leg," she replied. "Arthur's is made of metal and plastic."

"Have you seen it?" Jordan's eyes widened.

"Yes." But no way was she telling the boys she'd fished it out of the marina. "Now, stop staring and finish brushing your horses."

"How big do you think the explosion was?" Cody asked Jordan.

"I dunno. Do you reckon he was saving someone's life?" Jordan said.

Gretchen left them to their wondering. She'd have to warn Arthur he'd get questions. He might not be comfortable with them.

Over in the arena, Lara had Arthur trotting. His face was a picture of concentration, but his posture had relaxed somewhat as he shifted up and down. Impressive. The motion would probably rub on the cup.

Arthur winced and slowed. He rubbed below his knee and called a halt to the exercise. Good idea. He shouldn't overdo it.

"Finished," Jordan called. He and Cody had taken their horses back to the stable and closed the doors.

"Great. I just need to ask Faith about the weekend, and then we'll go." Most of the children had been picked up by now, and Faith was with Lara and Arthur.

Lara's cheeks reddened as they approached, and she shifted a little closer to Arthur, suddenly shy when Jordan was around.

"Nice riding," Gretchen said.

Arthur screwed up his nose. "Nothing like Lara."

"None of us are like Lara," Faith replied.

"What time are we due out at the Ridge on Saturday?" Gretchen asked.

"Around four," Faith replied. "We'll do a short ride at sunset before the sleepover and then a longer one in the morning, maybe to the beach, so don't forget to pack bathers."

She nodded. She'd agreed to help at the sleepover back when it was going to be during the school holidays, but it had been rained out. This weekend she was working at the shop on Saturday before taking both Cody and Jordan out to the Ridge. It felt good to be doing something for Holly for a change.

"Do you want a lift back to Sam's?" she asked Arthur.

"We'll take him," Lara said. "Won't we Faith?"

Faith smiled. "Sure, but it's up to Arthur."

Lara turned her pleading face to Arthur. No way was he going to refuse. Sure enough, he said, "I'd love a lift. Thanks Lara." He turned to Gretchen. "See you tomorrow?"

"Yeah." She waved, ignoring the disappointment, and rounded up Cody and Jordan. Better she keep her distance from him when possible. At least until she figured out how to deal with Kurt.

Arthur didn't need to be involved in her problems.

Chapter 7

The next day, Arthur was up before Sam. He stretched, feeling good aside from a slight ache in his stump in response to the trotting yesterday. No pins and needles. That was a first. Maybe the light walking and short horse ride had helped. Or perhaps it was the fact he hadn't dreamed, hadn't woken sweating from flashbacks of the explosion and spent hours staring at the ceiling, unable to go back to sleep. For the first time since he'd originally been discharged, he felt revitalised, eager for the day. He couldn't wait to read the journals again and sort through Amy's detailed notes.

The new challenge added to the relief from his pain made him giddy as he rubbed the scars and reached for his crutches. He needed a break from the socks and liners.

He shouldn't have ignored all his therapist's directions to exercise.

Arthur had been stupid. If he'd continued wearing his prosthesis after he'd been discharged the first time, he might have less pain and irritation, but he hadn't seen the point. He hadn't left the house and crutches were easier. Now, after a few minutes without pain, he could see more clearly.

In the kitchen, he examined his options. Holding mugs and using his crutches at the same time would be a little tricky. He settled on leaning the crutches against the bench and hopping around to get the items he needed. He'd just finished the coffees when Sam walked in. "Morning." He gestured to a mug. Better not to risk carrying it to him.

Sam's eyes widened. "Thanks, mate. Didn't you sleep well?"

Arthur shook his head. "I'm fine. I woke early."

Sam studied him. Looking for a lie.

He deserved it. He'd have to earn Sam's trust back. "Last night, I read the information Amy sent about the treasure. It's got me thinking. I want to read the journal again today."

"I've got a copy you can take on the boat. Just make sure you don't leave it lying around for anyone to read."

He worked better when he could write things down and see everything at once. He wouldn't be able to spread out in the cabin, not without risking someone seeing what he was working on. "I thought I'd stay here."

Sam shook his head. "You know the drill."

"The overdose was an accident."

His friend stared at him. "So you say, but the man I know doesn't accidentally take more than he needs."

Frustration filled him. "You don't understand the pain I was in. I wanted it to go away."

"How much pain are you in now?"

"Some." An ache had returned, but it wasn't the usual pins and needles.

"Then you're coming with me."

Arthur recognised the determination on Sam's face. Still, he tried. "Mate, I've been out every day for over a week. I need a break."

"Nope. Not until I see real progress."

Forced to do someone's will again. Though if he was honest, he'd made his choice both times. And he was grateful to Sam for not giving up on him. He rubbed the back of his head, unused to the length of his hair. "Listen, I ah, wanted to apologise."

Sam's eyebrows raised. "For?"

"For being such a dickhead to you. For shutting you out and ignoring you when you visited."

"Why did you?"

He huffed. "Because I resented you. You had everything I wanted, and you chose to leave the army. And I felt your pity every time you came in."

"It wasn't pity, Sherlock. It was concern. You weren't coping."

Arthur nodded. "I wasn't, but I treated you like shit, and I'm sorry." He took a deep breath. "Thank you for what you've done for me."

Sam slapped him on his shoulder, drawing him in for a brief hug. "That's what friends do, Sherlock." He smiled. "But you're still coming out on the boat today."

Relief swept through him at Sam's instant acceptance. They were OK. Sam didn't blame him or hate him. Arthur suppressed his smile and instead rolled his eyes and sighed. "Fine."

He sipped his coffee. At least he'd get to talk to Gretchen today. A highlight in his otherwise monotonous day. Speaking to her about his leg would allow him to get to know her better. Maybe find out who was contacting her, who put fear into her eyes. He'd told himself it was none of his business after she'd shoved her phone in her pocket at pony club, but later he'd remembered her reaction to the phone call after she'd fished his leg out of the marina. She had no family in town to help. Perhaps he should ask Amy if she knew what was up. He didn't want Gretchen to feel as if she was on her own.

Sam put his copy of the journal on the bench and Arthur picked it up, flicking through it. Stonefish Enterprises had triggered the whole event. They often used people in the community to do their dirty work. Gretchen was scared about something. "How much does Gretchen know about what's been going on?"

Sam frowned. "Nothing. She hasn't been involved."

Warning bells triggered. "She's friends with Amy, isn't she?"

"Yeah. They all go out together sometimes; Penny, Georgie, Amy, Faith, Dot and Nhiari."

"Could they have told her?"

"I don't know. What's this about?"

"It might be nothing." He didn't want to get Gretchen in trouble if he was making the wrong connections. "I'll look into it."

Sam finished his coffee. "OK. Let's get to it."

It didn't take long for them to get ready for the day and get to the boat. Arthur settled into the routine and the rhythm soothed him. Today, he'd packed his board shorts and a towel in his backpack. It felt like a huge, scary step forward over an abyss. He was yet to go out in anything other than long pants, not ready to face the questions and stares. The shorts were there if he was brave enough to swim. He'd be baring his soul and opening himself up for derision or pity.

Gretchen arrived, breathless as always. "I'm sorry. Jordan would not get moving this morning."

"It's all done." Finally, he could be useful.

"You're amazing," she gushed, slipping past him, a sweet, enticing fragrance like vanilla following her as she put her backpack in the cabin. "Thank you."

A warmth built inside him. He enjoyed helping her.

"I'm not usually this late," she continued. "Jordan's

going through a rough patch, which I'm hoping won't last long." She screwed up her face in apology.

"It's fine." But here was his opportunity. "It must be difficult without family in town."

A tiny flinch, but then she nodded. "It can be."

Maybe he could gain her trust by asking for something first. He considered his words. "Could you…maybe… help me with something."

"Sure." She raised her eyebrows in question.

"My leg didn't hurt much this morning. I thought maybe because I did more exercise yesterday."

She frowned. "How long have you had the prosthesis?"

"A couple of months."

"How much have you used it?"

He flushed. "Not much after I left the hospital."

"Didn't your therapist give you instructions?"

His face heated. "I didn't pay attention."

She smiled in understanding. "I'm not qualified to give advice yet, but I could write a schedule with some exercises and you could ask your therapist to approve it."

"That would be great." Not that he would go back to his therapist. He'd treated her poorly. But maybe he should call and apologise.

"When we get off the boat, I can look at your gait as well," she said. "Make sure you're walking the correct way."

He nodded. The shuffle he was currently doing wasn't great.

The bus arrived with passengers, and it wasn't long before they were motoring out of the marina. Arthur spread his notes across the table and compared what Amy had sent him with the journal clues. A few times she seemed to be reaching to make a connection, but he didn't know the Ridge like she did.

A nasty jolt over the waves made his stomach churn. He put down his pen and looked out the window at the horizon. Choppy was a nice word for the waves today. If he continued reading, he'd be sick. He should be back at the town house where he could get some actual work done. He sighed. No, he deserved Sam's caution. He'd treated his friend like shit when all he'd tried to do was help.

He gathered his papers and stuffed them in his backpack. Sam might have accepted his apology, but it would take more than words to show Sam he was healing. It was time to mend bridges. He carefully climbed the ladder to the top deck. A few other passengers had the same idea and were sitting on the seats chatting with each other. He debated sitting as well, but the canopy Sam stood under provided shade, so he stood next to him. Sweat trickled down his back. Perhaps he should wear shorts, even if it would reveal his prosthetic leg.

Sam glanced at him. "Everything all right?"

He nodded. "Too choppy to read."

"Yeah, the forecast is for the swell to die down by midday. I hope it's accurate." A brief flash of concern over Sam's face.

Arthur hadn't thought much about his friend's new venture. He'd been too busy feeling sorry for himself. "How's the business going?"

"Good so far, though I haven't really done anything. Rob was fully booked before I bought it. I'll have to see how it goes over the off season."

"What will you do?"

"I've already got a booking from the maritime museum, which starts next week after the season ends. Georgie discovered the Dutch wreck from that journal, and they're sending maritime archaeologists up to do some research. Guy in charge is called Oliver, and he wants to use my boat."

That could be interesting. He'd love to dive a wreck. "They didn't send anyone straight away?"

"The museum didn't have the resources to do more than a cursory examination. They've hired the boat for a week with the possibility to extend."

"Will you keep your entire crew on?"

Sam shook his head. "No, most have other jobs lined up. It's a seasonal thing."

Arthur glanced around the boat. "You can captain this thing by yourself?"

"I could do with a first mate, if you're interested."

He blinked. He hadn't thought about what he would do for work now, but it could be intriguing to be part of an archaeological investigation. "Yeah, all right."

Sam grinned. "Great. Thanks." He slowed the boat as they reached the snorkel spot. The swell had decreased, and it was pleasant. Arthur stayed on the top deck until the others were in the water. It looked cool and inviting. If he was quick, he could change into his shorts and go for a swim. He might even make it back on deck before any of the passengers, and no one would see his stump. "I might jump in."

Sam's eyebrows raised. "Go for it. You've got time."

He moved down the ladder and into the cabin. No one was around except Gretchen, who stood at the back of the boat near the marlin board watching the swimmers.

The problem was how to get changed quickly. Should he take off his leg now, or wait until he went into the water? The longer he spent debating his options, the less time he'd have for swimming. He needed it to walk to the stern of the boat.

Stupid.

He changed into his shorts and stared down at the fake leg; plastic foot, metal bone and silicone cup with its sock.

Freak.

"Are you going swimming?"

He flinched at Gretchen's voice. She stood in the doorway, an encouraging smile on her face.

He couldn't back out now.

"Maybe."

"What size flipper do you take?"

"Twelve."

"I'll grab you one." She hesitated. "Unless you want two?"

"One's fine." When she left, he got to his feet and walked onto the deck. Upstairs, Sam spoke with another crew member.

Gretchen brought over the fin and goggles. "Do you want me to hold your leg?"

This was awkward, but it helped she was being so matter-of-fact about it. "Yeah."

There was a step up from the marlin board, so he sat there, took off his leg, tipped out the sweat which had gathered in the cup and handed it to Gretchen. He rubbed his stump, conscious of the red scars, and quickly put the fin on his remaining foot.

"Here." Gretchen passed him suncream. "If you don't put it on your leg, it's likely to burn badly."

And that would make the prosthesis far more uncomfortable. Quickly he added the cream, then slipped on the goggles and slid into the water.

Refreshing. Cool enough to provide relief from the heat, but not cold enough to provide a chill. The water was clear and the clumps of coral teamed with life. He kicked in the opposite direction from the rest of the group. He tensed, the weirdness of only one fin powering him along, throwing him off balance. His other leg kicked, but did next to nothing to provide movement.

Arthur gritted his teeth. Get used to it. It was different, not bad. He exhaled and adjusted his rhythm to account for it. Then a turtle grazing on the coral caught his attention, and he forgot about his body.

He swam closer, the turtle unconcerned about his nearness as it continued to eat. Nearby, fluorescent blue fish darted around some stag coral and rainbow wrasse drifted with the sway of the water.

Beautiful. Peaceful. He could forget about his injury, forget about everything happening above the surface, and immerse himself in this world.

He dived under to peer beneath an undercroft where he could see a crayfish, some of its feelers exposed but the rest of its body blended with the coral. As he surfaced for a breath, another swimmer approached. He tensed until he recognised the bright blue of her bathers.

Gretchen.

Had Sam sent her to babysit him?

He lifted his head, and she took her snorkel from her mouth. "I hope you don't mind me joining you. Sam said I could jump in."

Arthur scowled. "Sam wanted you to monitor me."

She smiled. "Maybe, but it means I get an extra swim, which is always a bonus. I can go over there if you want."

That would only make him seem like an idiot. "No, it's fine. Did you see the turtle?"

Her face lit up with a grin. "No. Where?"

He pointed it out, and they swam together, side by side, as they made their way to the next clump of coral. Gretchen grabbed his hand to point out a sting ray gliding along the bottom. Though her touch was fleeting, it left a warmth behind. Connection. Something he had been a long time without.

A few large snapper swam near him, unconcerned

because this area of the reef was a no fishing zone and there was no danger. Some long pale pipe fish kept close to the bottom, swimming in small schools.

He shifted to look around and caught a dark shape gliding towards him. No, not gliding, almost flying with a dip and raise of its wings.

Manta ray.

He grabbed Gretchen's hand, and they floated side by side as the huge ray swam closer.

Epic.

When it had almost reached them, it did a loop, flashing its white underbelly as it did a full somersault in the water. Then, with a couple of flaps, it zipped out of sight.

Arthur let out the breath he hadn't realised he'd been holding. He met Gretchen's eyes. A connection sparked. A shared experience.

Gretchen surfaced and removed her snorkel. "Wow."

He nodded. There weren't many words to use. "Incredible." Could he capture its majesty on paper? It made him feel insignificant, as if his problems weren't worth much in the scheme of things. There was an immense world full of wonders which he should focus on rather than its horrors.

"It was like he was showing off for us," she continued. "That's pretty special."

"Do you see them much?"

"Mostly from the boat, but occasionally passengers get to swim with a manta as well as the whale shark or humpbacks." She smiled. "I rarely get a good look, because all the passengers are jostling for position."

He'd never considered it from her point of view. "I'm glad you got to now."

"Me too." She glanced over at the boat. "We should head back."

The other passengers were already climbing on board. Damn it. He'd wanted to be back in the cabin before they finished swimming. Now he would have to parade in front of them as he got out. They'd all see he was missing part of his leg.

His mouth set in a firm line as he nodded. As he replaced his snorkel, Gretchen touched his arm. "I know it's hard for you. I should have told you to go back earlier."

"Not your fault."

"I can board first and get your leg. They'll be too busy with food to notice you putting it back on, and then you can wrap a towel around your waist."

Her words released some of his tension. "Thanks."

By the time they reached the boat, everyone was on board. Gretchen lifted herself onto the marlin board with practised ease, her bathers stretching over her deliciously round butt. Arthur blinked, surprised by the wave of lust shooting through him. He floated nearby while she fetched his leg and wrapped a towel around it to hide it as she moved through the passengers. Thinking of everything.

He hoisted himself up, sitting back on the step and dried what was left of his leg and slipped the liner, socks and prosthesis on. Gretchen stayed next to him, his sentinel, until he climbed to his feet and wrapped the towel around his waist. It wasn't quite long enough to cover all of the leg, but it hid it somewhat.

No one paid him any attention. They stood in groups, holding plates of food, chatting about what they'd seen. He moved towards the cabin, eager to get his pants back on. On his way, he passed the food table where a woman was adding food to her plate. She turned and crashed into him. Fruit hit his bare chest, as did the cold liquid in her cup.

"Shit! I'm so sorry."

Arthur steadied her and as he did so, his towel fell to the ground, his leg exposed.

Damn. Before he could grab it, the woman dumped her plate and cup on the table and snatched some napkins, dabbing at his moist chest, her face bright red. Awkward.

Arthur grabbed her hands to stop her, as across from him a man murmured, "He's got a prosthetic leg."

The woman next to him replied, "Who cares about the leg? My eyes are on his glorious chest."

Arthur glanced up. The man who had mentioned his leg shot the woman an annoyed look, but the woman didn't notice, too busy staring at Arthur, or rather Arthur's chest. She grinned and waved. "Amazing pecs."

His whole body flushed. He had no words. There was no derision or disgust. She was checking him out. Before he could figure out what to do, Gretchen was there, gently turning the woman who was still dabbing at his chest. "It's fine. There's a shower where he can clean up." She handed Arthur his towel.

His brain still hadn't quite kicked into gear. He scanned the deck, but those who had noticed the incident weren't staring at his leg. In fact, several women were looking with appreciation at his chest.

Embarrassment of a different sort crept in. Usually, it was full of self-loathing and disgust, but this embarrassment held a little pride. He'd worked hard when he was in the army to keep his fitness up, but he had done little since the accident. But they didn't care he wasn't in as good shape as he used to be.

He hurried into the cabin, wrapping the towel around his waist as he did so. They weren't treating him like a cripple, but like a man.

Arthur sat, trying to come to terms with the shift in realisation.

His lips quirked as he glanced outside where a few women still looked his way.

Hell.

Sam walked in. "You're creating quite a stir with my passengers. You better put that chest away before someone gets injured." He tossed Arthur a shirt.

"Shut up." Arthur slipped it on.

Sam chuckled. "You're like a tomato right now. You were never great at dealing with attention from the ladies."

"I never thought I'd have that problem again."

"That's stupid. There will always be women out there who think your ugly mug is attractive."

Arthur snorted. He could always rely on Sam to make him laugh.

A tap on the door and Gretchen poked her head in. "Everything OK?" She handed him a packet of wet wipes.

Her smile again. Like a warm hug. "Yeah. Thanks." Now he thought about it, his chest was a little sticky.

"Great. I can't guarantee you won't get requests for photos later if you go swimming again." She hesitated and then added, "It might be worth using the wipes to clean any residual suncream from your leg, otherwise you might get a rash."

When he nodded, she headed back to the deck and began chatting with passengers.

"She's single," Sam said.

His heart jumped. "What?"

"She doesn't have a partner. Not sure what the story is about Jordan's father, though."

"He's out of the picture. Hasn't seen them in years." The words had left his mouth before he realised it was the wrong thing to say.

Sam smirked. "How do you know?"

"It's no big deal. Gretchen mentioned it yesterday

when she took me to the pony club."

"Sure." He continued to grin. "Anyway, she's a great woman—if you're interested."

He'd not considered getting romantically involved with anyone in a long time. The army had been his mistress and he couldn't be like his father and abandon his family whenever the army called. Better he be alone. "Don't you have a boat to steer?"

He laughed. "Yeah. Join me up top when you've recovered."

After Sam had gone, Arthur allowed his smile to show and started cleaning his chest.

Chapter 8

That night Arthur managed to convince Sam to take Penelope out for dinner and he was finally on his own. He spread his notes out over the table and flicked open his notebook, pausing at the sketches. The temptation to draw the manta ray he'd seen that day was strong, but so was the pull to solve the mystery of the treasure.

Mission first. That had been his mantra his whole life.

But he was no longer in the army. Was there a ticking clock to find the treasure? Was it arrogant of him to think he could solve it when no one else had?

Maybe he could do both. Set an alarm, spend an hour sketching while the image was still clear in his head and then move on to the journals. That way he could draw without worrying about Sam arriving home and interrupting him.

He smiled, set the alarm, and picked up his pencil.

The beep of his alarm sounded what felt like only moments later, but he had the full sketch of the manta ray done, its belly exposed as it did its backwards somersault. He smiled, feeling the motion of the animal in the sketch.

Satisfied, he put the drawing aside and went through Amy's notes again from the beginning. She'd printed off a satellite map of the Ridge and next to buildings she'd marked dates of when they'd been built. Then she'd highlighted all the possible options for shelters, like caves and outcrops.

In the margins she'd written *storm surge?*

He nodded. It was possible that the cyclone had exposed areas which had since been covered in sand, which would make finding it again next to impossible.

But Lilian must have left more clues.

He didn't know why she didn't just leave a map. They were isolated out here, even now, a hundred and fifty years later. It wasn't likely someone would walk into the house and steal it.

Lilian would have had a horse or camel, and maybe a cart for transport. They couldn't have carried it far, which meant closer to the coast was the best option.

He picked up his phone and rang Brandon.

"Hi, Arthur." Amy.

His attention was ripped away from the map. "Ames." Shit, he wasn't prepared for her. "I'm, ah, just going through your notes."

"What do you think?"

"They're meticulous." Easy praise. Their father would have been impressed. "How far is it from the coast to the Ridge on horseback?"

"Takes a couple of hours."

So quite the distance if they'd needed to get to the treasure in a hurry. But maybe they'd kept a few pieces on hand in the cellar in case. "Would they have kept the treasure close?"

Amy was quiet for a moment. "The mutiny sounds awful. If I'd been her, I would have kept it as far away as possible to keep my family safe."

His heart twinged at the word family. Did she include him? "The only others who knew about it were the pearl divers, right?"

"As far as we know."

"If they did steal the original Dutch journal, it might have taken them awhile to get it translated."

"Yeah, they wouldn't have trusted many, and the police were looking for the journal."

It could have taken them months or years to return to Retribution Bay. He tapped his pen on the map. "OK." He hesitated. "Ah, you've done a great job with your notes."

"Thanks."

What should he say now? He didn't want to get into anything personal over the phone. He should look her in the eye when he tried to patch their relationship. "Bye."

He pressed the hang up button milliseconds after he heard her say, "Why—"

Damn. Should he call her back?

His finger hovered over the button, his heart racing. What had she been about to ask? Was he ready for her questions?

He'd never be ready, but he had to face them. Not over the phone though. He'd speak to her on the weekend. He placed his phone onto the table and went back to work.

***

The weekend arrived far too quickly for Arthur's liking. He kept himself busy on the boat, interacting a little more with the passengers as they motored along, but in the back of his mind he knew he would be seeing Amy tonight. But he still hadn't figured out the words he needed.

Georgie picked him up from the marina.

"How was your day?" she asked as they drove out of town.

"Nice." He glanced at her. She was the only one who'd stated conditions on her acceptance of him and he appreciated her loyalty to Amy. "I've been reading the journals."

"Find anything new?"

"No. I'd like to look at the plaque with the names on it."

"We might get a chance to go down to the gulf this weekend."

Great.

"If not, I've probably got a photo of it somewhere." Georgie sighed. "I want to strangle Lilian some days. She hid the treasure so her ancestors had help when they needed it, but a fat lot of good that is if we can't find it."

The frustration in her voice made him frown. "How badly do you need it?"

She glanced at him. "What have Brandon and Sam told you of the situation?"

Cagey. He respected that. "Sam gave me a brief rundown on what Stonefish have been up to; the animal smuggling and poaching."

"That's not all. They've been trying to run the Ridge into the ground, and force us to sell. They even kidnapped Lara to try and get us to sign the lease over."

Arthur jolted. That he didn't know. "So you need the money?"

"Yeah. I've been trying to get out of my lease in town so I can save the money and move back to the Ridge. Faith and I are keeping it afloat right now."

Shit. He hadn't realised it was that bad. He needed to find the treasure for them. "How many others know about this?"

"Just the family, Sam and Penelope, and of course

Dot and Nhiari.”

“Dot and Nhiari?”

“Sergeant Dot Campbell and Senior Constable Nhiari Roe,” Georgie explained. “The local police.”

“Gretchen doesn’t know?”

Georgie shook her head. “We’re keeping it as quiet as we can. We don’t want anyone else to be a target for Stonefish.”

Unease stirred in his gut. “Are you two close?”

“She’s one of my besties,” Georgie said. “Why do you ask?”

He was quiet.

“Do you like her?”

“She’s nice.” OK, that was a fib. She was more than nice. He looked forward to seeing her every day, but with Georgie’s news, it might be wise to keep his distance. He’d have to ask Penelope if she’d spoken to Gretchen about what was going on. Gretchen could be a prime candidate for Stonefish’s manipulation.

“OK, it’s my turn to ask questions,” Georgie said.

He tensed.

“When are you going to apologise to Amy?”

Arthur rubbed his knee as the tingles started. How to explain? He looked out at the straggly bushes rushing past his window, the red dirt such a contrast with the bright blue sky.

“Arthur?”

He winced. “Sorry. I always spend too much time thinking before I speak.”

“So you’re not just ignoring me?”

“No, but I kind of want to.”

Georgie’s burst of laughter surprised him, but made him smile. “I don’t have the words to apologise.”

“Just tell her why you acted the way you did. That’s all she wants to know.”

“I’m not sure she’ll understand.”

"Well you won't know until you try, and hanging up on her isn't the way to start."

He groaned. "I didn't mean to."

"You could have called her back."

"I know." Her words weren't harsh and she was right. "I'm trying."

She smiled at him. "I know what you're going through is hard, but Amy went through similar hardship when she was only fifteen. You need to fix this."

Her words sank deep. He was still so self-absorbed. He had to do better. "I will."

***

Spending her day off chaperoning a group of mostly ten-year-olds was not what Gretchen really wanted to do, but she'd promised weeks ago. Back when Jordan was delightful and wouldn't mind his mum being there. She locked the small shop front the tour business had in town and headed to her car, glad she'd packed their things the night before. It was still warm, and she double-checked she'd packed sun cream before she drove to Cody's place to pick up both Jordan and his friend. Holly met her at the door.

"They're so excited, it's been hard containing them for the day. I had to send them to the oval to kick a football for an hour, so they wiped off some energy."

"Alone?" Kurt could have got to them.

"No, Ernest went with them."

Cody's father. Good. Before Gretchen could reply, the two boys stormed down the corridor, Cody with his backpack slung over his shoulder and Jordan carrying his sleeping bag.

"Hi, Mum. Are we going?"

Jordan's enthusiastic welcome cheered her. He'd been moody on and off for the past week about not being allowed by himself at home and what she'd said about his father. "Yeah. Are you ready?"

"Yes!" Both boys chimed and pushed past her to race to the car with Jordan yelling, "Shotgun."

"Better you than me," Holly sighed. "Good luck."

Gretchen laughed. "It will be fun." She hoped. She wasn't the best horse-rider. Was she supposed to go with the kids or just supervise the sleepover part? "I'll bring Cody back tomorrow afternoon."

"We should be home all day, so don't worry about the time."

Gretchen wanted to give back to Holly, so if the boys weren't too tired after the sleepover, maybe she'd take them snorkelling. She returned to the car where Jordan was sitting in the front seat. Though she let him sit there around town, she wasn't as keen about having him there for a long drive. "Hop in the back, mate," she said. "You'll be able to talk to Cody more easily."

He pouted but did as she asked.

Her phone beeped, and she took a second to check it. *I expect you to know everything about Stonefish when you get back to town or I visit Jordan.*

Kurt.

She rubbed her arms and cleared the message, glancing around to make sure no one was watching. Lindsay was watering plants in her front garden and Miss Simpson walked past with a beach bag over her shoulder. Gretchen's gut clenched. Kurt wasn't going away. Ignoring the matter wouldn't help. He knew all her plans. She had no desire to spy on her friends, but Kurt was serious. The urge to call Dot and Nhiari was strong. They were her friends, but Kurt had contacts in the police.

She drove on autopilot to the Ridge, the boys playing eye-spy in the back while she spent the hour imagining Kurt taking Jordan and her never seeing him again, never knowing what had happened to him. She gritted her teeth and forced the morbid loop out of her head as she drove through the station gate. Obsessing wasn't healthy. She would figure out some way to stop him.

Gretchen exhaled as she scanned her surroundings. Several kids were over by the horse yard with Lara as the centre of attention. Not all of them were from the pony club, so some must be from the families camping at the Ridge.

Almost before she'd come to a full stop, Jordan and Cody were out of the car and racing to join the kids. Right. No nerves there.

She retrieved their things and wandered up the steps of the homestead and rapped on the door frame. Amy and Faith were inside the kitchen, Faith cutting up fruit for a platter and Amy filling bottles with water.

"Come in!" Amy called.

"Do you need a hand?" Gretchen asked as she walked in. The kitchen smelled like freshly baked bread, and she inhaled, savouring the smell.

"We're just about done," Faith said. "We're waiting for a couple more kids and then we can go for the first ride."

"You can leave your stuff over there." Amy pointed to the line of bags against the wall. "We'll take them out to the shed later."

"Who else is coming?" She thought she'd be the last one here.

Faith finished arranging the fruit on a plate. "Mischa and Natasha aren't here yet." She glanced at Amy. "Neither is Arthur."

Gretchen jolted. "I'd forgotten he was coming. He would have been on the boat today." She checked her watch. "He's probably on his way."

"Georgie was picking him up." Amy didn't look at either of them as she spoke.

Then he'd definitely be here. Georgie wasn't the type to take no from him. Gretchen placed her hands on the back of a chair. "How are things between you two?"

Amy shrugged. "We've barely spoken more than polite conversation since he's been here."

Gretchen hesitated, but the sadness on Amy's face made her speak. "He's still coming to terms with everything. Sam said he wasn't the chattiest person to begin with."

"That's right, you've been on the boat with him," Faith said. "What's he like?"

"At first he wouldn't leave the cabin and rarely spoke. This week he went swimming. He's very self-conscious of his prosthesis, so it was a pretty big deal for him."

"How did people react?" Amy asked.

Gretchen grinned. "The women were too busy staring at his sculpted chest to notice his missing leg." It had taken her by surprise as well, and she'd taken a second look.

Faith raised her eyebrows. "That good?"

"Better than Sam's," Gretchen confirmed.

Amy shook her head. "It's weird to think of my brother that way."

Someone thundered up the steps. "Let's get this party started!"

Georgie.

Gretchen grinned. Always one to make an entrance. Faith rolled her eyes playfully. "We're still waiting on a couple of kids."

Behind Georgie, Arthur stepped cautiously into the room, eyes darting from Gretchen, to Faith, to Amy. Unsure of his welcome.

Gretchen moved towards him. "Hey, Arthur. How was the boat today?"

He looked a little startled, but gave her a small smile.

"Rough. You didn't miss much."

"Are you ready to ride?" Faith asked.

He shrugged. "I'm not sure I'll be much use."

"You'll be another set of eyes, and that's what we need," Faith told him.

He nodded and glanced at Amy who was busying herself arranging the water bottles on the table. "Hi, Amy."

She looked up and her smile was forced. "Hey, Arthur."

Awkward. Gretchen knew little about their history except Arthur hadn't come to Amy and Brandon's wedding, and they'd been estranged beforehand.

"Knock, knock," came the call from the door. Joan stood there with two backpacks on her shoulders.

Gretchen smiled at her. "Are you staying the night too?"

Joan shuddered. "No. I gave Natasha a lift because Kristy was too busy."

That sounded like Kristy. She always had more important places to be. Joan on the other hand often offered to help her with Jordan. "Can I bring Mischa back to town for you tomorrow?" she asked. "Save you another trip out."

"That would be incredible," Joan breathed. "Thank you. Kristy said she couldn't pick her up because they were going on a family picnic afterwards."

"No problem." It was nice to give back.

"If everyone's here, we should get started," Faith said. "It will take some time to get the horses ready."

As Gretchen followed Faith, Georgie and Arthur out of the house she said to Joan, "I'll call you before I leave so you know when we'll be back."

"Thanks."

Outside it was still warm although the sun sat low in the sky. The dozen or so kids were gathered around the horse yard and the horses owned by some of the kids had been tied to the outside. A blue heeler trotted from child to child lapping up the attention and a couple of sheep and a kangaroo also received their share of attention.

"All right." Faith clapped her hands. "Let's saddle up."

The kids all jumped to work. Gretchen went from horse to horse, helping the children place the saddles over their backs and then checking the cinches were tight. When she finished, she noticed Lara showing Arthur what to do to get his horse ready. It was sweet the way he listened attentively to the girl.

Faith wandered over. "With Arthur riding, we don't have a spare horse for you."

"That's fine. I'll help Amy get dinner ready." Horse-riding wasn't her favourite activity and Jordan would appreciate not having her hanging around.

After they made the final checks, they mounted and filed out of the yard with Faith leading, Arthur in the middle and Georgie bringing up the rear. Gretchen waved and then headed back into the house, with the dog, Bennett at her side.

Amy flinched as Gretchen came through the door and then relaxed. "Are they on their way?"

"Yeah. Are you all right?"

Amy shook her head. "I don't know what to do around Arthur."

It said a lot about how bad their relationship was for Amy to be uncomfortable.

She got salad makings from the fridge. "Part of me wants him to be the one to bridge this distance between us. He was the one who wronged me. But then I think that's just petty, and I should try, for Brandon. They're good friends." She handed Gretchen a glass of water.

"Do you want to tell me the story?"

"It's pretty short. My father is a major in the army and wanted his family to be as regimented. When he was away, Mum, Arthur and I would have a lot of fun, but when he came back, Arthur would do everything he could to please him." She peeled the carrot as if it had wronged her. "Arthur joined the army as soon as he turned eighteen. Not long afterwards, Mum was in a car accident. She got addicted to pain killers."

"I'm sorry." Amy would have been still at high school.

Amy shrugged. "I struggled to take care of her, but neither my father nor Arthur would help. She overdosed when I was fifteen. Only Arthur got leave for the funeral. Afterwards my father was going to put me in boarding school, but I'd had enough. I left home and started travelling, working wherever I could find a job. I hadn't heard from either of them until I discovered Brandon was Arthur's teammate at the beginning of the year."

Fifteen. That was young to be on her own. "Didn't you need ID?"

"I got a fake one until I turned eighteen." Another shrug as she chopped the carrot. "Most places were so desperate for workers they didn't care how old I was."

Gretchen hesitated. "I know what it's like to have a dysfunctional family. It's tough." She sipped her water. "I imagine Arthur doesn't know what to say to you. He seems a little socially awkward."

Amy rolled her shoulders. "That's what Brandon says too, but I don't know how I feel about it all. I want to know why he deserted me the way he did."

Gretchen smiled in sympathy. "Then you'll have to ask. One of you has to make the first move." She'd been the one in her family, but in her case it was to cut all ties.

"I asked him at the hospital, but he didn't answer."

Amy screwed up her face. "Maybe I should try again now he's had time to settle." She sighed.

Gretchen had witnessed how difficult it was for Arthur to interact with people. She would do what she could to help both of them. They deserved closure.

Chapter 9

Arthur braced himself as Faith called for the children to follow her in pairs. He was to be in the middle, which suited him. Georgie would notice if he needed help. In front of him rode Lara, Mischa, Jordan and Cody. Behind him, he heard the not so whispered sounds of a girl whinging about Lara being at the front. Childhood politics. They'd never been fun. He didn't deal with children, hadn't had to since he'd been one. On missions when kids had been involved, Sam or Dobby had taken point and Arthur had been happy to let them. So being with kids as well as riding a horse was not his finest hour.

But he'd figure it out.

He held himself stiffly astride a horse called Reg, which had been Lara's grandfather's. Reg seemed content to follow the horse in front of it in a swaying walk. They walked under an overhanging branch and Arthur had to duck or be hit in the head. It was then he remembered Lara had told him to relax, to settle into the saddle, and he'd be more comfortable. Following her advice, he shifted and became one with Reg's movement.

Around him, kids called to each other as they rode towards red sand dunes in the distance. He shook his head. He had never seen dunes this rich rusty red before. As they drew closer, he saw how fine the sand was. Animals left clear footprints in it, from tiny lizards, to birds, to the long curvy line of what could only be a snake.

His fingers itched for a paintbrush and some paper. Could he do the colours any justice? He breathed deeply. Perhaps he should see whether there was anywhere in town that sold paints and proper paper. He'd not brought anything up with him, and the notebook he took on the boat was almost full of his sketches. Maybe it was time he stopped hiding his passion. It would be nice not to have to sneak around, or make excuses to come out here and draw or paint.

He shook off the shame his father had instilled in him. Sam and Brandon wouldn't judge him. They'd be pleased he was doing something.

They moved around the base of the dunes, a mini desert amidst this mostly flat land, and then along a dry riverbed. Sweat trickled down his back and he wished he had a wide-brimmed hat like Brandon's to shade his face. The eucalyptus lining the riverbed provided a measure of shade from the harsh evening sun. Around them birds sang; the harsh squawk of a cockatoo, the high-pitched chirp of some little bird flittering amongst the branches and the occasional deeper song of something else.

His shoulders relaxed. Peaceful. Even the children's excited calls to each other as they spotted a bird or a lizard couldn't disturb the peace of this land. It was embedded in the vastness, the harshness, the remoteness of it all. He could understand why Brandon loved it here. It was a far cry from the tension and control of the army.

Arthur frowned. The rules and regulations of the army had told him how he had to act, even if at times it was against what he wanted.

He'd never liked the freedom to make his own choices, because he inevitably made the wrong one.

Up ahead, Jordan and Cody rode two abreast and leaned towards each other, whispering, and then glancing at him. What were they up to?

He found out after they arrived back at the horse yard and had unsaddled the horses. Cody nudged Jordan and said, "Go on, ask him."

Jordan stumbled forward. "Excuse me, sir."

At first Arthur didn't realise Jordan was addressing him. Since when had he become a sir? "Yeah?"

Jordan looked past him, as if not brave enough to meet his eyes. "Mum says you have a pro… pros… fake leg." He finally glanced at Arthur.

Arthur nodded. "I do." Where was this going?

"Me and Cody were wondering whether it was like a bionic leg, with gadgets and stuff, like you see in the movies?"

Cody grew brave enough and stepped forward. "Yeah, like does it have an inbuilt gun or something, so you can do sneak attacks?"

Arthur stared at them, surprise making him speechless. He'd never thought anyone would think his leg was interesting, but it was clear the boys had been debating it the whole ride. The shock morphed into delight at their imagination. He considered telling them the truth, but he didn't want to disappoint them. He gestured them closer and lowered his voice, staying serious. "That's top secret. If I told you, I'd have to kill you."

The boys' eyes widened. "Epic," Jordan breathed.

Arthur nodded, then turned away before he smiled. His gaze met Gretchen's, who was helping the boys unsaddle their horses. She grinned at him, having obviously overheard the conversation, and tapped her nose. His cheeks heated, but he couldn't prevent the smile from widening over his face.

"Time to wash up," Gretchen called to the kids. "Dinner is almost ready."

The sun hovered on the horizon above the ridge, still bathing the land in a soft glow of pinks and oranges. Faith made the rounds to ensure the children had finished packing up correctly, and she followed his gaze. "It's magic watching the sunset from up there, but trying to get a dozen kids back down the slope safely in the dark would not be fun." She smiled. "We'll have to take you up there another day."

"I'd like that."

Her eyes widened at his statement, but then she smiled. "Good." She tucked her arm through his. "Come on, we've got the horde to feed."

Faith led Arthur around the house to the side yard, where the scent of barbecue sausages and onions hit his nose. He inhaled, filling his lungs. The smell of good times.

Brandon and Darcy stood by the barbecue, Brandon with a pair of tongs in his hands. Arthur moved closer, not entirely sure of his welcome. He swallowed. It was past time he made the effort. "Isn't it dangerous to let Brandon be in charge of the sausages?" He inevitably overcooked them, which is why the team had banned him from cooking.

Darcy laughed. "I'm just letting him think he's in charge."

"That's a relief."

Brandon glanced at both of them, mock offence on his face. "I cook a mean sausage."

"If by *mean* you're implying nasty and burned almost beyond recognition, then yes, you do," Darcy replied.

Brandon shoved his brother and handed Arthur the tongs. "Let's see you do better."

Arthur gripped the metal tongs and stared down at the sizzling barbecue. It was almost as if the past few months hadn't happened, as if he was at a barbecue with his team mates and they were teasing each other as usual. Normal life. He'd been so caught up on losing his leg, he couldn't see past that. He should have been embracing being alive. But that was part of the problem. The army had been his life, and he'd been cut off as abruptly as he'd lost his leg. One second there, the next gone.

"You going to turn those things?" Brandon asked. "Or stare at them?"

Arthur shoulder bumped him, coming back to the sizzling barbecue. "I'm not taking advice from you," he retorted. "How long have they been on?" he asked Darcy.

Brandon harrumphed and stalked away. Arthur's lips curled up.

"Only need about a minute more."

Gretchen came over with an empty tray. "The mob's getting restless."

"It's coming right up," he said and filled her tray.

Sometime later, after the children had been fed, they moved over towards the shed where someone, probably Matt or Brandon, had built a fire in the fire pit. It now burned low, and the children sat around it on logs toasting marshmallows.

Or rather, burning them to ash. Arthur shuddered as another marshmallow went up in flames and the girl blew it out, gingerly taking the blackened goo off the long stick and shoving it into her mouth.

Gretchen sat down beside him. "You're not a fan of marshmallows?"

His father wasn't around to hear him now. "I love them."

"Then why the grimace?"

"Have you seen how they're toasting them?" He pointed as Jordan slipped an equally black glob from his fork.

Gretchen laughed. "Isn't the charred outside the best bit?" She placed a fresh marshmallow on her stick and stuck it right in the middle of the coals. It burst into flames and she grinned, pulling it out and blowing on it until the flames subsided. Then she touched it, checking its heat, and slipped it into her mouth. She closed her eyes. "So good."

Lust shot through him, as she moaned her appreciation and licked her lips.

Amy sat on the other side of Gretchen. "Have you shown them how it's done yet, Arthur?"

He glanced at her, surprised she remembered.

"He makes the best toasted marshmallows," Amy continued and handed him a long fork and the bag of marshmallows. "Will you make me one?"

Their eyes met and her hopeful expression took him back to their childhood, to the few rare times they'd been somewhere with an open fire and their father hadn't been around. They'd always toasted marshmallows then.

He wanted more good times with her. "Sure." He smiled a little tentatively and placed a marshmallow on the end.

Arthur turned his attention to the fire. He held the fork above the flames, turning it slowly, making sure each section got its share of heat before rotating it. The trick to a perfect marshmallow was a light browning on the outside and a deliciously melted inside. It might take a little longer, but it was worth it. After a few rotations, he pulled the fork away and offered the marshmallow to his sister.

Reverently, she slid the sugary treat from the end and popped it in her mouth. She sighed, pure pleasure, and after she swallowed, she said, "Thank you. I could never get the knack."

"You were never patient enough," Arthur responded.

She grinned. "True."

"Will you toast me one?" Gretchen asked. "That looked so good."

He toasted another marshmallow and, when it was done, he handed it to her.

Gretchen groaned. "Oh my God. You're right. It is so much better."

Her groan had him imagining her under him, sliding his hand up her side to her breast. He blinked. Not appropriate, especially not considering the setting. Arthur cooked himself a marshmallow and then tried to hand the fork to Georgie, who sat next to him.

She raised her eyebrows. "Oh, no you don't. You're officially the chief marshmallow cooker now. I'll take two please."

A thrill filled Arthur. Useful with a skill no one else had. One his father would consider useless, but everyone here appreciated. He nodded to Georgie and kept cooking.

"Story time!" Lara called when the marshmallows were gone. "Who can tell the scariest ghost story?"

As the kids all sat straighter, eyes wide, Faith said, "No scary stories at all, otherwise you'll never sleep tonight."

"With all that sugar, they're not likely to sleep anyway," Gretchen murmured.

Arthur chuckled as the children protested.

"Then we could play truth or dare," Lara's best

friend, Mischa, called.

"No dares relating to the fire or anything which will get you hurt," Darcy announced.

Another round of groans. Georgie stood up. "I've got some things to do. Matt, do you want to help?"

"Yep." The two of them hurried away.

"We've got an early start tomorrow," Brandon said as Mischa called truth or dare to one child. He and Amy quickly followed the others to the house.

"Do you feel we're being deserted?" Gretchen murmured.

Arthur nodded, but he didn't mind. It wasn't difficult keeping an eye on the kids.

"Darcy, you go too," Faith said. "We've got this."

"Are you sure?"

She nodded. "I'll see you in the morning." They kissed and Darcy said, "Call if you need anything."

They'd set up beds in the shearing shed, which was big enough for all the kids, and far enough away from the house so the farmers wouldn't be disturbed if the kids didn't sleep. It was kind of cool. Arthur had camped as an army cadet, but everything he did had been reported to his father, so he'd never been able to have any fun.

"Anyone want a cuppa?" Faith asked.

It would be nice to wash away some of the sweetness of the marshmallow. "Yes, please."

"I'll help you make them." Gretchen stood. In a low voice, she said to Arthur, "I don't want Jordan to feel as if I'm watching him."

How thoughtful and completely opposite to his own father.

Arthur settled back and stared at the glowing coals. The heat warmed his face against the chill of the night and the smoke wafted from the fire. He sat on the opposite side of the fire to the children, but they spoke loudly enough to be heard.

Their challenges comprised daring each other to run to various places, now in the dark, to show how brave they were.

"My turn," Lara called. "Truth or dare, Sherlock?"

Arthur jolted. Lara danced from foot to foot, biting her lip as she watched him. Oh, hell. What was going to get him in the least amount of trouble? "Truth."

At that moment, Gretchen and Faith arrived with the drinks. Gretchen handed him a mug. "Thanks."

Lara grinned. "Why do they really call you Sherlock?"

OK, so not too difficult. "It's my code name from the army. We all had them."

"Yeah, but why Sherlock?" Lara persisted.

"You don't have to answer," Faith said.

The disappointment on Lara's face made him feel like a heel. "No, it's fine." How could he put it so it didn't make him seem like an idiot? "I was always good with the detail."

"Like the detective, Sherlock Holmes?" Lara asked.

He nodded, though it wasn't quite accurate. His team had tired of him pointing out the obvious, and one day Brandon had said, 'No shit, Sherlock'. The name had stuck.

"That's so cool. I bet you had to unravel all sorts of info in the army," Lara said.

"Like spy stuff," Jordan added.

He didn't have the heart to tell them the spy stuff happened before they were sent in. It was Gretchen who spoke. "Why don't you play a game of spotlight?" She pointed to the torch they must have brought out with them.

"Yes," Jordan yelled and in moments the kids were on their feet and working out the boundaries of the game and who was going to be it first. After an initial count of thirty, the kids scattered.

Faith sighed and sipped her tea. "Great idea, Gretchen."

"I figured they needed some more exercise to burn off the sugar."

Arthur scanned the area. How much trouble could they get into? There were enough lights on the outside of the shed, the shearer's quarters and the toilet block for the campers that the kids could see where they were going. But they weren't great at hiding. In his quick scan, he spotted eight of the kids hiding behind trees or cars, or buildings. They were too impatient to stay hidden and kept popping up to see what was going on. Amateurs.

"What was that?" Gretchen asked.

Damn, he hadn't realised he'd spoken aloud. "Nothing."

Gretchen smiled at him. "They don't have your training."

"They don't need it. All they have to do is stay still. The movement gives them away." Sure enough, as he spoke, the torch illuminated Jordan's face and Cody yelled, "Gotcha, Jordan."

Jordan groaned and trudged over to the fire. "Why do I always get caught first?"

"Because you can't stay still," Arthur answered.

Jordan glanced at him as if surprised he'd received an answer. "What?"

Arthur gestured him over. "Scan the area. Tell me what you see."

Jordan scanned the area. "Nothing. It's too dark."

"Look again." He nodded towards the toilet block. "At ten o'clock."

"Huh?"

"It's military speak to tell you which direction. Twelve o'clock is straight ahead, so ten o'clock is to the left, like on a clock."

"Cool," Jordan breathed, and looked at the building as someone stuck their head around the corner. "That's Mischa."

"Would you have spotted her if she'd stayed behind the building?"

"No."

"OK, tell me who else you can see." Giggles erupted from behind a nearby ute. "Or hear."

"That sounds like Natasha," Jordan said. He slowly turned, surveying the grounds. "Lara's near the shed, Sophie is at the tree and Joe is at the shearer's quarters."

"Good job. Remember that when it's your turn with the torch."

It took another ten minutes before Cody had found everyone and then it was Jordan's turn to be it. He counted slowly, and the kids fled, some going to the same hiding places as before, others desperately trying to find new hiding spots before the count ended. When Jordan opened his eyes, he stepped away from the fire and panned the torch around. In about five seconds, he'd spotted those who'd hidden in the same spots.

"No fair," Natasha said. "You must have cheated."

Arthur hated it when people blamed others for things they were responsible for. "He didn't cheat. We were watching. You hid in the same spot."

Natasha crossed her arms and pouted, going to sit on the log away from him.

Within five minutes, they had found everyone. Jordan ran over. "You're so smart. That was easy." He held up a hand to high five.

Arthur stared at it for a second and then slapped it. Jordan grinned. "I know. My code name can be Watson." He ran over to the other kids.

Arthur exhaled. No one had ever wanted to be like him. He rubbed his chest.

"You've got a new fan," Gretchen said. "Thanks for helping him."

"It was nothing."

"It was for him."

He stared at the fire. Such a small thing, but he remembered being that age, remembered wanting to do anything he could to make his father praise him. Feeling so proud when he did something right.

"Maybe you should show them how it's done," Faith said.

"Yes!" Jordan exclaimed, overhearing her. "You should play, Sherlock. You can hide."

A small part of him wanted to, but he wasn't as nimble as he used to be. It would be mortifying if they caught him. "What are the rules?"

Jordan pointed out the boundaries.

"Please, Sherlock," Lara said. "It would be so cool if you played."

He had no hope with both Jordan and Lara pleading him. "All right." He got to his feet, hoping he wasn't making a big mistake. "Who's it?"

Chapter 10

Gretchen bit her lip to stop from interfering. Arthur was old enough to say no if he didn't want to play. The kids jumped around, excited because a trained soldier was going to play hide and seek with them. It was Natasha's turn to be it and as she began the count, the kids scattered.

Not Arthur. He calmly strode over to a nearby tree and climbed it. He had a little difficulty with his leg, but when he couldn't use it to get any purchase, he used brute strength to haul himself to the first branch.

Impressive.

He wasn't more than ten metres away, but the leaves didn't rustle and he blended into the trunk like he wasn't there.

"This is going to be interesting," Faith said.

Gretchen nodded.

Natasha called out, "Ready or not, here I come!" She swept the torch around and began her search. One by one, she caught all the kids, and they returned to the fire. At the last one she said, "Done!"

"You're missing someone," Gretchen called.

"Sherlock!" Lara exclaimed. "Did anyone see where

he went?" Everyone shook their heads.

It couldn't be comfortable in the tree, but there'd been no movement the entire time.

"Faith, do you know where he is?" Lara called.

Faith smiled. "I'm not telling. Why don't you all look for him?"

The kids scattered in pairs, each going to their favourite hiding places to check if he was there. Another fifteen minutes went by, and they gathered back at the fire. "Did he go inside?" Mischa asked.

"He's within the borders you set," Gretchen said.

Jordan sidled over. "Mum, you'll tell me where he is, won't you?"

Gretchen smiled. "That would be cheating. Why don't you keep searching? Maybe he'll come out of his own accord."

Another round of looking. Gretchen glanced towards the shed where Jordan and Cody were.

"I don't have any leaves on me, do I?"

She jolted. Arthur sat next to her, brushing a hand through his hair. Like a ninja. "No."

None of the kids had noticed he was back.

"Why not wait until they found you?" Faith asked.

He chuckled. "I figured it would be a while."

"There he is!" Lara shouted and ran over. "Where were you?"

"I never reveal a good hiding place," Arthur said.

"How could you just appear?" Mischa asked. "We were all searching for you."

"He's got skills," Faith said. "Now it's time you got ready for bed."

A chorus of groans, but the kids trooped into the shed and used the designated rooms to change into their pyjamas. Jordan hung back and walked next to Arthur. In a low voice, he said, "You'll tell me where you hid, won't you?"

Gretchen wasn't sure whether it was sweet Jordan was taking such an interest in Arthur, or concerning. He didn't have many male influences in his life.

"We'll see," Arthur responded.

That seemed to satisfy Jordan, and he hurried to join his friends.

Gretchen turned to Faith. "There's no need for you to sleep out here. Arthur and I can handle it."

Faith hesitated. "No, I need to. I'm responsible for them. But can you watch them while I clean up?"

"Sure."

The children found their sleeping bags and moved them around so they were next to their friends. The couple of older kids went in one corner of the room, the younger ones stayed in the middle and the adults' sleeping bags were at the other end. Gretchen helped a few who were having difficulties with their zips.

Faith did a head count when she returned. "The lights outside will be on all night," she said. "Toilets are across the way." She pointed. "If you need anything, Gretchen, Arthur and I will be here, and you can wake us for any reason." She switched on a night light. "Sweet dreams."

She turned off the main light, and the room plunged into darkness. The children gasped and Gretchen stayed where she was until her eyes adjusted to the light. The kids whispered to each other. They would talk for another hour or so, but eventually they'd go to sleep. She gestured for Arthur to follow her back to the fire. He limped a little, rubbing his leg. "Does it hurt?"

He nodded. "Twinged it when I climbed the tree, but it hurts most days anyway."

"Do you have any painkillers?"

He winced. "Yeah, but Sam's got them." He didn't look at her as he answered.

Because of the overdose. "I've heard massage can

sometimes help."

"Maybe."

Gretchen rubbed her arms. The temperature was dropping, but by the fire it was all right.

"Who's next for a shower?" Faith asked.

"You go, Arthur." It would take him longer dealing with his leg.

"The showers at the campground have accessibility features," Faith said. "You might find it easier."

"Thanks." He grabbed his bag and walked off.

They both watched him and when he entered the building, Faith said, "He seems to be relaxing."

Gretchen nodded. "What was he like before?"

She shook her head. "I don't know. Brandon said Arthur has always been the responsible, obedient soldier. They'd have to get him drunk, or in a life-threatening situation for him to open up."

How sad. What had led him to that? "I think others not making a big fuss over his leg is important."

"Neither Brandon nor Sam are likely to." Faith grinned. "Hopefully, he can find some peace here. There's something about Retribution Bay that's good for the soul."

Gretchen would have agreed before Kurt had come to town. She hesitated and then asked, "How are things out here?"

Faith sighed. "We're making ends meet—just. The campgrounds and Georgie's and my income are keeping us afloat."

Gretchen stared at her. "I didn't realise things were so bad."

Faith blinked and bit her lip. "Sorry, I forgot you didn't know about it."

Gretchen's skin prickled. Though she didn't want to ask, this might be what Kurt wanted. She heard Jordan laugh from inside the shed. She had to keep him safe.

She could choose whether she would tell her ex. "Know about what?"

Faith hesitated. "We've been having some trouble with a company who wants to buy the Ridge."

"What kind of trouble?"

"They pulled down a windmill, set our haystack alight, threatened people." Faith ran a hand over her face. "It's been a hard few months."

Kurt was involved. He had to be. The bastard was harassing not just her, but her friends, too. "Why do they want the Ridge?"

More hesitation. "They were smuggling native animals from the gulf, but it might be more than that. Seems as if they have their fingers in a lot of pies up here and they've decided the Ridge would make a good base."

Yeah, that sounded like stuff Kurt would be involved in. She would bet drugs were part of it, too. Perhaps she could tell Kurt about the company, without causing her friends trouble, because he probably already knew. It would buy her some time. "Sounds awful. What are the police doing?"

"There's not much they can do. It's a faceless entity. After each event we hope it's over, but then something else happens."

"Is there anything I can do to help?"

"We have no clue who's in charge, so it's like fighting a ghost. The less you know, the better."

Gretchen should tell her about Kurt, should tell her she was already involved. She opened her mouth to speak, as Arthur returned, dressed in track pants and a jumper, which read, *Be the Best*. It fit him well, and his smile distracted her for a moment. "Your turn, Gretchen."

She pressed her lips together. She'd implied to Arthur that she knew what was happening, so she could hardly ask more questions now. He might feel as if she'd lied to him—which to be fair, she had—but she didn't want him to know that. She stood. "Thanks."

She'd speak to Faith later. Maybe they could fight Kurt together.

After she showered, Gretchen returned to the fire where Faith and Arthur chatted. Faith smiled and then yawned at her. "Goodness, that's my cue to hit the sack."

She looked tired, but Gretchen wasn't. "I might stay up a little longer."

"Me too," Arthur said.

Faith entered the shed where the voices of the children had faded.

Arthur rubbed his leg again.

"Still sore?"

"Almost constantly."

"You want to describe it?"

He glanced at her. "Sharp pain down my leg or pins and needles, and then raw rashes around the prosthesis."

"Is the prosthetic leg temporary?"

He nodded. "The doctors say it will be another couple of months before everything settles and I can get a permanent one."

That reminded her. She retrieved a piece of paper from her backpack and handed it to him. "I wrote down some exercises for you, but you should check with your OT before you do them. I don't know enough about your case, and I'm not qualified. They're mostly to get mobility back into your knee."

"Thanks." He read it. "I don't want people seeing me without the prosthesis."

She understood. "I know, but going from not having one, to wearing it all day is not helpful. The area is sensitive and healing. It's not like the sole of your foot that has toughened skin. It has to get used to the contact."

He looked away. "I feel as if everyone is staring at me."

"It's just you and me now." She placed a hand on his knee. "Do you want to take it off?"

He glanced towards the shed.

"They're all asleep, and if someone comes out, I'll head them off."

He pulled up his tracksuit pants so they came over his knee. With a little finesse, he pulled his sock down and, with a grimace, pulled off his leg. The scar was still red and raised, and around the stump was a light rash.

"That's got to be uncomfortable."

"Yeah." He straddled the log they sat on so she could examine it in the firelight.

"Have you got cream for it?"

He shook his head.

"Then go to the doctor and get some," she ordered. "You need to take better care of yourself." She glanced at him. "Did your therapist massage it when you were in hospital?"

"Yeah."

"May I touch it?"

He inhaled, but nodded.

She brushed the scar. "Does that hurt?"

"No."

She pressed more firmly, massaging the area. "What about now?"

He winced. "It's tender."

"OK, that's fine." She continued to massage the scar and the surrounding area. She glanced at him to evaluate how much pain he was in and found him staring at her, his expression intense. Her fingers stilled. "Am I hurting you?"

He blinked at her question and pulled his leg away. "No. It's fine. Thanks." He began putting his leg back on.

She touched his arm. "Arthur?" Something wasn't right.

He paused, looked at her hand, and then up at her. Desire.

It hit her in the gut, and she inhaled. She had meant nothing sexual by her massage, but it had clearly been an intimate moment for him.

She bit her lip. If she was honest, she didn't mind the intimacy. He was an attractive man, and he wasn't her patient. If Kurt hadn't been in town hounding her, she'd be interested in exploring this attraction. But she couldn't while Kurt had demanded she do so. She shifted away. "It's time I went to bed, too."

She found her sleeping bag in the shed and lay down. It was a long time later before Arthur joined them.

***

Arthur was pleased when Gretchen went on the early morning trail ride with the kids instead of him. It had been a late night. Not that the kids had stayed up late talking. Most of them had crashed long before midnight despite their attempts to stay awake.

No, he'd spent the night fixated on Gretchen. Her touch, her smile, her understanding. She'd awoken hope and lust in him, and it disturbed him. He couldn't start any kind of relationship until he'd fixed the ones he'd broken.

After hours of deliberation, staring at the dark, he'd come to one conclusion. He had to speak to Amy.

He'd already left it too long and the longer he left it, the harder it would become. It was already difficult enough. He waved to Jordan and Cody as they rode off and wandered inside, where Amy was wiping down the kitchen table and Brandon was drying the last of the dishes.

"Good timing," Brandon said.

Arthur grimaced. "I was helping the kids saddle the horses."

"No judgement," Brandon replied, hanging up his tea towel. "Georgie won't be back for a while, so you can hang here."

Arthur shuffled his feet. "Actually, I was hoping to talk to Amy." He glanced at his friend. "Alone."

Brandon pressed his lips together. "Ames, you OK with that?"

Amy straightened and nodded. "Why don't we go for a walk?" She hesitated. "If it's not too painful for you."

She shouldn't be worrying about his pain. "It's fine." He followed her out of the house and east towards the red sand dunes. They walked in silence while Arthur tried to figure out the right words. Finally, when it stretched unbearably long, he blurted, "I'm sorry."

She looked at him. "For what?"

He sighed. "For everything." He ran a hand over his short-cropped hair, still not used to the length. "For not being there when Mum died, for not realising what you were going through, for not searching for you hard enough when you went missing, for not coming to your wedding, for not telling you about the accident." He sighed. "Basically, for everything I've not done for you since I turned eighteen."

She was silent for a long moment as they continued to walk. Finally, in a small voice, she said, "I don't want your apology, I want to know why. Why did you desert me?"

God, she might as well have shot him in the chest for the pain ripping through him. "I..." He had no excuses. "At eighteen, the only thing I wanted was Dad's approval," he said. "Just one word of praise."

Amy snorted. "You might as well have wished for the moon and the stars."

He nodded. He understood that now. "When Mum had her accident, I left training early to visit her. Dad found out and made me do five hundred push-ups and then do guard duty in the rain with no weatherproof gear."

Amy didn't seem surprised. "Sounds like Dad."

"I asked my commanding officer for permission to attend her funeral. The only reason I got the couple of days I did was because Dad didn't want to look bad in front of his peers. He was just shipping out."

"I begged for your help before that, Arthur. When she was addicted and not getting out of bed."

Arthur frowned. "I didn't get any calls from you."

"I emailed you," she said. "Almost every day."

He shook his head. That couldn't be right. He'd received nothing. "To what address?"

"The one you always had. The cloud-based one."

His jaw dropped. "Dad caught me using it one day and changed the password. He said the mail I was receiving was junk, and I didn't need to fill my head with it. The only email I had was my army one." No wonder Amy hated him. He'd never responded to her pleas. "I didn't even know you'd run away until after I got back from my six months overseas. I called the boarding school Dad said you were at, and they said you weren't a student there. When I confronted Dad, he said you were being childish and had run away, but you'd be back."

"He always thought he knew best," Amy said. "I never understood why Mum stayed with him."

Six months ago, Arthur would have jumped to their father's defence, but now he nodded. "I didn't know how to search for you. I checked social media, I called some of your friends, but I couldn't find you anywhere."

Amy rolled her shoulders. "I didn't have a computer for almost a year," she said. "My phone was the cheapest I could buy, so it wasn't a smart phone. I lived as cheaply as I could."

He should have looked harder. Should have hired a private investigator or reported her as a missing person to the police. He shuddered. His father would have been furious. "Where did you go?"

"Kalgoorlie at first. Spent a year working in a motel as a maid. No one looked too closely at my ID as they were desperate for staff. Then they had a change of management and I had to move on."

At fifteen. Arthur shook his head. "You're amazing."

She shrugged. "I did what I had to to survive."

There was one thing he still didn't understand. "But why run away at all? Why not go to boarding school and finish your education?" They reached the sand dunes, the fine red sand scattered with the footprints of small animals.

Amy sank to the ground, bringing her knees to her chest. "Defiance, I guess." Her fingers brushed the soft sand. "I was exhausted from caring for Mum, from all the funeral arrangements, and I was still grieving. I figured if Dad believed I was old enough to deal with all of it on my own, then I was old enough to do what I wanted." She picked up some sand and let it run through her fingers. "After that, it was stubbornness. No way was I going back for him to tell me I told you so."

Stubbornness was a strong trait in their family. "I wish I'd been there to help you, Ames. I'm so sorry you had to go through it on your own."

"It's done now."

But was there any way to repair their relationship? A small lizard scurried from a nearby grass clump, stopping to look at them before scurrying across the sand to the next clump a few metres away.

"Why didn't you come to my wedding?"

He let out a long breath. "Because I was too weak to stand up to Dad."

"What happened?"

"When Brandon called and told me he'd found you, I was excited. I made the mistake of thinking Dad would be too." He shook his head. "I don't know why. You were a forbidden topic, but in my head, I justified it because he was upset you'd left."

Amy snorted in disbelief.

She was right. He'd been foolish. "I guess I made excuses for his behaviour. He had a lot of stress and responsibility, he had to be beyond reproach."

"He hated anyone who didn't agree with him, anyone who didn't fit the mould he wanted."

Arthur nodded. "When I told him about you, he said he had no daughter." From here they were slightly elevated and could see over the Ridge land. Birds fluttered through the trees and insects buzzed. "Word must have reached him that the team had asked for leave to attend your wedding." He closed his eyes. "He ordered me to his office and told me he had a special mission for me." His view of his father had shifted when Arthur had told him about Amy, but it had really cracked that day. "When I mentioned your wedding, he asked where my loyalty was. He had stood by me my whole life and you had left us. He said if I didn't go on this mission, he'd see that my career would never advance." Arthur looked at Amy, hoping she would understand. "The army was my life. If I gave it up then, every decision I'd made where I'd put it ahead of you would have been for nothing. I would have wasted my adult life."

"Did Dad really have that power?"

"He knew everyone, and I guess I still wanted him to love me."

Amy sighed and squeezed his hand. "He really did a number on both of us, didn't he?"

Arthur looked down at their joined hands. Did she actually forgive him? "I was so stupid, Ames. So stubborn in my defence of him, in my reliance on the army as my identity."

"I understand. I clung to my independence, on the idea that I didn't need anyone else. It wasn't until I came here, and discovered what a real, supportive family was like, that I realised I didn't have to do it all on my own." She smiled. "A real family can argue, but still love and support each other."

"Brandon rarely talked about his family, but the one time he did, I saw just how much he missed them."

"It took him some time… no, it took everyone time to get used to having him back, but they all forgave him." She let go of his hand. "Why didn't you tell us about your accident?"

Us, not me. They were already a unit. "I wasn't strong enough. I assumed you wouldn't come and that would have broken me. My decisions to trust Dad would have been for nothing."

She bumped his shoulder. "You're such an idiot. Don't you remember what we were like when Dad wasn't around? Don't you remember how quickly I forgave you for being a douche bag after he left again?"

"It's been years, Ames. I didn't know who you'd become. And more importantly, I couldn't forgive myself, so I couldn't see how you could forgive me."

In a quiet voice, she asked, "Is that why you overdosed?"

The question speared him, and he shifted. "No. I was in pain, Ames. The nerves in my leg ached and stabbed all the time. It was exhausting. I just wanted it to go away." He sighed. "But if I'm honest, I didn't care what happened to me after I took the pills. I couldn't see a way out of the pit I was in."

"Sam tried to help."

"I know, but I resented him. He was whole, he'd voluntarily chosen to leave the army, he was living his best life."

She bumped his shoulder again. "It's easier with help." She tapped his leg. "What's the pain like now?"

Her question stopped him. "It hasn't been as bad since I've been here. The constant ache is less than it was." He'd heard the doctors suggest it could be partially psychosomatic, but he hadn't believed them. "Sometimes I get shooting pain, and the prosthesis rubs and because I haven't kept up with my therapy, I'm further behind than I should be."

"Can I help?"

A simple question, but one which carried so much weight. He shrugged. "I need to speak—no, apologise—to my therapist. I wasn't open to help before."

"But you are now?"

It would seem that way. He nodded. "This place… I don't know if it's the people, or the rugged beauty, or maybe it's simply not the hospital and the city… but I feel a little like the old me. The boy I was when Dad was away."

"I always looked up to that boy," Amy said. "I thought he was pretty cool."

Arthur snorted. "I was never cool."

"To me you were." She got to her feet and offered him her hand. "Do you still draw?"

The question shocked him, but he clasped her hand

and let her help him to his feet. "I can't believe you remember that.'

"Of course I do. You were brilliant." She tugged his hand, pulling him back down the dunes. He embraced her praise before saying, "I do draw, but no one knows about it."

"You shouldn't hide your talent. You're not alone any more, Arthur. You've got me and Sam, and the whole Stokes family behind you. If you need anything, all you have to do is ask."

Tears pricked his eyes. "I don't deserve it after the way I treated you."

"Bullshit. You were as traumatised by our father as I was. He just brainwashed you more." She hugged him and he clung to her, closing his eyes, fighting the tears.

"You're too kind to me, Ames." He swallowed as he stepped back. "But thank you."

"I'm glad to have you back, Arthur."

They walked in silence, side by side back to the house. Amy held the kitchen door open for him. "Come on. The kids will be back soon and they'll want morning tea before their parents pick them up. You can help chop."

"Sure thing." He smiled, the happiness welling up in him and bursting forth. He wasn't foolish enough to believe their relationship would be easy from here on, but now they had a chance. Amy had forgiven him.

She passed him a knife and a chopping board and he took an orange from the bowl.

"I'll be back in a second." She left the room as he chopped and when she returned, she held out a folded, aging piece of paper. He wiped his hands on a tea towel before he took it.

"What's this?"

"Take a look."

Carefully he unfolded it. A rough sketch he'd drawn

of Amy and their mother sitting on the couch, sharing a doona, eating popcorn during one of their movie nights. He remembered the night clearly, the storm outside shaking the trees, the warmth inside from the gas heater, and the movie was a thriller he hadn't been interested in. He'd spent the two hours trying to capture the two people he loved on paper.

Tears blurred his vision. "I can't believe you still have this."

"It's one of my most cherished possessions."

"Ames." His fingers trembled as he placed the drawing on the table and then dragged her into his arms. "I'm so sorry." The tears released as he held his sister in his arms.

He would be there for her always.

He would not stuff this up.

Chapter 11

Gretchen sighed as the horse yard came back into view. She shifted yet again in the saddle, her thighs and butt aching, and longed for a glass of cold water and some shade. Horse riding wasn't her idea of a fun time, and with the day heating, she was less inclined to spend her time on the back of a dusty, smelly animal. The highlight had been watching Jordan and Cody exclaim over animals and old farm machinery which lay rusting where it had ended its useful life.

She halted her horse outside the yard and braced herself before gingerly dismounting. She gave her butt a quick rub to get the circulation moving again and then helped the kids lift the heavy saddles from the horses. Arthur and Amy weren't around. Hopefully, they'd talked. The only reason she'd volunteered to go on the trail ride this morning was to ensure Arthur couldn't and so give him a chance to talk to his sister.

When the horses were brushed and tied in place with a bale of hay to keep them happy, she walked with the group back to the farmhouse. Someone, probably Amy, had set up a trestle table full of fruit and biscuits, with a big cooler full of drink outside on the lawn. The kids dived on it like locusts.

"Want a drink?"

Her body warmed at the sound of Arthur's voice, and she turned to find him holding out a glass of water full of ice. She'd hoped some distance would dampen the emotions which had awoken last night, but it wasn't the case. He appeared different, happier, which made him even more attractive. "Thank you." She held the glass to her forehead and then gulped a couple of mouthfuls. "You look happy."

He lowered his voice. "I spoke to Amy."

Her heart swelled. "It went well." There was no question about it, but he nodded. "I'm glad."

He moved on, taking another glass to Faith and Georgie.

Even the way he held himself was different. He stood straighter, but not in the ramrod pose of a soldier in front of his commanding officer, more like a man who was sure of his place in the world.

Jordan spotted Arthur and dashed over, one hand holding a cup of cordial and the other a piece of watermelon. He came to an abrupt stop, eyes wide, and while Gretchen couldn't hear his words from where she stood, she guessed he was asking Arthur about hide and seek last night. As Jordan gestured, liquid sloshed out of his cup, narrowly missing Arthur. Gretchen winced and stepped forward, but Arthur steadied Jordan's hand and kept talking.

He was good with Jordan. It was gratifying he didn't dismiss her son out of hand.

"He's not bad to look at." Georgie moved to stand next to her.

Gretchen rolled her eyes. "You're obsessed with matchmaking," she said. "I was watching my son."

"Honey, if I thought that look on your face was for your son, I'd be calling the cops."

Gretchen laughed. "Ew. That bad, huh?"

"Yep."

With no need to pretend any longer, she continued to study the man in front of her. "Does that mean he's no longer public enemy number one?"

"We had a chat on the way out. I get a good feeling about him."

"He spoke to Amy while we were riding."

Georgie smiled. "Good. Amy seems happier. What's your take on him?"

"Uncertain, yet sweet."

"He's good with the kids."

"Yeah. They don't judge him. The boys think he's amazing, and that has to be good for his ego." He'd had so many hits to it lately.

"You two look as if you're scheming." Matt joined them and Georgie slid her arm around his waist.

"Merely observing," Georgie replied with a smile.

His grunt of disbelief made Gretchen laugh.

The first parent arrived to pick up their child and there were choruses of goodbyes as one by one, the children left. Gretchen carried plates inside and stacked them to be washed. Arthur joined her.

"I hope Jordan wasn't being too insistent," Gretchen said.

Arthur smiled. "He's enthusiastic. He wants me to teach him how to hide. Thinks he'll be king of hide and seek if I do."

"I'm not sure he has the patience to stay in one spot for so long," Gretchen replied. "He'll want to be part of the action."

"If you're all right with it, I'm happy to teach him."

"Sure. Thank you."

Darcy entered the room, trailed by Lara.

"Can we call Mischa's mum and ask her if Mischa can stay longer?" Lara asked. "We could go to the beach. She hasn't seen the plaque."

"It's too late to call Mischa's mum. She'll be on her way."

Gretchen cleared her throat. "I'm taking Mischa home today."

Lara's eyes lit up. "Do you want to stay and go swimming?"

"I'm taking Cody and Jordan home as well."

The girl's cheeks reddened. "They can come swimming too."

A swim sounded nice, and she hadn't seen where the Ridge met the gulf, but Georgie had spoken about it many times. She glanced at Darcy to check whether it was something he wanted to do. He gave a small nod and smile, which she took for encouragement. "Let me call Joan and make sure she's got no plans this afternoon."

After a brief conversation, it was agreed they would all go swimming at the beach. Lara ran outside to tell her friends and Gretchen finished cleaning. In a surprisingly short amount of time, they were on their way to the beach in two utes, Brandon driving one, and Darcy the other, the kids sitting in one of the trays, the rest of the Stokes dispersed between them with Georgie, Matt and Arthur joining them too.

It was a bumpy half-hour ride over the red dirt track that led to the gulf. This part of the station had small trees and shrubs lining the track and occasionally they had to slow for a stray sheep. A final small hill and the aqua water glistened in front of them. Directly ahead was a large island a short distance offshore and to the left was a clump of mangroves with some kind of marker nearby. To the right, the beach curved around into the distance. The kids made a mad dash to the water as soon as the ute pulled to a stop, but Gretchen climbed out slowly, her muscles already protesting from the earlier ride.

"Are you swimming?" she asked Arthur.

He hesitated. "Maybe. I want to read the plaque first." He gestured towards the marker by the mangroves.

Gretchen frowned. "What is it?"

"It lists the names of those who were aboard the Retribution when it wrecked on the island out there."

Sounded interesting. "Can I come?"

"Sure."

They walked over to the plaque while the others unpacked towels and an esky of drinks. The way everyone worked in synch made it seem as if this was a regular occurrence.

Arthur got out his mobile phone and took a few photos of the metal plaque both from the front and back before he stepped closer to study it. The names had been engraved deeply enough on the metal to have been unaffected by rust. Two Stokes were listed: Lilian and Reginald, who had to be Georgie's ancestors. Then there was Da Lim. Da Lim was Ed's girlfriend, Tess's, ancestor. All the other names were unfamiliar, which was a little surprising because so many locations in Western Australia were named after people whose ancestors could still be found in the community. Though Retribution Bay hadn't been settled until years after the shipwreck.

Arthur studied the names, frowning.

"Is something wrong?"

"There're too many names."

"What do you mean?"

"Lil—" He caught himself. "Nothing."

He wasn't telling her something. Her muscles tightened, knowing by the way Arthur closed off that this was something secret, something which would interest Kurt. She bit her teeth to stop asking questions.

What she didn't know, she couldn't report back. Hopefully, what Faith had told her last night would be enough to keep Kurt from carrying out his threats. "I'll leave you to it. I'm going for a swim."

She hurried away, hoping she wasn't making a mistake.

***

Arthur watched Gretchen move away, enjoying the sway of her hips. Though he wanted to spend more time with her, he had almost told her about Lilian's journal. He needed to be careful what he said, especially if Stonefish had got to her. He'd have to figure out a way to broach the subject.

When she reached the towels, he studied the plaque again. He should have brought his notes with him, but he was almost certain Lilian had mentioned only twenty-five people on board the Retribution. This plaque listed thirty. He checked the photos he'd taken to ensure they were clear and examined the sign more carefully. The smooth metal pole had no markings on it. The back of the plaque, the side facing the ocean, was a little battered, but similarly unmarked. He would guarantee this wasn't the original plaque. Its condition was far too good to have been here for a hundred and fifty years. Which begged the question: did the original plaque have additional directions to find the treasure? Or had whoever erected this one copied it marking for marking?

Was the original plaque lying in a forgotten place in one of the outbuildings at the Ridge? He'd have to ask Amy if they'd looked for it.

Lara ran up, Mischa right behind her. "Did you find something?" she asked breathlessly.

Arthur glanced at Mischa.

"She knows about the treasure. I told her before

134

Dad said I couldn't tell anyone."

"I can keep a secret." Mischa mimed locking her lips and throwing away a key.

Be that as it may, the fewer people who knew, the better. "I'm not certain it's anything. I need to check my notes."

Lara danced from foot to foot as if the sand were hot. "Can you check them now?"

"They're at Sam's."

Jordan and Cody were walking towards them, and the others watched. If Stonefish had people tracking the Stokes's activity, he didn't want to stay in front of the plaque for too long. "Come on. Let's get back to the others." He scanned the surroundings, checking the sky for drones and the island for movement. Nothing he could see, but that didn't mean there wasn't something there.

He moved across the sand, noting Gretchen was stripping down to her bathers. What a body. Lean from all the swimming she did, but with only a partial tan because of the long- sleeved rashie she wore for work. Brandon went across to speak with her while the others headed for the water.

If he stayed in Retribution Bay, he had to get a waterproof prosthesis, or figure out how to get from the sand to the water on one leg. Hopping wasn't graceful, and neither was crawling, but relying on someone to be his crutch also wasn't ideal.

Lara and Mischa ran back to the boys, and they headed to the water to play Marco Polo. Arthur smiled. Some things never changed. He remembered playing the same game with his friends when they were kids.

Brandon turned to him. "Find anything?"

"Maybe."

Gretchen spoke. "Do you need a hand getting into the water?"

The gut clench was automatic. He didn't want to be the person people had to help, nor did he want her to view him as a charity case. "Brandon can help."

She nodded and moved towards the ocean.

Here was someone else he needed to make amends with. Brandon was the only one he'd told about Amy. Funny he should be the one to find her.

"You spoke with Amy."

Arthur nodded, unsurprised that Brandon should bring it up. He probably knew exactly what they spoke about.

"Thank you."

"It was past time."

Brandon nodded. "We all knew the major was a bastard, but I guess we didn't realise how bad he was."

Arthur shrugged. "He was my father."

"We can all do stupid things because of family."

Arthur didn't take offence at Brandon calling him stupid because he was including himself in that statement.

Brandon shifted his feet. "You seem to be less… more…" He waved his hand up and down. "Normal."

Arthur laughed. "Thanks, mate. You never thought I was normal."

His friend winced. "You know what I mean."

"I'm not wallowing in self-pity anymore," Arthur said. "Getting back into the world has been good for me."

"Took your time about it. You should have told us sooner."

He shook his head. "I couldn't. It was all too much."

Silence for a moment before Brandon asked, "What happened?"

"An IED." Arthur closed his eyes. "We were on patrol through a town and passing by an alleyway. A woman screamed for help." He turned to his friend.

"Genuine terror, not the kind you can fake." Or so he'd thought.

The sympathy on Brandon's face told him he understood. They'd been taught to ignore such things because insurgents often used women to lure soldiers into traps. "A child was being dragged away." The clarity of the vision seared on his mind took his breath away. He'd run through the scenario hundreds of times, trying to figure out what he might have missed, how he could have done things differently.

The dirt, the rotten refuse stench coming from the alleyway, the oppressive heat of the day, had all disappeared into nothing as he'd focused on the man dragging the child away. Arthur was an excellent shot, but if the woman had gone after the child at the wrong moment, he might have shot her.

"I took one small step forward to get out of the glare of the sun and into the shade of the building so I could see better." He shrugged. "The click was almost inaudible, but the explosion that followed wasn't."

"Fuck. Do you remember much of what happened next?"

"All of it." His teeth clenched at the remembered pain and his leg throbbed. "Someone dragged me away and put a tourniquet on my leg. They carried me to an extraction point and got me out of there." Sounded easy enough, but every step, every jolt had been agony, made worse because he'd glimpsed the woman smiling at him, no longer afraid—an actress to lure him forward into the alley. All he'd been able to think of was how disappointed his father would be that he'd made such a rookie mistake. "They triaged me at the base, then flew me home."

"Did the major chew you out?"

Brandon understood. It was a comfort. "Yeah. Ordered me not to return to the army."

"He doesn't have that power."

"No, but I'd never progress up the ranks." Arthur glanced at Brandon. "He's got connections."

"He's a bastard, but you shouldn't have let him win. We kept telling you he wasn't worth it."

"I wasn't ready to listen."

"And now?"

"I've seen the proof. I might be delusional, but I'm not blind." And the further he got from the army and the major, the clearer he could see.

Brandon clapped him on the shoulder. "I'm glad. We're your family now, and we won't abandon you."

Arthur swallowed past the lump in his throat and looked away, blinking rapidly. "I appreciate it."

"It's too hot to be standing around here. What help do you need to get into the water?"

He welcomed the change of topic, but there was something else he needed to say. "I'm sorry, Brandon. Sorry for swearing Sam to silence and not trusting you had my back. Sorry for how I treated Amy."

"I get it, and I forgive you for being a sulky little bitch." Brandon smirked and nodded to the water. "Now, how do we get you in there?"

Arthur chuckled, his friend's words making him feel light. "You're my crutch." He'd worn shorts under his pants, not ready to show his leg off to all the world yet. He slid his pants off and lowered himself to the ground.

Brandon crouched next to him and watched him peel off the layers. "There's more to it than I realised."

"Yeah. You get used to it." He removed the leg, pouring the sweat out. "It's still gross, though." Across in the ocean, everyone was playing Marco Polo, splashing and laughing. As he rubbed suncream on his limb, he said, "Not very stealthy."

Brandon laughed. "Shall we show them how it's done?" He stood and offered Arthur his hand.

Arthur clasped it. "Absolutely." Then he let his friend help him into the ocean.

***

Playing Marco Polo with only one leg made Arthur rethink his tactics. Next to him Brandon moved stealthily through the water, taunting Lara, who was it, by touching her hair and then moving away before she could catch him. But Brandon had two legs to balance on.

Arthur had to resort to swimming for his quick getaway. He also had to contend with two shadows in the form of Jordan and Cody, who had decided they needed to stick by his side and study everything he did.

It made things far less stealthy with all their whispered questions and splashing.

When Lara tagged him, Arthur wasn't surprised.

Before closing his eyes, he made note of where everyone was. But the question was, who should he go after? "Marco," he called.

Around him came the reply, "Polo."

He picked Gretchen's voice immediately and swam towards her before he reconsidered. As much as he liked the excuse to touch her, it wasn't his wisest idea. Maybe he should go after one of the kids, not that it would be difficult. Brandon would be a challenge though. He smiled. Possibly the safest option and one the kids would get a kick out of. He called again. "Marco."

"Polo." Brandon's deeper tones came from his left now, when previously he had been on Arthur's right. Yeah, this was going to be fun.

He swam to his left, calling out again. The reply had moved again, back towards where it had first been.

"He's going after Uncle Brandon," Lara whispered, though it was more like a shout. She was only a couple of lengths away from him, but he kept focused on Brandon.

"Marco."

"Polo." The response wasn't as loud, making it harder to pinpoint.

"Look out!" Lara called.

A swirl of water behind Arthur, and he spun, reaching out, just missing whoever it was. "Marco."

"Polo." Mirth. Brandon was enjoying this as much as he was.

"He's—"

"Lara, no helping," Darcy interrupted. "Arthur can do it on his own."

"Marco."

"Polo."

Gretchen was to his right, and it was tempting to change tactics and catch her. What would she feel like in his arms?

He pushed away the thought as he sensed someone approaching. Brandon was getting cocky, thought Gretchen would distract him enough not to notice. There was just enough water movement to pick the direction. Arthur moved in the opposite direction, luring him in. Closer, closer…

Now.

He lunged towards the movement and heard a gratifying grunt as his hand touched solid muscle. He opened his eyes and grinned at Brandon. "You're it."

Around him everyone cheered.

Brandon shook his head. "You haven't lost it. You were always more focused than me."

The compliment filled Arthur's soul, but before he could respond, the kids surrounded him.

"That was amazing!" Lara shouted.

"How did you know he was there?" Cody demanded.

"I was sure he was going to get you," Mischa said.

"Can you teach us?" Jordan asked.

Four hopeful faces peered up at him.

Beyond them, the adults were watching, waiting for his response. Gretchen looked worried. "Do you mind me teaching them?" he called.

Surprise lit her face. "Not if you don't."

He smiled. "Not at all." The kids were easy to be around.

The children cheered, and he put his finger to his lips. "The first thing you need to learn is to be silent. Any noise you make alerts the person you're trying to avoid."

"But we have to respond in Marco Polo," Mischa said.

He nodded. "So you respond, then move. No whispers to each other, no calls of encouragement or warning, no splashing as you move."

"Swimming is splashing," Cody said.

"Not if you use breaststroke and keep your strokes under the water." He demonstrated. "Any time you lift part of your body out of the water, you're going to splash. Slow and steady is your friend."

"What if you're being chased?" Lara asked.

"That depends on if your chaser knows where you are. In Marco Polo, get out of their reach and then go stealthy."

"And in real life?" She bit her lip.

Arthur stiffened. He'd forgotten she'd been kidnapped, forgotten for a moment the whole family had been terrorised by Stonefish. Perhaps this training would help her. "Same goes. If your attacker knows where you are, you want to run as fast as you can, duck and weave, put obstacles between you so they lose their line of sight. When that's done, you can hide, or quietly move away."

"But you found us all when we played hide and seek," Jordan pointed out. "We suck at hiding."

It would take a while to teach them everything they wanted to know. "One thing at a time. Hiding or stealth?"

"Hiding," they chorused.

He scanned the bush beyond the beach. "All right. Let's get out and I'll give you some tips."

It wasn't until he went to follow them that he remembered he didn't have both legs. He caught himself in the water and swore. Gritting his teeth, he swam to Brandon. "Can I get a hand out?"

"Sure." Brandon placed his shoulder under Arthur's armpit, and they moved up the beach in synch.

"Want to help teach the kids to hide?" Arthur asked.

"All right. Let's divide into groups." Brandon smirked. "Bet my group can find yours faster."

It was always a game, but today Arthur felt like playing. "You're on."

By the time they reached the towels, the kids were dry, dressed, and ready for action. Arthur lowered himself to the ground while Brandon explained what they were going to do.

It was a process to dry his stump, check no sand was left on his skin or the sock and then put it all together. When he was done, he found the kids watching him. His face heated, but the usual vulnerability wasn't there. "Sorry, it takes a while."

"It's epic," Lara said.

Jordan nodded. "It's so cool that it helps you walk."

"Cooler if it had a blade or a gun built in," Cody mumbled.

Arthur laughed. "I'll keep that in mind."

Brandon helped him to his feet, and he shifted to make sure the limb was settled. "Have we worked out teams?"

"We're with you," Jordan said, and he and Cody stepped forward.

"Boys versus girls?" Arthur smirked at Brandon.

"We'll take you down," Mischa said, and the three of them moved up the beach so Brandon could teach them.

"Mind if I watch?" Gretchen asked. She was towelling herself dry.

"Not at all," Arthur said. "This way."

He took them over the small dunes and into the bush, which would be their playground. He had thirty minutes to turn the boys into stealthy hiding machines.

"The first thing I noticed last night was you're all a pack of elephants," he said. "Thundering away when the person starts counting. You've got to start quietly, so they don't know which direction you've gone. Stay light on your feet, watch where you step." He glanced around. A lot of red dirt which would leave footprints and dry grass which would crunch. Not ideal. "Keep low and balanced." He lowered his centre of gravity. "Now show me what you can do." He moved fifteen metres away. "I'll face the other direction, but if I hear you, I'll turn around. First one to reach me wins." The additional competition would cause them to put speed over stealth, but it would be a good lesson.

He faced away. "Go."

One… two… crunch. He spun towards the sound and Cody cringed. "It was a leaf."

"Keep an eye out for that kind of thing." Jordan had frozen in place. "Try again."

One… two… thud. Again he spun to find Jordan only about five metres away. He must have run and landed heavily.

"All right. This time Cody is going to stand over here and I'll show Jordan what to do. Cody, you turn only if you hear us, all right?"

Cody nodded and took his position.

"Follow me." Arthur stepped carefully, picking out his path to get to Cody before he took a step. Then he moved slowly, conscious that occasionally his fake leg clunked when he moved, and making sure he kept his steps small so Jordan could follow. They crossed the ground together and Arthur hung back so Jordan could do the tag.

Cody jumped with a yell. "Oh my God. I didn't hear anything!"

Arthur explained his process and then the boys changed roles and he took Cody through it. With an eye on the time, he then showed the kids how to pick the best hiding places, how to backtrack, and to camouflage themselves.

After thirty minutes, they rejoined Brandon and the girls.

"Ready?" Brandon asked.

"Ready." They outlined the rules as the others joined them. The top of the small dunes was a good vantage point to watch the game play, so they sat while Brandon tossed a coin to choose who would hide first. The girls won.

Nerves ran across Arthur's skin. He hadn't covered how to find someone. He huddled Jordan and Cody together. "Think about what I taught you and apply it to finding them. Look for footprints, or damaged vegetation, listen for noises, watch for movement."

"We've got this," Jordan said.

The game started, and Arthur clenched his hands together to stop from fidgeting. Gretchen moved next to him. "Thank you. You're so good with the boys."

He gave her a brief smile before turning his attention back to the game. "I enjoyed it."

The count had finished. Lara and Mischa were well hidden, and the boys searched the ground for clues to which direction they'd gone. They must have picked up something, as they moved in the right direction. "That's it," he muttered.

"Do you and Brandon have a bet on the outcome?" Gretchen asked.

"Just bragging rights," Arthur said. "It's always good to have something to hold over him." The words were out before he considered how they might sound. He turned to her. "Not in a mean way. We just mess with each other, a long-standing thing from the army."

She smiled. "I get it. I imagine Sam will be sorry he missed out."

Arthur nodded, relieved she understood. "He'll be spewing."

The boys had split up, going in different directions to follow different trails. They were quiet, not calling to each other and Arthur felt a surge of pride. Jordan was close to where Arthur had last seen Lara. She had to be hiding behind one of those bushes. He checked his watch. Only two minutes had passed.

Mischa squealed as Cody found her and there was movement behind the bush Arthur was watching.

"Gotcha," Jordan called and Lara stood, pouting. They all trooped back and Jordan and Cody ran up to Arthur. "How did we do?"

"Two minutes, fifteen seconds."

The boys slapped hands.

"Your turn," Brandon called.

Arthur brought the boys into a huddle, conscious Gretchen was listening.

"Lara moved when Cody found Mischa," Jordan said. "That's how I found her, because she was hidden really well. We have to be still no matter what."

The earnest expression on his face made Arthur smile. He nodded. "Did you notice any good spots to hide when you were looking for them?"

He hesitated. "Yeah, but it's close to where they're counting."

"They might not look hard close by because they expect you to go further."

Both boys nodded and Jordan put his hand out. Cody placed his on top and they both looked at Arthur. Arthur added his hand to the pile.

"Team Sherlock!" Jordan yelled and thrust their hands high. The boys ran to the starting point and Arthur stared after them, his chest tight, no words to express his shock. They accepted him.

"Are you all right?" Gretchen asked.

He swallowed hard, not daring to look at her, his vision blurry. He nodded.

She squeezed his hand. "You're becoming his hero."

He blinked rapidly. No one had ever looked up to him. It made him want to do his best.

Lara and Mischa started counting. Jordan ducked behind a bush just to the left of the girls. A risky move because if they went either side of the bush, they'd find him. Then the boy lay on his stomach and tucked himself under, almost disappearing from view.

"Genius," he muttered.

"Is that some kind of burrow?" Gretchen asked. "Could there be snakes?"

"Any snake would have slithered off long ago." Arthur smiled at her. "It was probably washed out in a storm."

The count ended, and the girls began their search. They were equally quiet which was impressive given how much Lara liked to talk. Arthur started his stopwatch.

He held his breath as Lara moved near the bush where Jordan hid and didn't let it out until she'd passed by.

At the two-and-a-half minute mark, Mischa found

Cody. Arthur flashed Brandon a satisfied smile. "Beat you."

Brandon groaned. "Damn it. I'm impressed with Jordan's hiding place."

The girls continued to search, moving further and further away from Jordan.

"Should we end the game?" Gretchen asked.

"I'll call them back." Darcy yelled for Lara and Mischa. "He's over this way."

The girls ran back. "Where?"

"Between there and where you started," Arthur said. "No need to go so far."

"I'm going to get lunch ready," Amy said, and Faith, Georgie and Matt went to help.

The search continued. Cody came to stand next to Arthur. "Where is he?"

Arthur smiled. "Hidden."

They let the search run for another five minutes, but it was getting hot. "Shall we call it?" Arthur said.

Gretchen nodded.

Brandon cupped his hands over his mouth. "Game's over. Time to come out, Jordan. Lunch is ready."

No movement.

Maybe he thought Brandon was trying to lure him out. Arthur raised his voice. "You won, Jordan. Time to go."

Still no movement.

Arthur and Gretchen moved as one towards the bush where he'd been hiding, Gretchen breaking into a jog. "Jordan!"

Arthur jogged after her, flinching at the jolt in his prosthetic leg, and reached the bush as she'd squatted down to shake Jordan. "Jordan!" Her voice raised in a slight panic.

"Mum?" The sleepy voice assailed Arthur's concern.

"Game's over. It's time for lunch. Did you fall

asleep?"

Jordan yawned. "I guess so." He shifted and spotted Arthur. "Did we win?"

"Yeah, you chose a killer spot." He bent down and pulled the boy out from the little hole he was in and helped Gretchen brush the dust from his clothes.

"Stop it!" Jordan moved away, face red. "I can clean myself." He slapped at the dirt and looked around to check who was watching. The others were already heading back to the beach.

Jordan ran to catch up.

Gretchen sighed. "I'm being embarrassing again."

"You care. When he's older, he'll appreciate it."

"Did your mum ever embarrass you?"

The question took him by surprise, made him stop. He'd avoided thinking about his childhood for so long.

"Sorry, was that too personal?"

Arthur shook his head. "No, it's fine. I always thought Mum was so cool. She was fun, and loving, and such a contrast to my father." He kept walking. "I probably embarrassed her more than the other way around."

"I'm sure she was never embarrassed of you."

"I used to go through these stages when Dad was home and just after he left when I would try to emulate him." It was cringe-worthy. "I'd tell her how she should behave and sometimes I'd do it in front of her friends. She must have hated it."

Gretchen ran a hand over his arm. "I can tell you, as a mother, she would have understood where it came from, and she would have loved you anyway."

Her kindness undid him. "I wasn't a great son. I put Dad before her, I wasn't there when she needed me, I didn't even know she was addicted to painkillers."

She squeezed his hand. "It wasn't your job to be there for her. That was your father's role, and he failed her, just like he failed both you and Amy. That's all on him, not you."

Her words lessened some of the guilt, but he wouldn't absolve himself of all of it. "Thanks, Gretchen."

She smiled. "Any time."

They reached the towels where Amy had spread out an amazing feast. "This looks incredible, Ames."

"I made some melting moments for you." She offered him a container.

He took one, speechless. His mother had made them melting moments for afternoon tea sometimes, but he hadn't had any in years. He bit in and the flavour took him right back to those days. He forced himself to swallow and then he said, "It's just like Mum's."

Amy smiled. "It's her recipe. I'll give it to you when we get back."

"I'd like that." This was a new beginning for him. One where he never had to worry about what his father thought. He could draw and paint openly, read the books he wanted to read, maybe even try dating.

He glanced at Gretchen.

If he was brave enough.

Chapter 12

It was late afternoon before Gretchen rounded up the boys and Mischa to head home. "Time to go."

"Aw, Mum, do we have to?" Jordan responded.

"Yes. You've got school tomorrow."

They'd returned to the homestead after lunch and another swim, but the kids had wanted to practise what they'd learnt by playing hide and seek, so they'd stayed a little longer. Arthur had sat outside in the shade giving them tips, his notebook on his lap. She'd watched him for a while and realised he was sketching something. She glanced at him. "Do you want a lift?" Georgie probably wanted to stay at the Ridge with Matt.

"Yeah, that would be great."

His lack of hesitation surprised but warmed her.

"You can sit in the back with us," Jordan said.

Gretchen shook her head. "There's not enough leg room for someone Arthur's size."

"He can take one off," Jordan replied.

Gretchen gaped at her son, horrified at the suggestion, but Arthur burst out laughing, the joyous sound like a warm hug. His eyes sparkled with amusement. "I hadn't considered that."

Cheeks scorching hot, Gretchen said, "No. He'll sit in the front." Not waiting for an argument, she went to say goodbye to Amy and Faith.

"Thanks for your help," Faith said, hugging her.

"Thank you for putting it together, and for taking us swimming today."

"It was fun," Amy said. "You're welcome any time."

Gretchen moved aside as Arthur came over. "Thanks for the recipe, Ames." He hesitated and then hugged his sister.

She squeezed him back. "I expect some melting moments when I come to visit."

"Sure."

"Can I see what you drew?" Amy asked.

Arthur hesitated, glancing at the others, ending at Gretchen, uncertainty on his face. She smiled at him, trying for encouragement. He was silent for a moment and then braced himself and nodded, handing over the notebook.

Amy gasped and placed a hand on her chest. "This is amazing. You've captured the essence perfectly." She passed the notebook to Brandon.

Brandon's eyes widened. "You did this? I had no idea you could draw." He handed the notebook to Darcy and then said, "Wait a minute. You always had a notebook on missions. Were you drawing then?"

Arthur nodded. "The major said they were rubbish."

"Bullshit. This is excellent. I'd love to see what else you've done."

Arthur's mouth turned up in a small, pleased smile. "All right."

Finally the notebook reached Gretchen. Her mouth dropped open. He'd drawn the homestead, the detail intricate, the pencil sketch more like a photograph. "It's beautiful." He'd captured the hominess of the house, made her want to step inside. This is what he'd been spending his days doing on the boat. She handed the book back to Arthur. "You're very talented."

His cheeks reddened. "Thank you."

She wanted to see more of his drawings, but this was a big step for him. She'd wait until next week to ask.

It took another fifteen minutes for Gretchen to wrangle the three children into the back of her small car and Arthur hopped in the front with her. The moment they lost sight of the house, the boys and Mischa started peppering Arthur with questions.

"So, where did you hide last night?" Jordan asked.

"Were we better just now?" Mischa said.

"How can you hide footprints in the dust?" Cody demanded.

"Hey, settle down," Gretchen interrupted. "Give Arthur a break."

"I don't mind answering," Arthur replied. "Just one at a time." He shifted in his seat to face the children better. "Let's start with hiding footprints."

He explained options and was incredibly patient with all the interruptions and follow-up questions. A kind man. Far kinder than Kurt had ever been.

The thought of her ex made her tense. Would he be satisfied with the few bits of information she'd collected? She couldn't see how it would be of any value to him, but it might keep him from following through with his threats.

She couldn't obsess over it, couldn't let him take over her life again. Gretchen exhaled, pushing her concerns aside, and listened as Arthur answered questions all the way back to town. She dropped off Cody and then drove to Mischa's house.

As Mischa got out of the car, she said, "Sherlock, you're so smart, I bet you could solve the puzzle of the treasure in no time."

"Treasure?" Jordan yelped. "What treasure?"

Mischa paled and slapped a hand over her mouth. "Nothing. Forget I said anything."

"Mischa, you've got to tell me."

The girl set her mouth. "No. Jordan Wintie, you have to cross your heart and hope to die swear you won't tell anyone what I said."

"Only if you tell me more."

"Jordan!" Gretchen said. "That's no way to behave." He sounded too much like Kurt.

"Your mum's right," Arthur said. "A true man acknowledges when someone has made a mistake and doesn't punish them for it."

"All right. I swear." He slumped back in his seat and drew a cross over his heart.

Mischa exhaled. "Thank you. See you tomorrow." She slammed the door and ran up to her house. Gretchen waited until she was inside before she drove to Sam's place at the marina. Her stomach swirled. Was the talk of treasure just childish imaginations? Mischa seemed very serious, and Arthur backed her up quickly. Was this what Kurt wanted to know?

She had the urge to block her ears and pretend she'd never heard it.

Gretchen pulled up in front of the town house.

"Thanks for the lift. I'll see you tomorrow?"

She nodded as panic fought its way for control. She didn't want to betray her friends, but if it was between them and Jordan, she'd pick Jordan every time. Gretchen forced a smile. "Say hi to Sam for me."

"Yeah." He waved. "See you, Jordan."

"Bye, Sherlock. You can visit any time you want."

Arthur stepped back, surprise lighting his face, and then he smiled. "Thanks, Jordan. Same goes."

"Thanks. Can I come in now?"

Gretchen choked back a laugh, the panic receding. "No. Now is time for dinner and then bed. You've had a busy weekend."

Arthur nodded. "I've got to prepare for work tomorrow, otherwise my boss might get cross." He shut the door.

Jordan frowned. "Does Sam get cross, Mum?"

"I'm sure he does." She waved to Arthur and drove off before Jordan could ask Arthur more questions. She was looking forward to a cup of tea and an early night herself.

Gretchen unlocked the house and walked in, tossing her keys on the little table next to the door. Her phone buzzed as she entered the kitchen to put the kettle on. Jordan dumped his backpack on the ground and dashed for the television.

"Put your backpack in your room and go have a shower before any TV," Gretchen called.

Jordan groaned but did as she asked.

Gretchen opened the fridge. Perhaps toasted sandwiches would be suitable for dinner. They'd had a big lunch, and she didn't feel like cooking. Jordan loved toasted cheese sandwiches. She got out the ingredients and put the sandwich maker on to heat. By the time the kettle boiled, two sandwiches were sizzling and the water in the bathroom shut off, signalling Jordan had finished his shower.

She made her tea, cut the crisped-to-perfection sandwiches and placed them on two plates. Her phone buzzed again.

She picked it up and her cheerful mood vanished. *I want information.*

"Mum, I'm hungry." Jordan entered the kitchen wearing his superhero pyjamas, his hair damp and sticking out in different directions.

Love filled her. She had to protect her baby. "I made toasted sandwiches." She handed him a plate. "You can eat in front of the TV."

"Epic. Thanks." He left the room and a moment later, the television blared to life.

Normally she would tell him to turn it down, but she didn't want to risk him overhearing her conversation. Before she could call Kurt, her phone buzzed again, this time with a photo of Jordan and Cody, both in their school uniforms, obviously taken when they were walking home from school.

She slid into a chair, her legs not strong enough to hold her.

Could the Stokes or the police help her? If Stonefish hadn't been caught yet despite all the trouble they caused, it was hardly likely.

This was a test. Kurt expected her to call him. If she didn't, his threat was obvious. She glanced into the living room where Jordan was watching a cartoon. Dread and self-loathing filled her as she dialled Kurt's number. This was what he made her do, how he made her feel. The phone rang and rang. Just when she thought it would go to voice mail, he picked up. "What did you find out?"

She kept her voice low. "The Stokes have been having trouble with a company called Stonefish. They've been causing problems out at the Ridge."

Kurt grunted. "Tell me something I don't know."

Anger pushed aside her fear. "How am I supposed to know what that is?" she demanded. "You asked me to find out what was happening, and that's what they told me."

"Who told you?"

Gretchen hesitated. She didn't want to name names. But what choice did she have? "Faith."

"She's not a Stokes."

"She's engaged to Darcy." And as far as the Stokes were concerned, she was already family.

"You were at the beach today," Kurt said. "What did

they tell you about the Retribution?"

How the hell did he know that? The beach was in the middle of nowhere. There had been no boats, no other cars, no signs of civilisation at all. She shivered as she thought about the kids playing in the bush. What if one of them had stumbled upon the spy?

"All I know is that the Retribution wrecked on an island just offshore." Did he know about the plaque commemorating the passengers?

"Any mention of what happened to the cargo?"

He was fishing, but at least she could answer honestly. "No."

"What about stories about their ancestors?"

"Two of their ancestors were on board." But he'd given her an insight into what he was after. Could the treasure Mischa mentioned be part of this?

"You should ask questions. I want to know everything that happened on that boat the next time I call." He paused. "And because you failed, maybe I'll say hello to my son tomorrow." He hung up.

Gretchen's hand shook as she lowered the phone. A quick glance into the living room showed Jordan still happily in front of the television.

She couldn't live like this, couldn't keep wondering whether Kurt would carry out his threat and couldn't betray her friends. She needed help.

Her first thought was Arthur. He was military-trained and Jordan liked him, but she didn't want to get him involved. No, she had to call Dot, had to tell her everything.

Friends helped each other, they didn't betray each other.

Somehow, she would keep her son safe.

And she'd have a better chance with a team behind her. She dialled Dot's number.

"I need help."

***

Arthur let himself into the town house with a smile on his face. It had been an amazing weekend. He'd cleared the air with Amy and Brandon and spent time with Gretchen. Even his time with the kids had been a blast. He whistled a little ditty as he moved into the living area where he found Sam and Penelope in the kitchen.

Penelope was facing away from him, brushing down her top and Sam had shifted in front of her, blocking Arthur's view.

He'd interrupted something. He grinned. "Sorry, should I have knocked?"

Sam laughed. "The whistling did the trick. You look happy."

"I had a great weekend."

Penelope turned around, her cheeks not quite as red as her hair. "Hi, Arthur."

"Hey. I'll go to my room."

"No, it's fine. We were just making dinner." She reached for a bottle of pasta sauce and unscrewed the lid.

"Need a hand?"

Sam shook his head. "Take a seat. Tell me about your weekend."

"It was fun." He still couldn't quite believe how much fun. "The kids were enthusiastic about everything. I went on a ride with them in the evening and the Ridge land is incredible. It looks so barren, but there's life everywhere."

"Brandon loves it there," Sam said.

"You can tell. After dark, the kids played spotlight and they were terrible at hiding."

"Did you show them how it's done?"

Arthur grinned. "Yeah, and they wanted to know all my secrets."

Penelope looked between them. "Is Arthur good?"

"He was our number one sneak. He could infiltrate and hide for hours until it was time for action. The man's a genius."

Arthur blushed. "The entire team was talented."

"He's being modest," Sam said, stirring something on the stove.

Arthur took a moment to take in the praise. He'd been good at his job, but never as good as his father wanted. He should have never held himself to his father's unachievable standards. "Today we went to the beach after most of the kids had left. I taught Gretchen's boy, Jordan, and his friend, Cody, how to hide. Brandon taught Lara and Mischa."

"Who won?"

Arthur raised his eyebrows. "You have to ask?"

"Brandon's going to hate that." Sam laughed.

"How did the sleepover go?" Penelope asked. "I bet Faith and Amy are exhausted."

"The kids were pretty good." He hesitated. He had spent little time with Penelope, but Sam had spoken about her a lot, and he knew that most of what he'd told his friend, Penelope would know. "I spoke with Amy."

Both of their gazes sharpened on him. "How did it go?" Sam asked.

"Good," Arthur replied. "Really good."

"Told you it would." Sam smirked, and Arthur ignored him. "Take a shower and dinner will be ready when you get out."

Arthur was happy to do as suggested. He was still salty from the swim, and he wanted to clean his leg well, so no sand was left in a crevice where it could rub. Despite the bar in the shower, it still took far longer than he'd like. His balance was getting better, back closer to what it was pre-accident, but he should do more core exercises. Get back into yoga and tai chi. While he was drying himself, he massaged the scar like Gretchen had showed him. It took him back to the night before. There'd been nothing unprofessional in her touch. She'd massaged deep which had brought some pain, but seeing her hands on him had made his mind wander to other places he'd like her hands. While a part of him had been horrified about sexualising something that was a healing process, the other part of him celebrated feeling like a man again.

The only problem was, he couldn't work out whether the attraction was mutual.

He dressed and spent some time checking his leg was clean, and then he remembered Gretchen's advice about giving his leg time to rest. He managed to get himself into his bedroom where his crutches were, and then headed back to the kitchen. Penelope was pouring a glass of wine, and Sam was setting the table.

"Would you like a wine?" Penelope asked.

He wasn't supposed to drink alcohol on his medication, but he hadn't taken any painkillers over the weekend. "Yes, please."

"Have you taken your pills?" Sam asked.

"You didn't give me enough for the weekend," Arthur retorted.

Sam winced. "Sorry. How did you hold up?"

"Surprisingly well," Arthur told him. "The pain was manageable." He'd been too distracted to pay it much attention.

Sam grunted with approval.

They sat at the table and ate the ravioli while Arthur continued telling them about the weekend. When he mentioned the plaque, he stopped. He'd forgotten about the names.

"What is it?" Sam asked.

"I need to check Lilian's diary. There are too many

names on the plaque."

"Yes!" Penelope exclaimed. "I thought that too, and I forgot about it."

"When?" Sam asked.

"Just before we uncovered the weapons cache," Penelope replied. "Then I was too concerned about almost being blown up to remember."

Fair point.

Sam left the room and came back a minute later with his copy of the diary and a photo of the plaque. "Show me."

"I need my notes." Arthur grabbed his tablet and scrolled through to find the page he wanted. "Here. There were four civilians on board; Lilian, Reginald, Mr Smith and Mr Clarke. There were three convicts, three pearl divers and finally the sailors." He crossed off the names on the plaque as he read them out.

"But she doesn't mention the sailors by name," Sam said.

"No, but she mentions how many there are," Arthur countered. "Three took the one remaining lifeboat to get help." He marked three on the paper. "Three went looking for food and water and disappeared. Three were sent to search for those men a few days later." He wrote down another six. "Then the remaining six died in the mutiny. That's twenty-five people. The plaque has thirty names on it."

But who were the extra names and why were they there?

"I'd bet Tess has a passenger list somewhere," Sam said, reaching for his phone. "She's a history buff, and she wanted to find everything she could about the ship." He dialled a number and a minute later said, "Hey Tess, it's Sam. Have you and Ed been behaving yourselves?" He chuckled at the answer. "Yeah, all good here. Just wondering whether you ever found a passenger manifest for the Retribution when it left Fremantle." Another pause. "It might be nothing. Can you see what you can find?" He smiled. "Yeah. Say hi to Astro Boy for me." He hung up. "The passenger manifests had been loaned to the maritime museum for a project when she was last at the state library, but she's going to chase it up for us."

Arthur studied the names, hoping something would jump out at him. Some of them seemed more European, maybe Dutch or Celtic, though he was fairly certain most of the people in Western Australia at that time hailed from England. The extra names had to be clues—didn't they? Why else include them?

"Some names have alternative meanings," Penelope said. "Penelope means weaver. Could Lilian have known and used those in her clues? She was well read and intelligent."

Arthur nodded. "And the convicts were Irish. They could have used some Irish words." He grabbed his phone and searched for an Irish dictionary. Next to him, Penelope was looking up meanings of names. Sam put the kettle on.

"I can't believe it's taken this long to notice," he said. "We must have studied the plaque for clues dozens of times."

"We were all focused on clues in the journal," Penelope pointed out, looking up. "Lean means light or sun-ray for a girl."

"But in Irish, it means follow or continue," Arthur said, excitement tickling his nerves. How accurate was the internet? The convicts might have spelled things phonetically to hide the Irish origins of the word. This could be a haystack.

But at least it was something new.

He grinned and got to work.

Chapter 13

"Gretchen! Can you get the ropes?"

Gretchen jumped at the shout. Sam was yelling down at her from the bridge. Damn. They were almost at the pen. She grabbed the ropes and readied to tie the boat. Sam would start wondering why Rob had ever hired her at this rate. But how was she supposed to concentrate when Kurt had made such a threat?

The boat slid into the pen, and she tied it off as the rest of the crew prepared to disembark. Gretchen hurried back to the cabin to finish cleaning and checked her phone. No text from Holly. Jordan must be there.

Dot had said she'd keep an eye on him.

But they'd also agreed any sign of the police would tip off Kurt.

What had the sergeant arranged?

The not knowing was driving her crazy. She turned and crashed into a solid chest. Arthur steadied her, his hands gentle. "Are you all right?" His gaze searched hers.

She huffed out a breath as her heart raced. The urge to tell him had her opening her mouth, but then sense prevailed and she nodded. "Yeah, sorry." She wasn't bringing him into her mess. He had his own stuff to deal with.

She shifted around him and his grip tightened for a second before letting go. "Are you sure? You've been a little distracted all day."

She'd thought she'd done a good job at hiding it. She forced a smile. "Must be more tired from the weekend than I'd realised." She moved past him but felt his eyes on her as she straightened tubs and picked up stray rubbish. Thankfully, there wasn't much to do today. Arthur had spent some of his day on the deck, talking to passengers and had even worn shorts and gone snorkelling again. He'd cleaned up while she'd been stressing about all the possible outcomes of going to the police. Kurt was cruel.

Not that she'd spoken to Dot 'officially'. She just told her friend about an issue she was having with her ex.

But Dot had been very interested in learning about Kurt and how he was involved. It seemed they were short on leads. Not great.

Dot had promised to tell no one except Nhiari about the conversation, so Jordan should be safe.

Hopefully.

"They're forecasting a storm on Wednesday," Sam said, moving over to her. "Weather should be OK tomorrow still, but I'll let you know."

She nodded and raced through the rest of the clean-up, glad it wasn't her turn to drive the bus. She grabbed her bag. "See you tomorrow!"

"Gretchen, wait."

She closed her eyes and turned at Arthur's call. "Yeah?"

He clenched his hands, took a moment before he spoke as his eyes searched hers.

Again her heart raced, with anticipation this time.

Was he going to ask her out?

"Ah, say hi to Jordan for me."

Disappointment filled her. She nodded and waved. "Will do."

She half jogged to her car and threw her bag on the back seat. Then she sped through the streets to Holly's place.

Holly opened the door at her knock, her expression concerned. "Something happened today, and Jordan's upset. He and Cody have been shut in Cody's room since they got home from school."

Gretchen's heart lodged in her throat as she followed Holly through the house. Holly knocked on a bedroom door and when there was no response, she pushed it open.

The two boys were huddled on the floor, but both looked up. Jordan's eyes full of anger narrowed on Gretchen and her heart lurched.

"Why didn't you tell me Dad was in town?"

She clenched her hands as her legs went weak. "What do you mean?"

"Dad stopped us on the way home," Jordan said, his voice rising. "He was upset I didn't want to see him, that I didn't answer any of his emails. He wants to see me and *you've* been keeping me away. You lied to me!" He scrambled to his feet. "I hate you!" He pushed past them all and ran out of the house.

Shit. That was Kurt's game. The bastard.

"It's not nice what you did," Cody said.

Holly's eyes were wide, but she said nothing.

"I'll call you later and explain," Gretchen said, and hurried after her son.

Jordan was already halfway down the street.

She debated running after him and decided the car was the better option. She wound down the window as she approached and slowed to a crawl. "Jordan, please get in."

He folded his arms across his chest and kept walking.

"Don't you want to hear my side of the story?"

He flinched a little.

"We discussed your dad, remember?" But right now, it was Kurt's word against hers, and Kurt could be very convincing when he wanted something. "I know you're hurting." Her phone beeped. *This is just the start if you don't get the information I need.*

Still watching them. She gritted her teeth. No. He'd gone too far. She would not be manipulated, she would not let him use her child as a pawn in his sick games. This had to stop. She would stop it. And he would never hurt them again.

Maybe showing Jordan the text messages would help her cause. Though she hated to break Jordan's heart, it was safer this way. "Jordan, please get in the car."

Another car came from the opposite direction and slowed. Arthur and Sam. Damn it.

Sam wound down his window. "You need a hand?"

Her face flushed red. "We're all right."

Arthur leaned over. "Do you want me to walk him home?"

She'd told Arthur about some of the problems with Jordan, but she hesitated. "I don't know." Jordan was walking ahead.

"I can try." Arthur got out of the car and hurried to catch up with the boy.

Gretchen sighed when Jordan perked up at the sight of him. She turned to Sam. "I'm sorry. I'm not making the best impression. Jordan's going through a rough patch at the moment."

"It's all good." Sam smiled. "Tell me if you need more time, or different shifts. We'll make it work."

Gratitude filled her. "Thank you." Ahead, Arthur

turned and waved, which she took as a sign that Jordan was happy to walk with him. "Jordan and Arthur have hit it off."

Sam twisted to look behind him. "I'm glad. The kids seem to have a way of getting through to him when I couldn't."

"He seems happier."

Sam nodded. "Something's clicked. He can see ahead now. He's pretty excited about the journals."

Gretchen frowned. "What journals?"

He grimaced. "Just some family stuff." He glanced in his rear-view mirror. "I'd better stop blocking the road. Tell Arthur to call me if he wants a lift home."

There was definitely something going on. Something she wasn't privy to. Something Kurt wanted to know. But there was no way she'd be the one to tell him. Gretchen watched Sam go in her rear vision mirror and then put her car into gear and drove home.

She had whipped up a salad and had sausages ready to cook when Jordan and Arthur walked in. She poured two glasses of water and added plenty of ice because it was still warm out, and placed them on the table. Jordan took his, but didn't look at her.

"Have a nice walk?" she asked.

Arthur nodded, his expression serious. "Jordan and I had a good chat."

She could only imagine what Jordan had told him. "Sam said to call him if you want a lift home." Not that she was trying to get rid of Arthur, but she needed to speak to Jordan and clear the air.

"No. He's staying," Jordan said. "So he can hear what you have to say about Dad."

Arthur gave her a sympathetic look. "You can tell me later," he said to Jordan.

Jordan scowled and took a deep breath, readying himself for an argument.

"It's fine," Gretchen said. Though she hated airing her dirty laundry, she needed to get Jordan to listen, and if this was the only way he would, so be it. "Why don't you tell me what happened today?" She sat at the table.

Jordan stared at the glass.

"Watson, tell her what you told me," Arthur said.

Jordan straightened. "I saw Dad. He stopped us on the way to Cody's place."

A sliver of jealousy tickled her and she pushed it aside. It was good Jordan had someone to confide in, even if it wasn't her. "You recognised him?"

Jordan scowled. "Of course I did. I'm not stupid."

It had been five years, and they didn't have any photos around of Kurt, but she let the comment slide. "What did he say?"

"He said he missed me. He was sorry for being a bad dad, and had tried to email and call, but *you* wouldn't let him speak to me." His eyes glistened with righteous tears.

"Do you remember what I told you the other day?" Gretchen asked. "When you asked about your dad?"

"You lied!"

"I didn't." She placed a hand over his, and he snatched it away. She ignored the hurt. "I left your dad because he was involved with bad people, and I didn't want either of us hurt."

Arthur straightened at her words and pressed his lips together.

"He worked with Gram and Grampa," Jordan retorted.

"They didn't always follow the law." Something she'd been very late to realise. The only reason Kurt had been interested in her was to get to them. Her parents had thought Kurt was the ideal son-in-law, bringing him into the family business. Though Kurt wasn't as good as they were at separating home and work life. She'd overheard late-night conversations when threats were made, had people sneak into her backyard and leave packages in the cubby house, and smelled the perfume and smoke on Kurt's shirts. When she'd told her mother, she'd realised the family business was not what she thought it was.

At first, she'd stayed because her mother had told her not to make a fuss, and she had no money of her own. Over time she'd realised Kurt didn't give a damn about them and she wanted to remove Jordan from the toxic environment.

"I left him because he was bringing danger to the house."

Arthur's frown deepened.

"He loved me, and I loved him," Jordan retorted.

She shook her head. "After we left, I didn't hear from him," Gretchen continued. "Not until about a month ago when he arrived in Retribution Bay."

Jordan straightened. "And you didn't tell me?"

"He didn't ask about you. He wanted me to spy on my friends."

"Who?" Arthur asked.

She turned to him. "The Stokes."

He nodded as if that confirmed something for him. "And did you?"

She nodded. "I didn't want to, but he threatened Jordan. Said he would make him disappear on the way home from school."

Jordan slammed his hand on the table. "Liar."

Only one way to show him the truth. She got out her phone and pulled up the text messages from Kurt. "This is your dad's number." She handed it over to Jordan.

"Why'd he send a photo of you and Arthur?" Jordan asked as he scrolled through.

Crap. It would hurt him, but she was done with

hiding. She looked at Arthur as she responded. "Because he asked me to get close to Arthur in order to find out what was happening with the Stokes."

Arthur flinched, hurt showing in the slight widening of his eyes before he leaned back and crossed his arms.

She reached out to him. "I refused. I've enjoyed spending time with you."

His expression shuttered, closing her out. "You asked about Matt."

"I did." Damn Kurt. "Kurt told me about the situation, and said I needed to find out more. I hadn't decided if I would tell him what I learnt, but I needed to protect Jordan."

Jordan threw the phone on the table. "It's lies. That isn't his phone number."

Arthur picked up the mobile.

"It is," Gretchen said, but directed her next words to Arthur. "He rang after you lost your leg in the marina, and he's called a few times to tell me what I'm doing, to show he's watching me."

Arthur pressed some buttons, checking the call history.

"He knew Jordan was upset today."

"Sherlock, tell her to stop lying," Jordan demanded.

"The calls and messages line up with what she's saying," Arthur said.

"But Dad wouldn't want to hurt me."

Arthur sighed. "Not all fathers are loving," he said. "I spent my whole life trying to please mine, but when I had my accident and lost my leg, he only visited me once. He told me I wasn't welcome in the army any longer and I was a disappointment."

Gretchen gaped at him.

"No way," Jordan breathed.

Arthur nodded, his gaze on her son. "It took me a while to realise he never loved me. Not like my mum and Amy loved me. I was stubborn and refused to believe it, and I hurt others."

Jordan bit his lip. "How do I know who's telling the truth?"

"I guess you need to look at how they've both behaved in the past."

"Dad worked a lot. I didn't see him much."

"How was he today? Was he kind? Did he hug you? Did he speak to Cody?"

Jordan shrugged. "No."

Gretchen stayed silent. Defending herself and denigrating Kurt wouldn't win her any points.

Her phone rang and the caller ID said it was Kurt. What was he playing at now? Arthur handed it to her.

"Put it on speaker," Jordan said.

Her heart clenched. She didn't want to hurt Jordan, but it would show him the truth. "Only if you stay silent so he doesn't know you're listening," Gretchen said. Jordan hesitated and then nodded and she answered. "Kurt."

"I told you not to mess with me. Did you get Jordan in the car or have to follow him home?"

Gretchen put her finger to her lips. Kurt hadn't waited around to find out, which meant he didn't know Arthur walked Jordan home. "That's none of your business. What do you want?"

"I want information about the Stokes and so do my colleagues."

"What about Jordan? You said you wanted to spend time with him."

Kurt laughed. "Kids are so gullible."

Jordan's bottom lip trembled.

Gretchen stretched her hand across the table, but he pulled away. She hated this, but she needed to ensure Jordan understood the truth. "So you spoke to him after school just to cause trouble?"

"You need to understand I mean what I say. Jordan could disappear and you'd never see him again."

She wanted to be sick. "You would hurt your own child?"

"Those I deal with wouldn't hesitate."

"Can't you protect him from them?"

"If it's him or me, he's expendable."

Jordan paled, his face screwing up in pain. He'd heard enough. Gretchen hung up the phone and reached for him. Jordan wailed. "I hate him! I wish he'd die!" He flung back his chair and raced to his room, slamming the door behind him.

Gretchen's vision blurred as she got to her feet. Damn Kurt to hell.

Arthur placed a hand on her arm. "You need to call the police."

"I have. I called Dot last night, but I didn't expect it to escalate so rapidly." She glanced towards the bedrooms. "Will you stay? I'd like a chance to explain everything, and Jordan might want to ask you questions about your father."

He nodded.

She needed to make it up to this kind man. Had to tell him she wasn't being nice to him because of Kurt. "I was going to cook sausages for dinner. You could join us."

"How about I cook them while you speak with Jordan?" Arthur suggested. "I imagine he needs a hug."

She nodded, wiping the tears from her eyes. "Thank you."

She tapped on Jordan's door and pushed it open. Her baby lay face down on his bed, his bunny rabbit under one arm, sobbing his eyes out. Her heart broke for him. She sat on the edge of the bed and placed a hand on his back, gently rubbing it. "I'm sorry, baby."

"Go away." The voice was muffled and lacked any

real conviction.

"No. You could do with a big hug, so I'll wait here until you're ready. I love you, baby."

He shifted, his face peeking out from under his arms. "Dad doesn't."

"No," she agreed. "But your dad doesn't love anyone. He never loved me, and he doesn't love his parents. The only person he loves is himself."

"It hurts."

"I know it does. It hurt me for a long time too, before I realised we were better off without him. We've been pretty happy here in Retribution Bay. What do you think?"

"I like it here. Melbourne was boring."

"It was." She continued to rub circles on his back.

His sobs lessened. After a while he said, "Do you think Sherlock was telling the truth about his dad?"

Gretchen blinked. "Yes, I do."

"But Sherlock's so much cooler than me."

"I think you're pretty cool, but who you are has nothing to do with why your dad is the way he is. He's not a nice person."

Jordan shuffled to a seated position, his face red and tear streaked. "I'm sorry, Mum."

"So am I." She opened her arms, and he dived into them, squeezing her.

She closed her eyes, relieved he knew the truth, relieved he didn't blame her.

She would protect him, no matter what.

***

Arthur wanted to punch something, or more specifically, someone. An intense rage burned inside of him as Gretchen left the room to comfort her devastated child.

People like Kurt should be castrated.

To manipulate a child and be so callous about it. He'd questioned Gretchen putting the phone on speaker, but she'd been right. Jordan might not have believed it, if he hadn't heard it for himself.

Gretchen's phone buzzed. *You'll pay for hanging up on me.*

His blood ran cold at the threat. He would not let this bastard hurt this family. Not any longer. Kurt would find out he was messing with the wrong people.

He let out a deep breath and got to his feet. In order to rid himself of some of the anger, he ran through one of his Tai Chi flows, breathing slowly in time with the movements, and by the time he was done, he felt less murderous.

He moved into the kitchen, found the sausages in the fridge and dug around in the cupboards until he found a frying pan. He wasn't sure how long it would take for Gretchen and Jordan to come out, so he started heating the pan. The sausages would keep their heat if he covered them in foil when he was done.

The satisfying sizzle when he placed the sausages in the pan made him smile as he imagined one was Kurt. He adjusted the temperature and then checked the fridge and found a salad already prepared.

Monitoring the sausages gave him too much time to think. Kurt had ordered Gretchen to seduce him for information. That's what it boiled down to, though she hadn't said it in so many words. When he'd checked the dates of the calls and messages, so many of them had been when he and Gretchen had been together. That was why she'd reacted the way she had. She was being threatened by her ex.

An ugly voice in his head shouted he was a freak, and disgusting, and no one would want to be stuck with someone like him. He fought the urge to sink into self-pity. The whispers in his head weren't as hypnotising as they'd been in the past, but it was a struggle to fight them back.

Gretchen had called Dot even before Kurt had spoken with Jordan. That meant she wouldn't be manipulated by him. Perhaps their interactions had been real.

Besides, her attempts to dig for information had been half-hearted at best.

He shook away the thoughts. No matter what, he needed to tell Sam what had happened.

He grabbed his phone and dialled Sam.

"You need a lift, mate?" Sam asked.

"No." Quickly he outlined the events of the afternoon.

"Son of a bitch. Her ex has been stalking her?"

"Yeah. Kurt must be involved with Stonefish. He wanted her to seduce me." He bit his lip, cursing himself for saying it aloud. Damn his lack of confidence.

A pause. "Gretchen doesn't strike me as that type of woman."

"He threatened Jordan."

"Still, if you say she already told the police before Kurt escalated, it means she wasn't planning on obeying him."

Hearing Sam repeat his reasoning soothed him. "Thanks."

"No worries. We need to figure out how to protect her and Jordan. She'll be fine when she's on the boat, but the kid is an easy target."

"I can protect him."

"Not if you're on the boat."

"I don't need to be. I can walk Jordan home from school, stay with him until Gretchen gets home."

A long pause. "You sure?"

At least it wasn't a complete refusal like last time.

Perhaps he'd proven to Sam he was in a better place. "Yeah, I am."

"All right. I'll send you Dot and Nhiari's numbers in case you need them. Are you staying at Gretchen's a bit longer?"

"I'm staying for dinner."

"Call me when you're ready to leave. It might not be safe for you after dark. Not if Kurt sees you as a threat."

Though it rankled, Sam was right. Arthur wasn't prepared for a battle yet. He hung up and turned the sausages again. They were almost ready.

"Something smells good out here," Gretchen said.

She walked into the room with her arm around Jordan.

"Not hard to cook a couple of snaggers." He switched off the gas and transferred the sausages to a plate. "How are you, Watson?"

The boy shrugged. "OK."

Yeah, that was probably the best they could hope for.

Gretchen got the salad from the fridge and they sat down.

"Want a snagger?" The boy nodded and Arthur dished him up a sausage and then offered one to Gretchen. All at once he was struck by how cosy and natural it was, despite what had just happened. This was what it was like to be a family.

The deep yearning shocked him, and he reached for another sausage to cover his jolt. He'd never thought of having a family of his own, had always thought he'd be wedded to his job. But this felt... nice, comforting.

"Sherlock," Jordan said.

Arthur blinked. "Yes?"

"Will you tell me about your dad?"

Arthur's hand tightened around his fork. Gretchen

mouthed, *You don't have to*. Her understanding soothed and he relaxed his grip. Maybe his story would help Jordan. "What do you want to know?"

"Did he do things with you when you were a kid?"

"He was in the army, so he'd be gone for months at a time," Arthur said. "When he came back, he forgot we weren't his soldiers. He was very strict. We had to make our beds and keep our rooms clean, and tidy the house."

Jordan screwed up his face. "Did he take you to the zoo?"

A memory surfaced. "Once. Amy and I had a great day taking photos of the animals and reading the signs. But when we got home, Dad gave us a test about what we'd observed." He pressed his lips together. "Neither of us passed and Dad was disappointed. The next time he took us out it was to the museum, and I spent all my time taking notes and I forgot to have fun."

"He sounds mean."

"I guess he was, but I was young. I just wanted him to be proud of me." Now he was no longer blinded by that need, he could see how toxic their relationship had been. The barriers of defence he'd had for his father stripped away, leaving him raw. He swallowed the lump in his throat, blinking his eyes to stop the tears from falling. He'd clung to the naïve hope of that ten-year-old for far too long.

"Did he do anything for your birthday?"

"When I turned ten, he decided I could start training, so he took me on a five- kilometre run."

"No." Gretchen's disbelief made him glance at her.

"Yeah. I guess army drills were the only way he knew to communicate."

Jordan got up and moved around the table. "I'm sorry your dad was horrible." He hugged Arthur.

That this child should offer him comfort after just

having had his own heart broken killed Arthur. He hugged him back. "I'm sorry about your dad, too."

The boy hiccup-laughed. "It's all right. You turned out great, so I should be OK."

Oh, the child was something else. He made Arthur feel like some kind of superhero. He hugged him again. "You're already amazing."

When Jordan headed back to his seat, Arthur glanced at Gretchen. Her eyes glistened, and she dabbed at them with her fingertips. A rush of warm feelings filled him. She was incredible. He wanted to hear everything she'd been through, especially the stuff that wasn't fit for Jordan's ears. She'd raised such a wonderful son.

They did the dishes together and then Jordan went to watch TV. Arthur handed Gretchen her phone. "He sent another message while you were with Jordan."

Her face paled as she read it. "I need to call Dot."

He nodded. "I can walk Jordan to and from school."

"What about the boat?"

"I spoke to Sam. He doesn't need me, and I can protect Jordan."

The relief and gratitude on her face made him feel unworthy. "Thank you." She made the call and Arthur shifted closer to the television to give her a measure of privacy, and to make sure Jordan wasn't eavesdropping.

Jordan was watching a show about shipwreck hunters. At least spending his days at home would give Arthur a chance to investigate the extra names. He'd have to get Tess's number from Sam and ask if she'd tracked down the passenger list.

Though he wanted to tell Jordan about the discovery, it would only expose him to further risk.

Jordan glanced at him. "These guys should investigate the Retribution, don't you think?"

"It seems like they're searching for undiscovered

shipwrecks," Arthur said. "Everyone knows where the Retribution is."

"Maybe there's another one out there," Jordan insisted.

"Maybe. There have been a lot of shipwrecks off the coast over the years."

Jordan looked past him. "Who's Mum talking to?"

"She rang Dot."

Jordan tilted his head. "Sergeant Campbell?"

"Yeah." Though he wasn't sure Gretchen would appreciate him telling Jordan, the boy had a right to know. "Your dad made a threat."

Jordan shifted to face Arthur. "What kind of threat?"

"He didn't like your mum hanging up on him."

"Will he hurt her?" The fear on Jordan's face made Arthur move around the couch and sit next to him.

"We don't know if he'll try, but we're doing everything we can to protect her. She'll be safe at work. Sam's ex-army and it's unlikely your dad will follow them out to sea."

"What about after work?"

"We're still working that out, but I'll walk you and Cody home from school."

His bottom lip trembled. "Am I in danger too?"

"We won't take any chances."

Jordan glanced towards the windows. "You should move in," he stated. "You'll have to stay with me after school, and we'll be safer with you here."

The idea had merit and appeal. "Let's wait to find out what Dot has to say." He gestured to the TV. "Where are they looking for a shipwreck?"

"At the Abrolhos Islands," Jordan said. "Where's that?"

"It's off the coast around Geraldton," Arthur told him.

They watched the rest of the show and as it was finishing, Gretchen joined them. Jordan turned off the television. "What did Dot say?"

Gretchen sighed. "There's not a lot she can do. She'll get her officers to keep an eye out for Kurt, and search for where he's staying. If she can find him, she can question him."

There weren't as many tourists in town any more with the season almost ended. Someone should have seen him unless someone was helping him. Sam had mentioned they'd thought Stonefish was an international entity, because they'd had contacts in Perth and overseas, but last month they'd caught someone local who was high on the pecking order. Maybe he wasn't the only one.

"Arthur's going to walk me home from school," Jordan said. "But he should move in so he can protect you."

Gretchen gaped at him. "I'll be fine."

Jordan shook his head. "You said Dad knows bad people. They might try to hurt you, but not if Arthur's here. He knows army stuff to protect us." He turned to Arthur. "Do you have a gun?"

He did, but it was back in his apartment in the city. "Not here."

"Does Sam?"

"I don't think so."

"Guns aren't the solution," Gretchen said.

"I'm happy to stay here, if you want me to," Arthur said.

"We don't have a spare bed."

"I can sleep on the couch, or the floor. I'm used to sleeping rough." And he very much wanted to protect this family.

Gretchen hesitated. "I don't want to take advantage of you."

He didn't mind in the slightest. In fact he kind of wished she would. "The other option would be to come and stay at Sam's. He's got a spare bedroom."

Gretchen glanced at Jordan. "Here would be better. Jordan has all his things and Kurt will know something is up if we move."

Arthur smiled. "I'll call Sam and tell him not to expect me home tonight."

Gretchen bit her lip. "Are you certain you don't mind?"

"Not at all." He would make sure no harm came to them.

Jordan cheered. "You can stay in my room. Cody sleeps on a mattress on the floor when he stays over."

His enthusiasm was sweet. "Probably best I stay out here. That way I can monitor both doors."

"Right. Of course." Jordan nodded as if he knew it all along.

There was something else they need to consider. "We should talk about what Jordan should say if his dad approaches him again," Arthur said.

"I won't speak to him."

Arthur glanced at Gretchen. "Kurt doesn't know Jordan overheard what he said. We could use that to our advantage."

"I am not letting him anywhere near Jordan."

Arthur held up a hand to placate her. "Kurt's going to be suspicious if Jordan suddenly hates him, and I'm his bodyguard."

"It's too much to ask of Jordan."

"Do you mean I'd be like a spy?" Jordan asked, his face shining with excitement.

Not good. "No. It means you're not giving the enemy valuable information. You need to act like you did today when you saw him, but you shouldn't seek him out."

"This is a bad idea," Gretchen said.

Kurt might not give them a choice. "We need an excuse for why I'm walking Jordan home from school."

"You need gentle exercise with your prosthesis," she said.

He nodded. "And you're helping me." He glanced at Jordan. "What about me staying the night?"

Her cheeks reddened. "Kurt wanted… that to happen."

Yeah, seduce the cripple.

Gretchen cleared her throat. "Jordan, if you talk to your dad and he asks about Arthur staying here, say he's my new boyfriend."

Jordan looked between the two of them. "Is he?"

"No, but your dad will believe it."

He nodded slowly, a little confusion on his face. "All right."

"Good, now time for you to go to bed," Gretchen said. "Go brush your teeth."

He pouted but said, "Fine."

Arthur smiled as Jordan left the room. "He's a great kid."

"Yeah, he is. Let me grab the mattress out of his room."

Arthur followed her so he could help, but he was distracted when she got on to her hands and knees to pull the mattress out from under the bed. He got a very nice view of her round backside. As she shifted, he blinked and hurried forward to help her, pain stabbing his leg as he did so. "Ah!" He fell onto the mattress she'd pulled out and clutched his thigh. Damn thing.

"Are you all right?"

He nodded, gritting his teeth as he rode it out. Finally he exhaled. "Just some nerve pain. It can hit out of the blue sometimes."

"Have you been doing those exercises?"

"Yeah." He needed to be ready for anything Kurt might throw at them. He took the hand Gretchen offered and let her help him to his feet. They carried the mattress into the living area.

Jordan came out to say goodnight, and he hugged Arthur. "Thank you for protecting us."

"You're welcome." He was half in love with this kid.

Gretchen went to tuck Jordan in, and Arthur arranged the mattress where he would have a good view of both the front and back doors. Kurt would have to be pretty bold to try something, but Arthur wouldn't discount it. He filled the kettle more to give himself something to do than from any real desire for tea.

Not long after, Gretchen returned and sighed, running her hand through her hair. "What a day."

"Do you want a cup of tea?"

"Yes, please." Fatigue weighed on her shoulders and her eyes were dark.

"Go sit on the couch. I'll bring it over."

She stared at him a long moment. "You're too sweet."

Her words made his chest sing, and he smiled as he made them both a mug and then carried them over to where she sat curled up on the couch.

"I don't think anyone has ever brought me a cup of tea," she said as she took the mug.

He frowned. "Never?"

She shook her head. "Kurt never did and before him, I lived with my parents. They weren't cup of tea people."

Even he could remember times when his mother or Amy had made them all drinks. "Well I hope it's up to scratch."

She smiled. "It will be, because it's nice not having to make it myself."

How rough had her childhood been that she hadn't

had something as simple as a cup of tea brought to her?

"Thank you for staying," Gretchen said. "If it was just me involved, I'd be fine, but I'm scared he'll do something to Jordan."

Arthur shook his head and placed his mug on the coffee table. "You need protection too," he said. "You deserve it."

He caught her gaze and something passed between them. A definite 'more'. He should have asked her out that afternoon before any of this happened, instead of chickening out. Now he was here, but in the role of protector, he couldn't. It wouldn't be right.

Gretchen shifted, moving a little closer, and her hand cupped his face. "Arthur, I don't know what to do about you. You say the sweetest, kindest things and it wraps my heart in knots."

His heart thumped and he couldn't stop himself from holding her hand in place with his own. "I feel the same about you."

She smiled. "Well then, I guess there's only one thing left to do." She leaned closer and her lips brushed his. Sweet, just like she was.

He closed his eyes, savouring her touch, her taste, but when she pulled away, all he could think was more. He pulled her back, deepening the kiss and she opened for him with a small moan. Their tongues danced, and he slid his arms around her waist, needing her body close to his. How long since he'd felt this kind of passion?

Gretchen pulled up the bottom of his T-shirt, sliding her soft, warm hands along his skin and he groaned. All he wanted was to drag their clothes off and bury himself deep within her.

A sound, a kind of thud, dragged him back to his senses, and he pulled away, placing his finger over her lips when she went to speak. He scanned the room, checking for movement from Jordan's room, glancing at the windows to make sure the curtains were all shut, and finally the doors. Nothing. Still his instincts wouldn't let him rest until he'd checked things more thoroughly. "I heard something," he murmured, and then because he couldn't help himself, he brushed another kiss over her lips before he stood. "Stay here while I check."

She nodded, concern on her face.

He went to Jordan's room first, but the boy was already fast asleep. Then he moved from room to room, closing curtains if they were open and checking the latches were all secure. It was a new house, double brick, and the master bedroom even had a walk-in robe. The locks were new and as he mapped the floor plan in his head, he made contingencies for ways out and where they could hole up if they needed to.

He checked the back door, opening it to peer out at the night, the outside light illuminating the yard. A border of hedges and trees around the outside, a small garden shed in the corner and a small patch of lawn. The fence was intact and none of the neighbours could see into the yard. Empty. He threw the deadlock and then went to the front door. A large pot plant was on its side. Too big to have been blown over by anything but a very strong gust of wind, and there wasn't any wind tonight. He scanned the neighbourhood, feeling like a target in the light's glare, and then bent and picked up the pot. He moved back inside and locked the door.

Gretchen hovered in the living room. "Anything?"

"The pot plant blew over."

She frowned. "There's no wind."

"It might have been teenagers having fun." It was an effort to make her feel better, but she clearly didn't believe him.

"I'm glad you're staying." She came over and kissed him again, this time short and sweet. "As much as I enjoyed what we were up to, I'm exhausted."

"Go to bed. I've got this."

She kissed him again. "I know. It's the only reason I'll get any sleep tonight."

And with those simple words, Arthur fell completely in love with her.

Chapter 14

Arthur barely slept, so when Gretchen started moving around in her bedroom, he got up and made breakfast. Part of the reason for his lack of sleep was his damned leg. He'd debated taking off the prosthesis like he normally did when he slept, but he wasn't sure how quickly Kurt would act on his threat. He wouldn't have time to go through the process of putting on his leg if something happened in the middle of the night. The extra weight and discomfort made sleeping difficult.

Then there was the added fact that he was on edge. Every new sound had him alert and ready; cats fighting, leaves brushing against the roof, dogs barking, cars driving past.

What he wouldn't give for a strong coffee right now, but there were no signs of a coffee machine on Gretchen's bench. Instead, he filled the kettle and got out the makings for tea.

Jordan needed lunch for school, but he didn't know what the boy normally took.

Gretchen came out, already dressed in her work uniform of a polo shirt and shorts. He handed her a mug of tea.

She took the mug, her eyes wide. "Thank you."

"Is something wrong?" He'd made it the same as she'd had it the night before.

She shook her head. "Sorry, I'm not used to having someone in my kitchen." She smiled. "It's nice."

"I would have made you breakfast, but I wasn't sure what you ate."

"You don't need to," Gretchen said. "It's enough that you're staying here." She pressed a kiss to his cheek.

"I want to. I like to be useful."

She kissed him on the lips then, long and slow. "Thank you."

If that was his reward, he'd make dinner as well. "What does Jordan usually do for lunch?"

"He makes his own sandwiches and takes fruit for a snack." She screwed up her face. "He never eats what I make him."

Arthur couldn't imagine not eating something his mother had made him. His father wouldn't have stood for it.

"He loves porridge for breakfast," she said. "I throw some dates in for sweetness."

Arthur smiled. "I can make it." He took the oats she handed him and started cooking. "What does Jordan do before school?" Gretchen was at the boat by seven thirty.

She grimaced. "I drop him at school and he helps the teachers. They have a school garden, so he does the weeding, or he'll help collate workbooks and such. He doesn't like it, but I rely on Holly enough as it is. She's got three kids to get ready in the morning and she doesn't need Jordan added to the mix."

He'd never considered how hard it was for a single parent, especially one who didn't have a support network around her. But he imagined Jordan would hate being the first one at school. "I can take him to school later," he said. "What time does he start?"

"You don't have to."

"I want to," he reiterated. "Jordan's fun to hang out with."

She sighed. "He starts at eight twenty."

"Great. I'll make sure he's there on time."

"I'll tell Miss Simpson he won't be there early today." She made the phone call then she went to wake Jordan while Arthur finished cooking breakfast.

The boy came out, his blond hair sticking up in different directions and wearing pyjamas with superheroes on them. "Morning," he grunted and slouched into a chair at the table.

Not a morning person.

Arthur dished up the porridge and Gretchen poured Jordan an orange juice. As she placed it on the table, she said, "Arthur's going to walk you to school today, so you don't need to go in so early."

Jordan perked up. "Really? Can I watch cartoons this morning?"

"Not until you're ready to go. That means lunch is made, bag is packed and you're dressed with teeth and hair brushed and shoes on."

Arthur hid a smile. She knew what to expect from Jordan.

"Sure!"

Maybe the lure of cartoons was enough to perk him up.

"*And* you have to go when Arthur tells you, even if the cartoon isn't finished yet."

"OK." A little less enthusiasm now.

Arthur calculated the distance to school. It wasn't far, but Jordan didn't walk fast—at least he hadn't yesterday. It would take about twenty minutes, which meant he'd have to leave just before the hour when any cartoon would be finishing. He'd be the bad guy.

When they finished breakfast, Gretchen handed Arthur a key to the house. "Come and go as you please." She hesitated and then showed him a photo on her phone. "This is Kurt."

Kurt was smirking, but his eyes were hard. He wore a black singlet which showed off the rose tattoo on his shoulder with a name scrawled underneath. Jordan looked about three and played with some blocks on the ground behind him, but was smiling at the camera. They were in a living room and the massive television in the background took up most of the wall.

Arthur committed Kurt's features to memory. "Thanks." He walked her to the door and, after checking Jordan was in his room, Arthur kissed her. "Have a good day."

She smiled. "You too."

He waited on the step until she drove away and scanned the neighbourhood. Not much movement. An older woman he recognised from the grocery store walked her dog, and a couple of school kids rode their bikes. No Kurt. He went back inside, locking the door behind him. Jordan was already in front of the TV, still in his pyjamas. Arthur grinned. "Didn't Gretchen say something about being ready for school before watching television?"

Jordan peeked over his shoulder, a very guilty expression on his face. "Just one?"

It was so very tempting to say yes. He didn't want to be inflexible and exacting like his father, but he also wanted to respect Gretchen's wishes. "You can keep the tele on while you make lunch."

Jordan nodded and headed for the kitchen.

While Jordan took ages putting together a sandwich, spending most of his time staring at the television rather than at the bread he was buttering, Arthur took off his prosthetic leg. He sighed in relief as it came away and he rubbed the raw skin.

"Does it hurt?" Jordan had finished preparing his lunch and returned to the living area.

"Sometimes." He massaged the scar like Gretchen had shown him. "It's nice to let it breathe."

"Do you sleep with it on?"

"Not normally, but I did last night."

"Why?"

"I wouldn't be much use protecting you if I had to take five minutes to put on my leg."

Jordan cocked his head. "It didn't take that long at the beach."

"No, but it's also not as quick as jumping to my feet." He waved Jordan towards his room. "Go, finish getting ready and you can time me when you get back."

The boy ran off, the cartoons forgotten as he'd been tempted by something far more unusual.

Arthur sighed. This was his new normal. He needed to accept and get better at preparing himself, taking care of the site, and strengthening his muscles. Gretchen's and Jordan's lives could depend on him.

The thought gave him motivation, and he moved through the mobility exercises Gretchen had given him.

Jordan jogged into the room, his hair damp and wearing his yellow and brown school uniform. "Did I miss it?"

Arthur shook his head. "No. Have you brushed your teeth?"

Jordan spun around and ran back to the bathroom.

Arthur chuckled. The boy was great. He waited until Jordan returned before he explained each element of his prosthesis.

"There's so many layers," Jordan exclaimed as he started the stopwatch on Arthur's phone.

"Yeah. Some of it is to pad the limb, and other bits

are to help the suction stay in place."

Jordan's eyes widened. "Does it ever fall off?"

Arthur nodded. "Your mum had to fish it out of the marina for me the other day."

He grinned. "She's the coolest."

"She is." Arthur checked the time. "We'd better get to school."

Jordan fetched his bag and Arthur turned off the television and tidied the house.

It was a cool, clear morning, the blue sky stretching into the distance, the sun rising towards its zenith, and birds calling to each other in the garden. Other children were walking or riding their bikes to school, and Jordan waved to a couple but stayed next to Arthur. Arthur scanned the road ahead. No parked cars where people could hide and most of the front yards were simple patches of lawn. Parents waved their children off to school and a couple of joggers ran past.

Normal life.

"Thanks for staying with me," Jordan said. "It's nice going to school at a normal time."

"It's my pleasure. You're helping me by making sure I get some exercise. I've been lazy."

"Aren't you supposed to be super fit?"

"I was when I was in the army. But I spent a lot of time in hospital and haven't got back into the swing of things."

"We could exercise after school," Jordan said. "You could show me and Cody army drills on the oval."

Arthur hesitated. Should he encourage Jordan's interest in the army? Right now, he saw only what he thought was cool, but there were so many elements to it. And he shuddered when he remembered his father's drills. "We'll see. I'll have to chat to Cody's mum."

That seemed to satisfy Jordan, and they chatted until they got to school, where they met up with Cody.

"Hey, Sherlock!" Cody waved.

"Morning."

"Sherlock's staying with us at the moment," Jordan said. "He's going to walk me to school every day."

"Epic!"

"I'll see you after school," Arthur reminded him. "I'll walk you both home."

"Awesome," Cody said.

The bell rang, and the boys ran inside.

Arthur scanned the schoolyard, and then the carpark and surrounding road. There were a couple of cars containing harassed-looking parents who shooed their children out and then drove away. No one who didn't belong there. Jordan would be safe inside the school for the day. Still, it was harder than he expected to walk away.

He was invested.

Arthur exhaled and headed for Sam's place. He could do with a shower, and wanted to change the liners on his prosthesis. This was his first day alone since he'd been discharged. Excitement tickled his skin. He could do whatever he wanted. His first thought was to research Kurt. The more he knew about his enemy, the better. Then, if he had time, he wanted to dive into the research of those extra Retribution passenger names.

Two worthy missions, both of which he was qualified to do.

He wouldn't fail.

***

Arthur's alarm blared, and he jolted, switching it off and checking the time. Two o'clock. Time to pick up Jordan. Good thing he'd set an alarm. Time had disappeared as he'd submerged in his research, finding little about Kurt online, but a bit about Gretchen's parents. Nothing seemed out of the ordinary. He'd turned his attention to the puzzle of the Retribution and lost all track of time so that he'd forgotten to have lunch. His stomach rumbled.

He'd taken Gretchen's advice and spent part of the day with his prosthesis off, so he reattached it and then quickly threw some clothes into his backpack and grabbed an apple from the fridge. The work he'd done on trying to decipher the meaning behind the extra names still lay on the table. Easy for someone to see if they broke in. He bundled it together, careful not to get anything out of order, and added it to his backpack before heading outside.

A dry heat sapped any moisture from his skin as he left the house. He checked the time. Not enough to go back and look for sun cream. He'd make do and stick to the shaded paths where he could. No way would he be late.

Arthur considered jogging, but he hadn't tested his leg at any fast pace. Definitely something he needed to do, but he'd do it later when Jordan was with him.

The first kids were walking towards him as he reached the school's street. Arthur picked up his pace, scanning the faces for Jordan or Cody. Gretchen had mentioned Cody walked with his sisters as well.

As he reached the gates, Jordan and Cody crossed the yard together. Behind them, a young, female teacher watched all the kids from near the classrooms.

"Hurry up, Cody," a girl who was maybe thirteen yelled from nearby.

She had the same dark hair as Cody and similar facial features. She had to be his sister. Sure enough, Cody ignored her as he walked up to Arthur. "Jordan said you're going to show us army drills this afternoon."

The older girl studied Arthur.

"I'm Arthur. I'm a friend of Jordan's and his mum."

She gave a slight smile and said to Cody, "Come on." A girl younger than Jordan followed her, and the boys fell in step with Arthur.

"Is that your teacher?" Arthur nodded back to the building.

The boys turned. "Yeah, it's Miss Simpson," Jordan said. He screwed up his face. "She asked me heaps of questions about why I was in later today."

Arthur started walking, his interest piqued. "Like what?"

"Whether Mum was sick, and how I got to school."

"What did you tell her?"

"I said you walked me to school."

"Did she ask who I was?"

"Yeah. I told her you were my friend."

Was Miss Simpson just being nosy? She might be a gossip, but he made a mental note to ask Gretchen about her.

"So, are you going to show us some drills?" Cody asked.

Arthur smiled at the boy's impatience. "Let's ask your mum first."

As they walked, the boys asked him questions about the army. He kept his attention on them as much as possible while also being aware of his surroundings, but no one looked out of place.

When they arrived at Cody's place, Arthur waited at the door while Cody fetched his mum. Arthur didn't want to startle Holly by being a strange man in her house. She walked down the corridor, smiling at him. "You must be Arthur."

He nodded. "Did Gretchen call you?"

"Yes, she explained everything."

Great.

"Mum, can we go to the oval with Arthur?" Cody asked. "He's going to teach us army stuff."

At Holly's concerned expression, Arthur explained, "The boys wanted to learn my fitness drills. But I can do it in the backyard, either here or at Gretchen's." He preferred the privacy, so anyone watching didn't know what he was capable of. Far better if they saw him as a cripple.

"We can go to my place," Jordan said. "Then the girls won't get in the way."

Arthur raised his eyebrows. "Girls are quite capable."

Holly nodded. "But in this case, the dog would drive you crazy. If you don't mind taking them to Gretchen's, that would be great."

"Sure."

The boys cheered.

"I'll have Cody back by five."

They left the house and continued along the footpath towards Gretchen's place. Arthur resisted the urge to scratch his leg. The prosthesis was itching and rubbing, but there was nowhere he could sit to readjust it. He should have asked Holly if he could come in for a second, but he wasn't quite ready for strangers to see him take off his leg.

It wasn't far to Gretchen's place.

The street was empty now except for the occasional school child dragging their feet on their way home.

The boys peppered Arthur with questions about what they'd be learning. "You'll see when we get there." After he'd figured out what he could show them. Jordan would benefit from learning how to escape holds in case his father tried anything.

They were passing the park, and Arthur scanned it for a bench where he could sit. He winced as his leg continued to rub and he slowed, trying to adjust the sleeve so it sat better. Jordan bumped him as he bent over and his weight was just off centre enough that he fell, his leg popping off, and as he windmilled to get his balance, it flew out of his hand and down the incline into the park. Arthur lost his fight against gravity and sprawled unceremoniously on the ground.

Shit.

He shifted to a seated position. Jordan stared at him with horrified wide eyes, while Cody yelled, "I'll get it!" and ran into the park to fetch Arthur's leg.

"I'm sorry!"

Arthur smiled, though his palms stung from hitting the pavement. "It's fine." Cody had reached the leg and was examining it.

Jordan's eyes teared up. "Are you OK?"

"Yeah, it happens sometimes."

"Jordan! Do you need a lift home?" The voice was rough, male and came from a black four-wheel drive which pulled up next to them.

Arthur couldn't see the driver from where he sat, but Jordan's worried expression told him all he needed to know. Fuck. "Cody! I need my leg." Cody looked up and jogged towards them.

Hurry.

Jordan glanced at him and then back at the car. "No thanks, Dad. Arthur's walking us home."

"Doesn't look like he's getting far." The car door slammed and footsteps sounded on the bitumen. Short, solid, and covered in tattoos, the man assessed Arthur and clenched his hands before relaxing. A fighter. And a cocky son-of-a-bitch.

Revealing himself to Arthur, trying something straight after the warning. Was Kurt assessing him, or had he already dismissed Arthur, and was sending a message to Gretchen? Either way, Arthur was vulnerable down here. Cody handed Arthur his leg, and he slipped it on, rolling up the sleeve.

"You don't mind if I give my son a lift, do you?"

Kurt asked.

Arthur smiled as he held up his hand to get Cody and Jordan to help him to his feet, as if he couldn't do it on his own. After making sure the prosthesis was seated correctly, he replied, "Actually, I do. We've got plans." He held out his hand. "I'm Arthur."

"Kurt." He squeezed Arthur's hand as he shook, as if testing his strength. "I'm only in town for a short time."

Arthur faked his surprise. "Gretchen didn't mention it."

"I'd like to spend time with Jordan. I miss him."

"I can appreciate that, mate," Arthur replied, keeping his tone jovial. "But I've got responsibility for Jordan at the moment, and I'm not comfortable letting a stranger take him."

Kurt scowled. "I'm not a stranger. I'm his dad, aren't I, Jordan?"

Arthur spoke before Jordan did. "You're a stranger to me, but I can call Gretchen now."

Kurt ignored the suggestion. "Jordan, you want to come with me, don't you?"

Bastard.

Jordan glanced between the two of them, uncertain, but he shifted a little closer to Arthur.

"I need Jordan's help," Arthur said, placing a hand on Jordan's shoulder and giving it a gentle squeeze. "I don't get around as easily as I used to."

A brief smirk as Kurt glanced at Arthur's leg.

Jordan nodded. "Sorry, Dad. I promised Mum I'd help him."

Kurt smiled, though it barely reached his cheeks, let alone his eyes. "Fine, maybe tomorrow then." He pivoted and strode back to the car.

They all watched him drive away, and then Cody clapped Jordan on his back. "Your dad is kind of scary."

Jordan nodded and glanced up at Arthur, worry and sadness in his eyes.

Arthur smiled and squeezed his shoulder again. How much had the boy shared with his friend?

"Hey, Sherlock," Cody said. "What's that over there?" He pointed to a plaque in the centre of the park, which was surrounded by a small brick wall.

"Probably an ANZAC memorial," Arthur replied. "Most towns have them. They engrave plaques with the names of their men who fought in the wars to honour them."

"Can we go look?" Cody asked.

Jordan was still subdued. "Maybe tomorrow. Let's get home." Kurt had escalated quickly. He needed to prepare Jordan.

They had a lot of training to do.

Chapter 15

Gretchen waved to the last passenger and sighed in relief when they finally got on the bus. This lot had been chatterers, and it had been difficult to get them off the boat, because they'd wanted to rave about the tour. Normally she loved talking with them, but today all she could think of was Jordan with Arthur. She wasn't worried Arthur wouldn't take care of her son, but she didn't want to miss out on the time they spent together.

Arthur had sent her a text to say they were home and Cody was with them. She liked the idea of them all playing in the backyard.

She finished tidying the boat in record time.

Sam pulled her aside. "Are you all right?"

She stiffened, though she'd been waiting for this conversation. Gretchen nodded. "I will be."

"We'll help you," he said. "You're not on your own."

The relief was instant, and she smiled. "I know. Thank you."

"Arthur's good at what he does. He'll be able to protect you." He sounded almost as if he was trying to convince himself.

She frowned. "I know he can." Was it simply doubt about Arthur's leg, or his mental state? "We'll help each other."

Sam nodded. "This will be good for him. It will give him a mission."

Gretchen gathered her things. She didn't want to be just a mission to him.

"Tell him to call if he needs anything," Sam added.

"I will."

"Good. We should be right for the tour tomorrow. The storm isn't due to hit until tomorrow night and the swell should be reasonable."

"Great." She honestly didn't care about the weather at the moment, but she understood his concern. He'd have to cancel the tour and disappoint a lot of people if the storm arrived early.

Finally, she escaped and drove home. The slam of her car door echoed in the garage and Gretchen frowned. She'd expected to hear them playing in the backyard. Concern skittered over her skin and she hurried inside. "I'm home."

Nothing.

She checked Jordan's room to find it empty, and then she headed outside.

No one.

Where were they? Arthur had said they'd got home safely.

"Jordan!" Unless someone else had sent the text from Arthur's phone.

Panic built inside her and she scanned the garden for evidence they had been here. The small garden shed in the corner was closed, the shrubs against the fence line rustled in the wind, the grass was clear and in need of a mow.

"Boo!"

Gretchen shrieked and spun to find Jordan right

behind her, grinning from ear to ear.

"I hid so well you didn't even spot me!" He danced from foot to foot in excitement.

"Boo!"

Gretchen jumped again to find Cody next to her. She put a hand to her heart as Arthur walked over, an apologetic smile on his face.

"Sorry. The boys wanted to test their skills. I didn't know they were going to scare you." He raised his eyebrows at Jordan.

Jordan grinned. "Sorry."

Yeah, she really believed him. Her relief outweighed the fright, and she hugged her son. "Seems like you've been busy this afternoon."

Jordan nodded. "Sherlock's the best. He wouldn't let Dad take me."

What? Her breath left her, and she spun to Arthur. "What did he do?"

Arthur held up a hand. "He wanted to take Jordan home, but I told him I was responsible for Jordan and couldn't let him. He didn't push it."

But he'd still tried something when Arthur was right there. What had he hoped to achieve? Had he been assessing Arthur's ability to take care of her child, or was he trying to prove some misguided point?

"I was worried because Sherlock lost his leg, but he put it back on fast," Jordan said.

She blinked, trying to catch up. Was Sam right? Should she be concerned about Arthur's ability?

Her heart still raced as Arthur said, "I'll tell you all about it later."

"Sherlock's been teaching us how to get out of holds," Cody said.

"Grab me, Mum." Jordan thrust out his arm. His wrist was red and a little bruised.

Still not sure about any of this, Gretchen took hold

of Jordan's wrist. In only a second, he'd pried back her fingers and freed himself, wincing a little.

Impressive, but, "I think that's enough. Your wrist looks sore."

Jordan rubbed it and grinned. "The bruise is from the cable ties." He pulled out a couple of cable ties from his pocket.

"What?" Doubt crept in as she glanced at Arthur.

He rubbed the back of his head. "They asked about how to free themselves if they were tied up. I could only find cable ties in your shed."

The reality of the situation hit her hard. Jordan might need these skills with Kurt. "Did Arthur's technique work?"

Cody nodded. "It was hard, and hurt, but we got free."

The thought of either boy in a situation where they were cable-tied made her heart race, but she forced a smile and mouthed, *Thank you* to Arthur. "Looks like you guys have learnt a lot," she said. "I'm going to head inside and make dinner." And try not to completely freak out about Kurt.

"You should learn too, Mum," Jordan said. "In case Dad is mean to you."

She was too tired to concentrate now. Her heartbeat still hadn't slowed to its normal pace. "Arthur can show me later." When he told her all about what had happened. She checked the time. "You finish up here. I'll take Cody home in half an hour." She headed inside to prepare dinner.

It wasn't until after Jordan had gone to bed that Gretchen asked Arthur about the afternoon. She set a mug of tea next to him and sat on the couch. "What did Kurt do?"

Arthur rubbed a hand over his face. "It was after we

left Cody's place. My leg fell off and while I was reattaching it, Kurt pulled up and offered Jordan a lift."

Gretchen was careful not to let her expression change, but it was difficult. Arthur's leg was a disadvantage. Kurt would target it to disable Arthur in any kind of fight.

"I told him no, and that I needed Jordan's help to get around. Eventually he left."

Smart. Making Kurt think he was less capable was a good strategy, but if Kurt was watching them all, he'd soon see that Arthur was extremely capable. "Why would Kurt make himself known like that?"

Arthur sipped his tea. "I think he was testing the waters. Trying to figure out what you'd told Jordan about him, and whether you'd told me."

"How did Jordan react?"

"He was great. He said he'd promised you he'd help me, but he looked a little worried. I'm not sure Kurt noticed. He was too busy sizing me up."

"I don't like this."

Arthur placed a hand on her knee. "I know. Jordan and Cody are great at hiding, and they're much better at getting out of holds. By the end of the week, they should have all the tools they need to escape if Kurt gets to them."

That only made her feel marginally better. The thought of Kurt kidnapping either child gave her chills. "Maybe I should stop working," she said. "It's almost the end of the season. I can be with Jordan when he's not in school."

Hurt crossed Arthur's face. "I know my leg's a disadvantage, but I will take care of Jordan."

Appalled, Gretchen shuffled closer to him. "No. That's not what I meant. I'd feel the same no matter who was with Jordan." She sighed. "Having him out of my sight makes me nervous."

"And Jordan will hate you hovering over him."

"I know." Her gut twisted and she sighed. "I feel so helpless."

"I'll protect Jordan with my life."

The thought worried her. She didn't want it to come to that.

But that was out of her control. "What can I do?"

"You can be vigilant. Report any contact with Kurt, or anything that seems odd to the police, document everything. With enough evidence, you might get a restraining order."

"That won't stop him."

"No, but breaching it might get him thrown in gaol for a while."

Fat lot of good that would do when he had others who could do his dirty work. Still, Arthur was trying to console her. "Thanks." She finished her tea and took both their mugs into the kitchen to wash. Before she sat down again, she went to check on Jordan. He slept curled into a ball, the sheets clutched around him, and hugging the stuffed bunny he'd had since he was a baby.

Safe.

She brushed a kiss against his forehead, and he didn't stir. Sleeping peacefully.

When she returned to the living room, Arthur was doing some exercises she'd given him.

"How are you finding it?" Gretchen asked.

He grunted. "I should have been doing these all along."

"Why didn't you?"

"I didn't see the point." He didn't look at her as he spoke. "Couldn't see past the loss."

"It must have been difficult."

"I was selfish, only thinking about myself." He glanced at her. "I can see that now. There's more to life than the army and making my father happy."

The intensity in his eyes drew her in. "I'm glad." The kiss they'd shared the night before came back to her with clarity. His passion had surprised her, possibly because of how sullen he'd been when she'd first met him. She swallowed and asked, "Do you want a hand with your exercises?"

He hesitated and then nodded.

She knelt on the ground and took the end of his leg in her hands, massaging it, pressing into the scars to soften them and help the blood circulate. Arthur hissed and she glanced at him. "Too hard?"

"No, it's fine."

From this position on her knees, she could think of other things she'd like to do with him. He hadn't lost all his muscle through his inactivity, and her fingers itched to run under his shirt and across his chest. His eyes widened and she smiled, before concentrating back on his legs. He knew what she was thinking.

Arthur let out a shaky breath. "If you'd been my therapist, I would have done my exercises diligently."

She grinned. "If I'd been your therapist, I wouldn't have acted on these thoughts I'm having."

His lips twitched. "What thoughts would they be?"

"These." She slid her hands further up his legs, skirting his groin, and shifted to a crouch so she could straddle him and run her hands under his shirt.

His hands clenched her hips and held her in place. "I like your thoughts."

She dipped her head and brushed a kiss against one cheek and then the other. His hand went to the back of her head, and he held her in place, turning their heads so their lips met. She'd been expecting a rush of passion, but he was slow, methodical, teasing her lips open, taking small soft kisses as if he wanted to taste every millimetre.

Gretchen let him lead even though she was on top. Her heart fluttered at his thorough exploration before he slipped his tongue between her lips and tasted her.

She sighed, floating away on the pleasure, being so expertly seduced by him. She moved her hands, rubbing soft circles over his nipples. He groaned and pressed into her, deepening the kiss. More. She wanted his lips all over her body, and she wanted to touch him everywhere. She broke the kiss. "Bedroom."

In one swift movement, he pressed up, keeping his grip on her butt, standing.

Then he swore and teetered, letting go of her. Her feet hit the ground and she caught him before he fell. Arthur's face flushed red. "Are you all right?"

They'd both forgotten about his leg.

"I will be as long as you don't stop." Gretchen wrapped her arms around his neck, sliding one hand onto the back of his head, and brought him close. She wouldn't let this minor hiccup ruin the night.

His kisses were more perfunctory and she broke away. "Arthur, don't let it bother you."

"How am I supposed to get to the bedroom without my prosthesis?"

She imagined it wouldn't feel sexy if she helped him. "You could put it back on." But would it hinder his pleasure or be a reminder of what he'd lost? She glanced around and thought about when she knelt beside him. She ran a finger down his chest. "You know, I don't mind a man on his hands and knees."

There was a spark of interest, but it didn't light him up. Hoping she was doing the right thing, she stepped away and slid her polo shirt off, so she stood in her bra and shorts.

His eyes widened in appreciation and scanned her body, lingering on her breasts. "You want to see these, you need to come after me." She undid her bra, turning and sliding it off so all he saw was her back. She tossed it at him and he caught it, running his fingers over the material. Her body tingled in anticipation, and she slipped out of her shorts, leaving them on the floor. She glanced over her shoulder. "I'd really like you to see the rest of me." She walked into her bedroom, hoping he would follow.

***

Arthur absent-mindedly stroked the soft fabric of Gretchen's bra as she disappeared into her bedroom. The self-loathing and feelings of inadequacy fought to take over, and he struggled to push them down. What was wrong with him? He had a beautiful woman inviting him to her bedroom, and he was too caught up in how he'd made a fool of himself to go after her.

All he'd wanted was to carry Gretchen to her bedroom and make love to her.

Until he almost dropped her. She'd rescued him. Again.

With the humiliation battering him, he focused on the scrap of warm fabric in his hands. This had been touching her breasts. *He* could be touching her breasts if he got over his loathing and just dealt with his changed circumstances.

The thought gave him the strength to push down the rest of the negativity. What were his options?

Did he want to put his leg back on? Would it feel unnatural and be in the way in the bedroom, or would it help him balance? Too many unknowns and time was wasting. He grabbed his leg and crawled awkwardly after Gretchen. Just before the doorway of her bedroom, he lifted himself up and hopped into the room, closing the door behind him, leaning against the door so he could work out his next move. Gretchen lay sprawled in her underwear on her bed, looking like a temptress. He hardened as she smiled at him. "I'm glad you joined me."

So was he. Now to get from the door to the bed without looking like an idiot.

The room was simply furnished; a single bed-side table which didn't match the frame of the bed, and what looked like a touch lamp from the nineties on top of it. A few clothes hung in the walk-in-robe, but that was all there was. Simple and cheap. Probably all Gretchen could afford. Arthur had the sudden urge to buy her nice things, not as a bribe or as a show of power, but because he wanted her to have whatever she wanted.

"Are you going to stay there all night?"

The sultry tone brought his attention right back to Gretchen, where it belonged. Two hops got him to the edge of the bed. He placed his right knee on the bed and stretched over to lean his prosthesis up against the bed-side table in case he needed it. Then he gave his entire attention to Gretchen.

"You're a little overdressed, aren't you?"

He ripped off his T-shirt, obeying her every command, unspoken or not. He scanned her body, from her painted pink toenails to her dishevelled blonde hair. Where to start?

He was always one to savour and save the best to last, but he wasn't certain what the best would be. He started at her feet. She needed to be worshipped.

His lips brushed the tops of her feet, kissing them as his hands massaged the balls of them. She let out a soft moan. "That feels so good."

He smiled. He would pleasure every inch of her body until she couldn't remember her own name. She would know the joys of being pampered.

Slowly he worked up her body, rubbing one foot and then the other, before turning her over so he could nibble on her calves, and kiss and lick her thighs. Beneath him she became a boneless mass of relaxation and her quiet groans sent blood straight to his groin. At her bottom, he slid his finger under her panties, tracing the curve of the fabric around her thigh, and felt the heat of her wetness.

"Please, Arthur." She pressed closer to his hand.

He fought for control, every part of him wanting to rip her underwear off and plunge into her.

Slowly.

He slid her underwear off and threw it on the floor. Then, unable to resist, he slid two fingers between her thighs and stroked.

She bucked into him. "Yes."

Arthur rolled her onto her back and her eyes full of desire almost undid him. He tasted her sweetness from his fingers and she lifted her hips towards him and reached for the condom on her bedside table. "More."

His erection pushed against his shorts, wanting out. "There's no rush." Still, he pushed his remaining clothes off. Brushing a thumb against her mound, he then kissed his way up her stomach until he reached her breasts. Small, plump and just the right size for his hand.

He licked and sucked first one nipple and then the next.

Her moans grew louder. "Arthur, you're killing me."

His name on her lips made him feel strong, powerful. "I need to savour you."

"I've been savoured." She grabbed the back of his neck and pulled him close so she could kiss him.

Her passion and desire sent a surge of lust through his body. He met her kiss with equal passion, and he groaned when she rubbed herself against his cock.

"I need you inside of me."

He fought for control, taking the moment to kiss

and nibble her neck while his hand searched for the condom on the bedside table. Finding it, he made quick work of sliding it on. Then he swept kisses across her face, ending on her mouth and as she opened for him, he slowly slid inside of her.

Their moans mingled. Home. It was as if he belonged here with her. He relished the moment and then moved, slowly at first, almost unwilling to remove any part from her, and then faster as the urges built.

"Yes." She met him thrust for thrust until she shuddered, clenching tighter around him and he was lost.

Chapter 16

Arthur was gone when Gretchen woke the next morning. The last thing she remembered after being so thoroughly pleasured was him holding her in his arms and telling her to go to sleep. She cringed. How embarrassing to have immediately fallen asleep after the best sex of her life. Her hand ran over the empty, cold side of the bed. What an experience. She stretched, enjoying the pull of her muscles, and checked the time. Just before six. She had to be up now, anyway. As she stood, she noticed the clothes she'd worn yesterday were folded on her bed-side table. Tidying up in case Jordan had woken first. She smiled and quickly showered and dressed for the day before heading out to find the man who had made her feel so wonderful.

He stood in the kitchen stirring something on the stove as if he did it every day.

Her heart twinged. She could get used to him being there, get used to being cared for. She'd had to be self-sufficient her whole life.

He glanced back and his slow smile warmed her insides. "Good morning."

Yes, it was. "Hi, you didn't have to make breakfast."

"I wanted to." He switched off the stove and moved over to her. "Did you sleep well?"

Her cheeks flushed. "Yes. I'm sorry for falling asleep on you."

"I didn't mind." He kissed her. "What do you want to tell Jordan about us?"

Us. It sounded so simple. "I don't know." What were they? "I hadn't thought about it."

He stepped back. "I don't have to kiss or touch you in front of him. We can pretend we're friends."

She shook her head. That wasn't fair to anyone. "I'll talk to him. Tell him we're…" She looked at him to fill in the blank.

Arthur shrugged. "Together? Dating?"

She nodded. Jordan could understand that. "I'll tell him tonight, so he has time to process it. Will you walk him to school?"

"Of course."

That meant she didn't have to wake him until she was leaving for work. He could sleep a whole extra hour.

As Arthur dished up the porridge, Gretchen checked the weather and sighed.

"What's wrong?"

"Storms are forecast tonight. We'll probably have to cancel tomorrow's tour, which will disappoint people."

"How far ahead do you decide?"

"Sam will decide today. If it's too rough, or visibility is bad, it won't be pleasant."

"And if you get the day off?" His tone was a little wicked.

She grinned. "I'll set aside some time to study for my exam." She sipped her coffee. "But if it's raining, it might be a good time to be tucked up in bed with company."

"I hope it rains a lot."

Gretchen laughed. It would be a relief to be in town closer to Jordan. She got out her phone and messaged Dot. *Any update?*

Not yet. We can't find where he's staying.

Maybe he was camping somewhere, but Kurt never liked to rough it. She showed Arthur the message and checked the time. "I need to wake Jordan."

Love filled her as she entered his room. Somehow, he'd ended up with his sheets around his head, his legs sticking out below, and his stuffed bunny on the floor. Gently she uncovered him. "Jordan, it's time to wake up."

He grumbled.

She kissed his brow. "Come on, sweetheart. I need to get to work, and Arthur will walk you to school."

His eyes flashed open. "Arthur's here?" He didn't wait for her answer, leapt out of bed and ran into the living room.

Well, she knew her place. She pushed the slight jealousy away. She was his mum, his everyday constant. She couldn't compete with the excitement of an ex-soldier in the house.

And to be fair, she'd wanted to run out to greet Arthur when she'd woken this morning, too.

She made his bed and by the time she returned to the living area, Jordan was sitting at the table, eating porridge, chatting to Arthur, completely at ease.

"I'm off to work." She kissed Jordan, lifted her backpack, and smiled at Arthur, even though she wanted to kiss him as well. "I'll see you this afternoon."

"I'll walk you out." Arthur stood and joined her at the door.

Jordan was busy eating, not paying them any attention. She kissed Arthur. "Have a good day."

He smiled. "I will now. You too."

She waved, smiling, her heart full of hope as she

headed to work.

***

Arthur locked the front door after Gretchen drove away and turned to find Jordan staring at him, confusion on his face. "Something wrong?"

"Mum kissed you."

Oh. Damn. "Yeah, she did."

"Are you like, really her boyfriend now? Not pretend?"

Arthur sat at the table. "I'd like to be. I think your mum is pretty special."

"Is that why you're being so nice to me?"

He leaned back, shocked. "No, of course not. I like you too. You made me feel better about losing my leg."

Jordan frowned. "Huh?"

"When I moved up here, I was feeling pretty bad about my leg." He tapped the prosthesis. "I thought I was worthless. But you and Cody saw me as a person, not an injured soldier, and that made me feel much better. It gave me the confidence I'd lost."

The boy was silent for a moment as he processed the information. "I helped you?"

"A lot," Arthur confirmed. "I like you as much as I like your mum."

"Are you going to stay here forever now?" Jordan asked. "Like Faith moved in with Lara's dad."

The image of staying here forever warmed him, but it was far too early for that. "I don't know. It depends on how your mum feels, and how you feel."

"Me?"

"Yeah. Your mum loves you so much, so if you don't want me around, I won't be around."

"I like you. I like you're teaching me stuff, and that I don't have to go to school early."

Arthur smiled. "I like that too."

"I don't mind if you're Mum's boyfriend. You're cool."

Arthur nodded solemnly, though inside he cheered. "I appreciate it." He checked the time. "You'd better finish your breakfast and brush your teeth." There wasn't time to make lunch. "I'll give you some money for the canteen."

Jordan's face lit up. "Really? Thanks!" He rushed his bowl to the sink and then ran to the bathroom. Arthur cleaned the kitchen and Jordan returned carrying both his school backpack and Arthur's bag. As he handed Arthur's bag to him, a pile of notes fell out.

"Sorry!" Jordan bent to pick them up.

Arthur cringed and tried to grab the notes before Jordan read them, but he was too late. Jordan held a sheet, his eyes wide. "Treasure?"

Damn. He gently pried the paper away from Jordan. "It's nothing."

Jordan shook his head, expression hurt. "You're looking at clues to the treasure Mischa told me about. It's real, isn't it? Where's the plaque?"

Hell. He finished gathering the pages and put them back in his bag before facing Jordan. "We don't know for sure," he said. "But this is a big secret. You can't tell anyone, not even Cody or your mum."

"Mum doesn't know?"

"No. There are bad people looking for it and the fewer people who know, the better."

"Like Dad?"

The kid was smart. "Maybe. I need you to promise me you won't tell a soul."

His indecision was clear.

"No one, Jordan. This is a top-secret mission. Telling people might endanger them."

Jordan nodded. "All right. I promise."

Arthur let out a breath. "Thank you." How long

would Jordan be able to hold out? Mischa had slipped up, possibly because she hadn't understood the seriousness of it like Lara had. Jordan was likely to tell Cody and it wouldn't take long to spread through the school. The clock was ticking.

"You'll keep me up to date, won't you?" Jordan asked.

"If it's safe to do so."

That seemed to satisfy Jordan. "OK."

"Come on, let's get you to school."

An hour later, Arthur was settled at Sam's kitchen table. It felt safer here, as if he wasn't endangering Gretchen and Jordan by investigating the clues at their place. A sense of urgency filled him.

He went back to examining the names on the plaque. What he needed was the passenger list. He flicked through his notes until he found Tess's number. He didn't know the woman, but Sam and their teammates, Heath and Dobby, had spoken highly of her. A few nerves tickled his skin as he dialled.

"Hello?" The soft female voice was a little unsure.

He cleared his throat. "Tess, this is Arthur Hammond. Amy's brother."

"Oh." He couldn't quite read her tone.

"I was wondering whether you have found the passenger list for the Retribution yet?"

A pause. "I don't want to be rude, but I don't know you. You could be someone from Stonefish pretending to be Arthur."

She had a good point.

"Amy knows the answer to your question. I spoke to her last night. I need to get to class." Tess hung up.

He appreciated her caution. He should have thought of it himself. Arthur dialled Amy's number, and it wasn't until she answered that he realised he hadn't thought about what he should say to her. "Hey, it's Arthur."

"Hey, I hear you're staying with Gretchen and Jordan." Her pleased tone helped release the sudden tension in his shoulders.

"Yeah, her ex is making threats. I'm walking Jordan to school and picking him up afterwards."

"And where are you sleeping?" Her teasing made him smile.

"On a mattress in the living room." For now.

"Thank you for protecting my friend."

"It's a pleasure." Before she could ask him any more questions, he said, "I called Tess, but she wouldn't tell me anything. Did she find the passenger list?"

"Yeah, she emailed it to me yesterday. Give me a second and I'll forward you a copy."

Sounds of typing in the background. "I had a quick look and narrowed down the names, but I haven't cross-referenced anything."

"I'll do it today," Arthur said as he turned on his laptop. "Jordan found my notes and while he promised not to tell anyone, I'm not sure whether he'll be able to resist telling Cody."

"Crap," Amy said. "Those kinds of rumours will spread faster than the flu at school."

"I know." The email arrived in his inbox, and he scanned the contents, pulling out his list and circling those names that weren't on the passenger manifest. He lined them up with the notes of meanings and anagrams he'd already come up with and grinned, his heart racing. "They're directions."

"What?" Amy gasped.

"I'd guess the starting point is from the plaque," he continued, scribbling his best guess on a clean sheet of paper. As the excitement built, he gathered his notes and laptop, and placed them in his bag. "Can I come out?"

"The others will be disappointed if we do it without them," Amy said. "We've been looking for this for months."

The urgency still beat at him. "I might be wrong," Arthur said. "There are a couple of possibilities, and we can narrow them down while the others are at work. Save some time." He'd have a couple of hours at the Ridge before he had to pick up Jordan from school.

"Do you have a car?"

"Sam's is here." And while it was an automatic, he hadn't tried to drive it yet. It would be tricky with his leg, but he might be able to use his left foot instead. The road was fairly straight and there wouldn't be much traffic. He hesitated, but the urgency still prodded him. He'd work something out.

"Why don't you meet me at the gulf?" Amy suggested. "There's a track you can take that will lead you there, so it won't take as long. I'll send you a mud map."

"I'll be there soon." Arthur found Sam's car keys and dumped his bag in the back seat. Then he added a couple of shovels to the tray and a few other tools they might need. He checked his phone and found the map Amy had sent. Shouldn't take too long.

He hung up and grinned. He was going treasure hunting.

***

Arthur bumped along the track, running through the clues in his head, trying to figure out the best way to put them together. When he arrived at the gulf, he saw a dust plume coming from the direction of the Ridge. Amy was almost here. He set an alarm on his phone, so he didn't forget when he needed to leave to pick up Jordan.

He got out and scanned the surroundings, taking his time, noting the empty beach, no movement on the island except for shrubs swaying in the breeze, and nothing except the dust plume on the land. In the distance to the west, the sky was dark, probably clouds forming for the storm that was forecast tonight. He frowned. He wouldn't have expected them to form this early, but he wasn't familiar with the climate up here. Opening his phone to check the weather app, he found he had no reception.

Damn.

Arthur wandered over to study the plaque again. The additional names were on opposite sides of the plaque, and their locations could be an extra clue.

Amy pulled up next to Sam's car and got out, striding over to him. "Explain it to me."

He showed her his notes and pointed to the names. "They might be the pacing from the plaque."

She shook her head. "No, look at the way they're laid out. More likely they're a mirror of the instructions."

She was right. "Are we going to test it?"

Amy hesitated only for a second. "All right, but no digging." She slipped her hand into his and squeezed it.

A rush of love filled him. This was their adventure, their opportunity to do something together, just the two of them, and maybe build their relationship. They counted the paces, turning right and then left, and ended up about thirty metres away from the ocean, on a small mound behind the dunes and staring out at the scrubby trees and grasses. Amy brushed away some sand, but there was nothing but more sand.

The urge to dig was strong. "What do you think?"

Amy screwed up her face, her temptation clear. She sighed. "Lara would disown me if I did this without her."

"There's no proof it's here," Arthur said. "Or it might be a dozen steps away from here. We don't know how tall Lilian and Reginald were." He glanced back at the plaque and noticed the dark clouds were closer now. Maybe that storm was going to hit sooner than forecast.

The radio on Amy's belt squawked. "Ames, are you there?"

She lifted the radio. "Yeah, what's up, Brandon?"

"Just got an emergency broadcast. Storm's coming. It might even form into an early cyclone. Faith's picking up Lara from school and coming home. Can you batten the hatches?"

Arthur's heart lurched. Jordan. If Faith was picking up Lara, it meant the school was closing. He had to get back.

They moved back to the cars as one. "I'm at the gulf, but I'll be back soon," Amy said.

She might need him. His loyalties were conflicted. "I have to get Jordan."

"Faith could pick him up."

"No, Gretchen will want him near." And he wasn't leaving her alone in town if the storm was going to be bad.

"All right. Stay in town. There will be enough people at the Ridge when the others get back. Gretchen and Sam will need you."

They were both still on the boat. He checked his phone again, but he still had no reception. He hugged his sister. "Take care."

"You too."

Arthur waited until Amy was on her way before he drove as fast as he dared back to town. He kept his eye on the phone reception and as soon as he came into range, he rang the school and explained who he was.

"The children have all been sent home," the

receptionist said.

He slammed his hand on the steering wheel and hung up. Gretchen wouldn't forgive him. He called her, but it went straight to voice mail.

Finally, he hit the bitumen and sped down the straight road to town. The dark clouds were moving fast towards him. By the time he raced past the town welcome sign, the wind was gusting. His phone rang. Gretchen. "Where are you?"

"On our way back, almost at the marina. Have you got Jordan?"

He hated the worry in her voice. "Not yet. I was out at the Ridge. Just reached town now." He slowed as a car pulled out in front of him.

"Call me when you have."

The trees shook helplessly against the wind as he drove past the school and followed the path Jordan and Cody took home. No children were in sight. He stopped at Cody's place first and ran to the front door. Holly answered his frantic pounding. "Is Jordan here?"

Her eyes widened. "No, Cody told his sister they were going to Jordan's place. I haven't picked him up."

The oldest sister he'd seen yesterday walked up. "They were talking about finding treasure."

Shit. Surely Jordan could see this storm was bad. "I've been out," Arthur explained. "They're probably already at Gretchen's." He raced back to the car and arrived at Gretchen's in record time. The wind buffeted him as he unlocked the front door and bellowed, "Jordan!"

Nothing. He swept through the house, checking the rooms before heading outside. "Jordan! Cody! Now's not the time to play hide and seek."

No response. Dread filled him. He'd seen no trace of the boys on their usual route. Where the hell were they? He blocked the panic and focused. Cody's sister had mentioned treasure. Maybe they'd decided to look for it, but where?

He dug out his notes, scanning them to see if there was something Jordan might have seen as a clue. He tapped a word on the notes. Plaque. Cody had asked him about the one in the park. Maybe they thought that's what the document was referring to.

He raced back outside as Gretchen called again. Damn. He put the car into reverse and answered. "Jordan and Cody are both missing."

Her anguished gasp skewered him. "Holly said they went to your place, but the boys aren't here. I might know where they are, though."

"Kurt."

"There's another option. They might have been looking for treasure." He drove through town to the park, his hands clenched on the wheel as the wind pushed the car around like it was nothing.

"What?"

There wasn't time to explain. "Where are you?"

"We're just tying up."

"Get home. Move things inside. I'll call." He screeched to a stop outside the park and leapt out of the car, his leg twinging. Don't fail me now. He adjusted the prosthesis and yelled, "Jordan!" The plaque stood in the centre of the park surrounded by a gabled wall. No one was there.

The wind whisked his words away and rain pelted him in a barrage of drops.

He stumbled through the wind, praying his instincts were right. "Jordan!"

This time a head popped up from behind the wall, followed by a second one. Relief flowed through him. He waved the boys over and they ran to meet him. Jordan yelled something at him, but the wind was too loud. Arthur placed a hand around both of them and steered them back to the car, helping them inside.

"I'm sorry," Jordan said, tears running down his face.

"It's fine. Let's get you home." He passed his phone to Jordan. "Call your mum."

He drove as fast as he dared, stopping to drop Cody at his house to a relieved Holly and then continuing to Gretchen's. She had the garage door up and he drove straight in and she lowered it behind them.

"What were you thinking?" Gretchen exclaimed, dragging Jordan into her arms.

"Inside," Arthur ordered. This was no ordinary storm. It was almost as dark as night and the windows were bowing under the pressure of the wind. "Have you got torches?"

"I've got a cyclone kit." She pointed to a tub on the shelf.

Arthur grabbed it and hustled them further into the house, locking the door behind him. He called Sam while he checked the windows and doors and made sure nothing outside could become a projectile. "You safe?"

"Yeah, Penelope and I are at my place. Have you got my car?"

"Yeah. Will the Ridge hold up?" That farmhouse was ancient.

"They've got the cellar to shelter in."

Not reassuring. "Take care." He hung up and looped through the house to make sure it was secure while Gretchen towelled Jordan. "Let's get you into dry clothes."

Arthur exhaled as he checked the cyclone kit; a small gas cooker, tins of food, water and a first aid kit, torches and other essentials. The house shuddered as the wind roared around them.

Gretchen sent him a worried look as she handed

him a towel. "It's wild out there."

He nodded and switched on the radio. It was tuned to the emergency station, where a broadcaster was urging people to prepare for the worst. The storm was predicted to rage until the morning. While they might be safe in their bedrooms, he preferred to be away from the windows.

The walk-in robe. It had no windows, was in the centre of the house and would be the most secure. They wouldn't have to worry about flying glass or projectiles from outside.

Arthur strode into Gretchen's room. She didn't have a lot of clothes, but he moved any long items to one side.

"What are you doing?" Jordan asked. They'd both followed him.

"Making a shelter," he explained. "This is the safest place for us to stay during the storm." He had to shout to be heard. "Let's drag a mattress and some rugs in here."

Jordan smiled. "We're camping in Mum's closet?"

"Yep."

Gretchen was already around the other side of her bed, ready to lift. They carried it into the room and it just fit. "Everyone go to the toilet and then gather supplies," Arthur said. The less they had to leave the room, the better.

He carried the cyclone kit in, along with his bag, and he grabbed Jordan's bunny rabbit from his room. Gretchen brought in snacks and Jordan fetched some games. They made a pile, and he surveyed it before going to the fridge to get two bottles of water. He might be overreacting, but he would keep his family safe.

Though the clouds blotted out the sun, darkening the day, there was still enough light to see, and he didn't want to run down the torch battery and candles until he had to. He sat by the door, ready to slam it shut if necessary.

Finally he exhaled, facing Gretchen and Jordan. They both stared back at him, a little wide-eyed. Suddenly self-conscious, he asked, "What?"

"You are epic," Jordan threw his arms around Arthur's neck. "Thank you."

Gretchen nodded, her eyes damp. "We're used to having to do everything ourselves."

Arthur swallowed the lump in his throat. "Well, you don't have to anymore."

Jordan smiled and sat next to Arthur. "You chose the best boyfriend, Mum."

Gretchen's eyes widened.

It felt like days ago that Arthur had spoken with Jordan. "Jordan saw us kiss this morning and asked about it."

"Oh. I'm glad you approve, sweetheart."

They all jumped as something banged outside. Probably a fence ripping off. Gretchen rubbed her arms. "I can't believe how quickly it arrived."

Neither could Arthur. He hoped Amy and everyone else were safe. It was far too early in the season to be a cyclone, so perhaps it was a late winter storm. But the ferocity would do damage, no matter what kind of storm it was. It would be a long night.

Chapter 17

The constant roar of the wind grated on Gretchen's nerves. It had been unrelenting for hours now, making it difficult to hear each other. They'd played cards and board games until they were sick of it. She'd considered getting her laptop to watch movies, but the battery didn't last long, and the power had gone out almost as soon as the storm had hit.

"I'm hungry," Jordan called.

They'd had plenty of snacks throughout the afternoon, but something more substantial might make them sleepy. "Do you think it's too confined to use the gas burner in here?"

"It'll be fine by the door. Do you want me to cook some soup?" Arthur asked.

"Yes!" Jordan said.

Gretchen let Arthur take charge. She could get used to having someone help her. His earlier declaration about them not having to do it on their own any more sounded almost like a promise, a commitment. It had tickled all of her senses and made her yearn for more. He was quickly becoming part of her life, and she liked it. She'd had to do it all for so long, even when she'd been with Kurt. Having someone to share the load was nice. Gave her a bit of respite.

In very little time, the soup was ready, and Arthur poured it into the two bowls from the cyclone kit. He didn't have one. She'd never considered there'd be more than her and Jordan. "You can have my bowl."

"No need. I'll use the pot."

Where had this easy-going man come from? Nothing fazed him, yet when they'd first met, he'd snapped at her every suggestion. It was lovely to see the true man underneath.

When they were done, she cleaned the dishes with wet wipes and packed everything away. They'd switched on the LCD lantern about an hour ago and the pale glow lit the whole room.

Arthur shut the door and the roar lessened. "No point having it open now it's dark."

"How much longer will it last?" Jordan asked.

Arthur switched on the radio. "Let's find out."

He took Jordan's questions seriously. Was it any wonder her heart expanded every time she saw him?

The broadcaster looped through the same information they'd heard the last time. The storm was over Retribution Bay and nearing Coral Bay in the south. Winds weren't expected to ease until morning.

Jordan pouted. "How am I supposed to sleep when it's so noisy?"

"How about we read a story?" Gretchen suggested.

He brightened. "Arthur can tell us about the treasure."

At Arthur's grunt, Jordan slapped his hand over his mouth, eyes wide.

"What treasure?" Jordan's very guilty expression made her turn to Arthur, her heart racing.

"Nothing, Mum. Don't worry."

Arthur had mentioned something about treasure

when he'd been looking for Jordan, but she'd been too worried about Jordan's safety to focus on it. And now she thought about it, Mischa had said something about treasure the other day as well. "Would this be the treasure you were looking for instead of heading home to safety?"

Jordan screwed up his face. "Maybe."

She waited for either male to explain and when neither spoke, she said, "I'm waiting."

Jordan looked at Arthur and, with a sigh, Arthur nodded.

"There's treasure at the Ridge," Jordan blurted. "Arthur's been looking for it."

Her eyebrows raised. She glanced at Arthur. Was this a game he was playing with the kids? "Really?"

He nodded. "We believe it might be what Stonefish is looking for."

She waited for a smile, or a twitch of his eye to show he was kidding, but it didn't come. Unease prickled her skin. "Would you like to explain?"

Arthur rubbed his hand over his face. "I don't want to endanger you or Jordan. If—" he cast a look at Jordan. "—*people* think you know about it, they may try to force you to tell."

They were back to Kurt again. So that was what he was after. It made perfect sense why he didn't give her details. He wasn't sure whether the Stokes knew about it.

"Do you mean Dad?" Jordan asked, his voice so quiet she could barely hear it above the noise.

Arthur nodded.

"He really didn't come to town for me, did he?"

"I'm sorry, sweetheart. No, he didn't." She hugged him close to her, wishing she could take away his pain. Was this a way they could get rid of Kurt? If she could get him arrested for breaking and entering... She'd ask

Arthur about it later. Jordan shouldn't hear her plotting to have Kurt arrested, no matter how much the bastard deserved it.

"I can tell you about the Retribution," Arthur suggested.

"Everyone knows the story of how it was wrecked on the island and Lara's family set up a sheep station there," Jordan said.

"But do you know the part about the mutiny?"

Jordan shifted closer. "No."

Gretchen held up a hand. "Is this likely to give Jordan nightmares?"

"No."

Jordan left her side and curled up next to Arthur so he could hear better. Arthur patted the mattress on his other side and smiled at her, so she joined them. He slid his arm around them both and her heart ached. This was what family was supposed to be like.

"This is the Stokes's family history, so you need to keep it a secret unless Lara says it's OK to say something."

Jordan and Gretchen nodded.

"Lara's ancestors were Lilian and Reginald Stokes. Lilian married Reginald just before they sailed to Australia, and he wasn't a very nice man."

"Why did she marry him?" Jordan asked.

"In those days, women had to marry whomever their parents chose for them," Gretchen explained. Her own parents had encouraged her to stay with Kurt.

"That's stupid."

Arthur continued. "When they arrived in Fremantle, Reginald bought the ship and planned to set up a shipping business between the Fremantle port and the Kimberley. They were on their first voyage when the cyclone hit."

How unfortunate.

"Everyone survived the night, but the ship was ruined on the reef. They sent a party in a life raft to get help, and while the rest waited, Reginald spent his time with a man called Mr Smith. They were searching for something and in the end, they found it."

Jordan leaned forward. "What was it?"

"A small chest of jewels."

"They've already found the treasure?" He slumped back.

"Some of it. The sailors wanted their share, and in the scuffle there was a mutiny, and most of the remaining survivors were killed, including Reginald."

Gretchen frowned. "That's impossible, unless Lilian was already pregnant. But then how could he have set up the Ridge?"

Arthur smiled. "There were three convicts on board who were assigned to a stockman who died from a snake bite. Lilian had fallen in love with one of them, who looked enough like Reginald to pass for him. He took on Reginald's identity, and no one was any wiser when they were rescued."

She had so many questions, but Jordan was faster. "What about the treasure?"

"Lilian split it amongst the survivors; some pearl divers, the convicts and herself. They used the money to help set up Retribution Ridge."

"Where did the treasure come from in the first place?" Gretchen asked.

"Another ship which was wrecked there about a century earlier," Arthur answered. "It was carrying treasure from the Dutch East Indies."

"And there's more?" Jordan said.

"We don't know for sure."

That was enough. They didn't need to know more, not if Kurt was looking for it. "Great story," she said. "Jordan, how about you tell us what you did at school today?"

"But I've got questions."

"Not tonight." She didn't like him knowing so much.

"What are you learning about?" Arthur asked.

"Miss Simpson wants us to do our family tree, and then do a report on something interesting our ancestors did." Jordan glanced at Gretchen. "Do we have anything interesting in our family?"

Maybe in a hundred years they would find the business her parents ran interesting, but right now it would just get them arrested. "I'll think about it."

"What about you, Sherlock?" Jordan asked.

"My dad's side is full of military men with stories," he said. "I'm not sure about my mum's side. Maybe we can research our families together."

"Yeah." Jordan's eyes drooped as the pull of sleep dragged at him.

"It's time for bed," Gretchen said to Jordan.

"But Mu-um."

She shook her head. "Hopefully when you wake, the storm will be over."

He pouted but shuffled to the side of the mattress he'd claimed as his. Gretchen clicked the lamp, so it dimmed to the lowest setting and kissed Jordan before tucking him in. "Good night."

"Night, Mum. Night, Arthur."

"Sweet dreams, Jordan," Arthur said.

Gretchen moved back next to Arthur and leaned into him as he pulled her closer. "How much of that story is true?"

"All of it," he replied. "They found Lilian's journal, outlining the events."

Fascinating. "I'd love to read it one day."

"I'm sure Amy will give you a copy."

She appreciated he wasn't promising anything, as it

wasn't his to promise. She yawned.

"We could both do with getting an early night," Arthur said. "There's not much to do, and I imagine there's going to be a big clean up tomorrow."

He was right. She lay down on the mattress next to Jordan and Arthur lay on her other side. Jordan shuffled so he was curled into her, and Arthur spooned her from behind. She closed her eyes, feeling the warmth and comfort of being loved and protected.

Despite the storm raging outside, she fell asleep immediately.

***

A thump on Gretchen's back woke her with a start. She gasped and blinked, trying to see, but it was pitch black. Outside the wind still gusted, but not as fiercely as before. They were in her closet, sheltering from the storm. A loud groan and another slap coming from Arthur. "Arthur?"

No response.

Was he having a nightmare?

"Move back or I'll shoot." His snarl made her gasp, and she moved fast, shifting her and Jordan away, and flicking the lantern on. Jordan blinked sleepily next to her. "Mum?"

Her heart pounded as she pulled him close and shifted down the end of the mattress. Arthur was covered in sweat, arms flailing. She'd covered a little about PTSD during her studies; it could be dangerous to wake him.

"What's wrong with Arthur?"

"He's having a nightmare." She called softly, "Arthur, wake up."

He kicked out, just brushing her arm, and she jerked back.

"Arthur, you're safe here." She kept her tone gentle,

not daring to touch him. His eyes flashed open, but unseeing. Fear slipped through her. "Arthur, it's Gretchen and Jordan. You're in Retribution Bay. There's a storm outside."

He made no sign he heard her but continued to yell incomprehensible words.

"Mum?" The fear in Jordan's voice made her slip an arm around him.

"Sometimes soldiers have really real dreams that they're still in a war zone," she explained. "Arthur's having one of those now."

"How can we help him?"

"I don't know." All the documentation she'd read said to talk calmly to them. She knew enough not to get too close in case he mistook her for the enemy and accidentally hurt her.

"Singing always helps me feel better when I'm scared," Jordan suggested.

It was as good an idea as any. "What do you want to sing?"

"There's this song Lara sang the other day." He broke into a familiar old song about not worrying and being happy. Gretchen joined in and Arthur's twitches became less violent. When the song finished, they started again from the beginning. His eyes closed and his hands unclenched.

"It's working," Jordan whispered.

It was. Arthur's breathing slowed, and Gretchen said, "Arthur, honey. Wake up for me." She didn't want him to slip back into his nightmare the moment they stopped singing.

She continued singing and at the end of the second round she called, "Wake up, Arthur."

His eyes flicked open again, but this time they focused on her. "Gretchen, what's wrong?"

Jordan crawled over. "You were having a nightmare,

but we couldn't wake you, so we sang to you."

Arthur sat up, swept a hand through his damp hair, and then his eyes widened with fear. "I didn't hurt you?"

She shook her head.

Jordan crawled onto Arthur's lap and hugged him. "It's OK, Sherlock. You're safe here. It was just a dream."

Gretchen smiled at the words she'd said so many times coming out of her son's mouth. Arthur hugged Jordan, closing his eyes. "Thank you. What were you singing?"

Jordan sang the chorus, and Arthur's eyes widened. "My mum used to sing that all the time."

"Lara taught it to me. She said Amy sings it."

"It's a good song. It always used to make me feel better." Arthur reached out and clutched Gretchen's hand. "You're really all right?"

"Yes. We were just worried about you." She moved closer and joined the hug.

Arthur squeezed them, his voice rough. "I love you."

Gretchen stiffened and glanced at him.

His expression was earnest. "So much, Gretchen. Both of you."

"We love you too, don't we, Mum?"

Her heart thumped at a million miles an hour. This wonderful, damaged man loved them. Was it too soon for emotions as intense and heady as this?

She gazed into his eyes and saw her answer. "Yeah, we do."

His mouth met hers and they kissed, but Jordan moved away with a disgusted, "Ew."

They both laughed.

"Is it morning yet?" Jordan asked.

Some light peeked in from underneath the bedroom

door and Gretchen checked her watch. Six-twenty-five. "Yeah. Shall we go out and assess things?"

Arthur helped her to her feet, kissing her again, and then moved forward, stopping Jordan from ripping open the door. "Let me go first, mate."

Jordan hung back and Arthur exited, scanning the room with the torch before motioning them out. Gretchen didn't want him taking all the risks. She joined him, and together they walked through the house, checking windows and the roof for leaks. The sun was only just rising, and Gretchen pulled open curtains and blinds to survey the damage outside. Slowly the sun lit the world and revealed the mess. Tree branches were strewn over the road, rubbish and assorted things that people hadn't tied down littered the area.

Arthur came back into the kitchen carrying the gas cooker and the radio. He switched the radio on. *—and now it's time for the news. The town of Retribution Bay is without power today after a fierce storm hit their shores. Authorities are not sure how long it will take to restore infrastructure, but the premier has already called a state of emergency and is arranging supplies to be flown in. Residents are cautioned to take care around fallen power lines.*

Gretchen checked her phone. A couple of bars.

"Can I call Cody?" Jordan asked.

"It's a bit early," Gretchen said. "We can stop by later." She sent a message to Amy, Penelope and Holly to see how they had all fared. They might be too busy dealing with damage to talk.

She moved to the back door and opened it. The wind still blew, but the rain had stopped. A few plants had been ripped out and her shrubs were almost leafless, but aside from that, there was little damage. She moved further into the garden and glanced back at the roof. No loose panels that she could see. She went out the front to check from that side, but she was lucky. Everything was in place.

One less thing to worry about.

Arthur handed her a mug of tea and Jordan a warm Milo. "Let's have breakfast and then go for a drive. I'd like to see how Sam and Penelope are, and maybe head out to the Ridge."

"What about school?" Jordan asked.

"There won't be school today," Gretchen told him. How had the Ridge fared? All the buildings were so much older, and they had animals and fencing to deal with, too.

"Yes!" Jordan exclaimed. "Do you think the school was damaged? What about the shops?"

He peppered her with questions as they ate. Finally Gretchen said, "Enough. We'll go out after we've showered."

Jordan ran to the bathroom. At least they had hot water because of her gas hot water system. She checked her phone. A message from Penelope. *All fine here.*

Arthur's phone rang and from his side of the conversation, it sounded as if he spoke to Sam. He glanced at Gretchen. "Sam says he's cancelled the tour today."

She wasn't surprised. It wouldn't go ahead tomorrow either if the weather stayed bad.

When Arthur hung up, he said, "Penelope has to go to work to assess the damage, but Sam wants to go to the Ridge after he's called all the crew and passengers."

"Jordan and I can come too, in case there's a lot of work."

Arthur smiled. "That would be great."

She checked her phone. Still no response from either Holly or Amy.

They cleaned up from breakfast and then climbed into Sam's four-wheel drive and headed out.

Gretchen scanned the road for damaged power lines, but aside from having to stop to remove broken tree branches or debris, this street was fine. Along the way, they spoke to neighbours who had various levels of damage.

At Cody's place, the front fence had a gaping hole where panels were missing. Jordan knocked on the door, and Holly answered.

"How is everyone?" Gretchen asked.

Holly smiled. "We survived. A few broken fence panels and some overflowing gutters, but everyone's fine."

Jordan pushed past her and ran inside, looking for Cody.

"Do you want to come in for a chat?" Holly invited.

"No, we need to check on some others," Gretchen said, knowing Arthur was concerned about his sister. She called for Jordan, and they headed to Sam's, having to detour around some power lines. More fences were gone, and some houses had lost roofs, with people trying to cover the gaps with tarps. The State Emergency Service were visible in their bright orange clothing and Gretchen stopped to chat to Dot and Nhiari as they made their rounds to check everyone's safety.

"Have you heard from the Ridge?" Nhiari asked.

"We're heading there after we pick up Sam," Gretchen said.

"Let me know. I've left a couple of messages."

"Will do."

They pulled up in front of Sam's town house. All the buildings by the marina were new and were undamaged. Arthur knocked and then let himself in.

"What a night." Penelope came forward to hug them, already dressed in her Parks and Wildlife uniform.

"You're OK?"

She nodded. "Bit of water over from the canal, but nothing serious. Have you heard from Amy or Faith?"

Gretchen shook her head, and they exchanged worried glances.

Sam came downstairs and he and Arthur did that back slap hug thing men did.

"Have you checked the boat?" Gretchen asked.

"Went down at first light. Had to tighten a couple of ropes, but no damage there."

Gretchen sighed in relief.

"I need to get to work," Penelope said. "Assess the damage."

"It's too rough to head out on the water," Sam said and from Penelope's gentle smile, it was clear they'd had this discussion before.

"I won't," she promised. "We'll focus on the mainland before we check how the islands fared." She kissed him, and with a wave, she left.

Worry covered Sam's face. "Penelope knows how to take care of herself," Gretchen said.

"I know. I'd feel better going with her, but she wants me to check on the Ridge. She's hoping Georgie will be at work and can update her."

"Got any gear they might need?" Arthur asked.

Sam nodded, and they headed to his garage to fetch an old tarp and some rope. "We'll stop by the hardware store on the way out, see if they've got any supplies left."

Sam slowed as the hardware store came into view. The carpark was full and there was a line of people out the door. He kept driving. "No point stopping."

The store would probably run out of stock before it was their turn to buy anything.

Not far out of town, water ran over the road with the depth gauge showing it was a metre deep. It flowed swiftly, coming from the ranges in the west, and Sam stopped. "Think we can get through?"

"Let's look." Arthur and Sam got out of the car and approached the river. Jordan quickly followed.

Gretchen unstrapped herself and moved to the centre seat to watch. She'd seen a lot of water crossings gone wrong videos on the internet thanks to Jordan's interests.

Sam waded in and stood his ground. That was a good thing. If he could stand the force of the water without being washed off his feet, then the car should.

The men returned and Jordan jumped in first. "We're giving it a go."

Sam moved the car slowly, aiming for the right side of the road, probably to give them more space if they got washed off. They hit the water and kept a steady speed as they crossed the river to the other side.

Only three more to go. When they crossed the final bit of flooded road, Gretchen let out a sigh. Sam slowed as he went past the airport, but the damage didn't look too extensive. Already machines were clearing the runway and shifting planes. There shouldn't be any trouble flying supplies and volunteers in.

By the time they arrived at the Ridge, Jordan had fallen asleep, face pressed up against the door of the car, the interrupted night catching up on him.

"The sign's missing," Sam said, concern on his face. "We'll have to look for it. Charlie made it. He was the brother who died."

So the sign had special significance. Gretchen hoped they could find it.

The campgrounds were deserted. All the guests must have headed out of the storm's path when it was announced.

The shed was missing its roof and one of the ablution blocks leaned drunkenly against a tree. The house appeared in one piece aside from a broken window, which had already been boarded up. Metal panels and other debris were caught in the trees and bushes nearby, and a fence in the horse corral was down, the horses missing. Hopefully they'd sheltered somewhere safe.

As they drove around the side of the house, Gretchen gasped. The roof over the kitchen was missing.

"Shit," Sam swore. He parked, and they all leapt out.

Amy came out of the house. Her clothes were crinkled and her hair tied back in a messy bun. She looked exhausted. Gretchen hurried to greet her and hugged her. "Is everyone safe?"

"Yes. We sheltered in the cellar. Darcy and Matt have already left to check the sheep and fences. Georgie got called into work and Brandon, Faith, Lara and I are cleaning up this mess."

"Where are the horses?" Jordan asked.

"In the shearing shed," Amy answered. "Lara and Faith are down there now, making sure they're all right."

Jordan glanced at Gretchen, and she nodded. He ran towards the shed.

"I thought you might need some of these," Sam said, carrying the tarps from the ute tray.

Amy smiled. "Thank you."

Arthur stepped closer. "I'm glad you're all right. We were worried when your phones went straight to voice mail." He hugged his sister and Amy's eyes widened and then hugged him back.

"We lost power early. None of our phones keeps its charge well. They're all flat."

Gretchen sent Nhiari and Dot a message to say everyone was safe. Then she smiled at Amy. "Where do we start?"

Chapter 18

Amy was as efficient as a drill sergeant. It shouldn't surprise Arthur after having grown up with the major, but somehow it did. He'd thought she'd abandoned everything to do with their father. She'd made a list of everything that needed repairing and assigned jobs methodically. Jordan and Lara were assigned kitchen duty to mop, clean and dry everything that had been soaked when the roof had blown off. With them was Gretchen. Sam and Brandon set to work climbing onto the roof to secure the tarps in place, and Amy and Arthur searched for the missing roof panels, while Faith checked out how they might rebuild the horse corral.

The corrugated panels weren't difficult to find. They'd blown against a wall of shrubs a couple of hundred metres away, where they lay slightly bent but otherwise undamaged. Amy pulled the ute up alongside and sighed. "I hope we can get those bends out."

The sheets of metal shouldn't be too expensive. "Can't you get more in Retribution Bay?"

She shrugged. "Maybe, but we don't have the extra funds until the insurance comes through and it might take weeks."

"Finances are that bad?"

"Yeah. Brandon's parents made some poor decisions."

Arthur had compensation from his injury. "I can pay."

She glanced at him. "We'll manage. We always do." She smiled. "Though finding the treasure would be helpful right about now."

"We should dig for it," Arthur said. "After we've got everything watertight, let's just try. If nothing else, it will be something to cheer everyone up."

Amy raised her eyebrows. "You doing something just for fun? Dad would be appalled." She grinned.

She was right, but he loved the idea of shocking his father. "Good."

Amy lifted one side of the metal sheet. "Now let's get this metal back to the house."

They worked hard all morning. Matt and Darcy reported in, saying an entire line of fencing had been damaged, but the sheep were contained. They'd be back when it was fixed.

Faith and Arthur repaired the horse yard and returned the horses to it, with Lara's pet sheep, and Maggie the kangaroo venturing out of the shearing shed where they'd been hiding.

With every portable fan on high in the kitchen drying it out, and the section of roof back in place, they ate lunch outside where the sun was pushing through the clouds. Gretchen raised her face to the sky. "Hopefully this will help dry out things."

The shed and the ablution block were tackled after lunch. Arthur worked side-by-side with his sister, reinforcing the walls of the toilet block, and then they cleaned the building thoroughly. By the end of the day, the shed had been cleaned, the generator was working, and a tarp was in place over the area where the metal sheets had been too damaged to be replaced. Sam had ordered new sheets, which would be delivered when the supplies arrived. Stock was being flown up tomorrow.

The one thing they hadn't found yet was Charlie's sign.

Arthur's leg was throbbing as he walked up the steps and into the kitchen. Another hour and it would get dark. Amy was peering in the fridge, muttering to herself.

"What's up?" Arthur asked.

She glanced at him. "Trying to figure out what we've got for dinner."

"We'll head back to town," Arthur said. No way would he be an extra mouth to feed if things were as tight as she'd said.

Her relief said it all. "Thank you."

The others made their way into the kitchen and Darcy and Matt arrived back, dirty and sweaty. Darcy left his boots outside and hung his hat on the hook on the wall. "It's done. It's not pretty, but the fence won't move."

Lara hugged him. "We've fixed most things here."

Penelope and Georgie walked in, looking equally tired. Sam made a beeline to Penelope. "How was it?"

"Mostly clean-up work and taping off areas until we can get supplies to fix them," she said.

"Have a seat," Amy said, filling up the kettle.

Arthur moved over to his sister. "That includes you. I can put mugs and milk on the table."

Her eyes filled and she nodded. They'd had it rough out here and the stress of so little money would be wearing on her.

When the kettle boiled, he filled the teapot and set it on the table. Everyone sat around it, silent, lost in their own contemplation.

They needed something to cheer them up.

He glanced at Amy. Should he mention his theory about the treasure, or would it devastate them further if it wasn't there? "Is now a good time?"

She frowned, and then when she realised what he was asking, she smiled and nodded.

Arthur cleared his throat. "I might have some news." He poured milk into his cup.

"What?" Lara asked.

"I might have figured out Lilian's clues for where the treasure is."

Georgie dropped the spoon she'd picked up, and everyone turned to look at him.

His face heated. "I might be wrong, but you know those extra names?"

"What about them?" Faith asked.

"They might be directions."

Lara clapped her hands together with a squeal. "We have to go! Please, Dad."

Darcy rubbed his face, eyes already dark with fatigue. "We can wait one more night."

Lara's face fell.

Brandon ran a hand through his hair, looking as exhausted as Darcy. "We should check the fences down that way."

"It will be dark soon," Matt said.

"We've got spotlights on the ute," Brandon said.

Darcy sighed and forced a smile. "All right. As long as I don't have to do any more digging."

In very little time, they were on their way to the gulf with Sam following Amy in the ute. They'd thrown some tools in the tray of one ute in case fences were down, and Lara and Jordan sat in the back of the other one.

Arthur slipped his arm around Gretchen and she leaned into him. Georgie's eyebrows almost disappeared into her hairline when she noticed, but she said nothing and simply smiled.

Just over the road they found Charlie's sign. It was dented and had a scratch right down the middle. They all got out to look.

"It's ruined," Georgie whispered.

Arthur stepped closer, examining it, and shook his head. "No, it's not. We can knock the dents out and I can touch up the paintwork."

"You paint now?" Sam asked.

"Haven't you seen his notebook?" Brandon asked. "He's incredible."

Sam glanced at him. "The notebook you hid from me?"

Arthur nodded. "It contains my drawings. I, ah, don't like to show people."

"Dad told him they were worthless," Amy added.

"Which probably means they're art gallery worthy," Sam said, nodding in understanding. "I'd like to see them."

Arthur nodded and helped Darcy lift the sign into the back of the ute and they continued their journey.

They had to stop a few more times to remove debris from the track, but they finally reached the gulf.

What a difference a day made.

The water churned a milky beige and mangrove branches were scattered along the shore. The concrete base of the plaque had been exposed, and the pole leaned towards the sand. Even the dunes had almost been washed away by the surge of the swell and though it was low tide, the water lapped high on the shore.

Arthur got out and his gaze was drawn to where he suspected the treasure had been buried. The small dunes had eroded away and in their place were a few limestone rocks jutting out. His pulse increased.

"Ames," he called and jerked his head toward them.

Her mouth dropped open.

Lara ran over to the plaque with Jordan and together they pushed it so it was standing upright again.

Arthur took the shovels out of the back and Georgie demanded, "So, what are the clues?"

They all walked over to the plaque, and Arthur pointed out the fake names. Then he explained how he'd translated them. "Which puts the treasure right near those newly exposed rocks." He pointed.

"Where shelter, water and food collide, you will find the treasure hide," Lara quoted. She ran over. "There's water here!"

Sure enough, the exposed rocks now held a pool of water from the rain.

Arthur held up a shovel. "Who wants first go?"

Lara grabbed one and Jordan peered up with hopeful eyes at Arthur. He handed the other shovel to the boy and the two children began attacking the sand with gusto. They hit rock quickly, so started scooping sand from the front.

"Why do they get all the fun?" Georgie grumbled.

"They'll tire soon enough," Gretchen said.

Little by little, with others taking their turns, they exposed a cave, the limestone rock that had been exposed forming its roof.

Brandon switched on the ute spotlights, and people murmured to each other, but everyone watched avidly. Faith and Georgie passed the shovels to Darcy and Matt, Darcy forgetting his fatigue. It was likely the cyclone that had wrecked the Retribution would have exposed this cave. Lilian might not have known time would cover it with sand again, or maybe that had been the whole point.

The sand flowed out of the cave now much of the entrance had been cleared. Darcy thrust his shovel in and... *thunk!*

Definitely the sound of the shovel hitting something that wasn't rock.

Lara danced from foot to foot. "It's there!"

Darcy wiped his brow and handed the shovel to Arthur. "You should uncover it. We wouldn't have found it without you."

Arthur lost the ability to speak as he took the shovel. He glanced at Amy, who nodded, and then Gretchen, who grinned at him. "You deserve this."

His heart skittered in his chest, but everyone was waiting for him to step up. He exhaled and moved forward, shifting the sand until through the falling particles he spotted wood.

No freaking way.

He dropped the shovel and shifted the remaining sand by hand.

A wooden chest, slightly rotted with age but in remarkable condition.

"Epic," Lara breathed.

He glanced back, eyes wide. Jordan appeared frozen, staring with disbelief. Gretchen was equally shocked, but Georgie summed it up best. "Well, shit."

Amy laughed. "Let's get it out of there. I want to see what's inside."

Arthur moved out of the way to let Brandon and Sam drag the heavy chest out of the cave. The thick brass lock broke with a tug, and Arthur felt a slight twinge of guilt over the history they might be destroying, but this family had been through a lot because of this. They deserved whatever was inside.

Brandon paused, hand poised to lift the lid. "I don't know if I can do it."

Arthur understood his reluctance. If nothing was inside, it would be gutting.

"Move over then." Georgie pushed to the front. Brandon laughed and together they lifted the lid.

"No fucking way," Georgie breathed.

Arthur couldn't see the inside from where he stood.

"Spill it, Georgie," Matt demanded.

She reached in and withdrew a handful of silver and gold coins, letting them run through her fingers.

Lara screamed. "We're rich!"

Brandon took out a red jewelled necklace. "Do you think these are rubies?"

Darcy's eyes teared up. "This will save the Ridge." They were all quiet for a moment. Arthur scanned their surroundings. More clouds were rolling in from the west and the final rays of light were disappearing below the horizon.

"Let's get this back to the house," he said. "Then we can take our time to see what's inside."

He didn't want to be stuck here if it started raining again. Plus, if Stonefish were watching as closely as they seemed to be, there was a chance they'd be around.

Brandon nodded. "Let's move."

Gretchen couldn't believe it. Real, honest-to-goodness treasure. She stood back while Sam and Brandon lifted the chest gingerly from the back of the ute and carried it into the kitchen. The wood creaked and groaned and she tensed until it was lowered to the floor. Everyone gathered around the kitchen, silent, wide-eyed, as if they couldn't quite comprehend it.

Penelope cleared her throat. "I hate to be the one who asks but, what are the legalities? Who owns the treasure? It's illegal to take anything from a shipwreck in Australia."

"We didn't take it," Georgie pointed out. "It was removed by the survivors themselves and Lilian found it, but she never said where she found it."

"And it's now on Ridge land," Sam replied.

Was it far enough from the shore to count as Ridge

land rather than Crown land? The Stokes needed the money, but some necklaces and jewels might have cultural significance, or be family heritage for someone.

"We need some advice," Arthur said. "We can't carry a handful of coins into the bank and bank them, and melting the gold is going to raise notice as well."

"I researched it," Faith said. "It goes to the true owner unless they can't be found, and then it goes to the property owner."

"So we have to find the descendants of the Dutch East India Company?" Darcy asked.

"No." Amy walked over to a drawer and withdrew a notebook, flicking to a page. "It went bankrupt in 1799 and was dissolved. The possessions were taken over by the Dutch Batavian Republic which, as far as I can tell, ceased to exist during the French Revolution."

"French, Dutch, Australian. This is getting messy," Matt said.

"Can't we just keep it?" Lara played with a gold coin. "No one needs to know."

Darcy smiled. "It's the right thing to do, Pumpkin. People would start wondering where we got the money from, and if Stonefish knew we had it, they'd try and take it."

Kurt.

He was still out there somewhere. He would have sheltered during the storm, but who knew what kind of trouble he was stirring up? This was exactly the kind of thing he'd want to get his hands on. She glanced at Jordan. He took a necklace from the chest and showed it to Lara. She lowered her voice. "Can we let them know?"

Everyone turned to stare at her. "What?" Georgie asked.

"Set a trap," she explained. "Somehow leak to them we've found the treasure, and then have the police ready to arrest them."

Georgie smiled. "I like the way you think."

"It could be dangerous," Matt said.

Darcy nodded. "Who knows what they'll do as retaliation?"

"Lee does," Georgie said. "Maybe we can ask him."

Gretchen glanced at Arthur, but he looked as clueless as she did about who Lee was. "Who's Lee?"

"He works… worked for Stonefish," Amy said. "We don't actually know what his end goal is."

"And that makes him potentially dangerous." Brandon crossed his arms.

"He saved Tess's life," Georgie argued.

"We don't know where he is," Matt said.

Georgie glanced at the ground and curled a piece of hair around her finger.

"Georgie!" Matt growled. "What have you done?"

She sighed. "Nothing. I occasionally run into him when I'm in the ranges. I don't go looking for him."

"You don't avoid him either," Darcy surmised.

She pressed her lips together.

Gretchen fought her smile. This appeared to be a long-standing argument. "How dangerous is he?"

"Deadly," Sam said. "He's got to have military training."

"But he hasn't physically hurt us," Georgie argued.

"Yet." Darcy walked over to the kettle and switched it on.

"How about we decide about the treasure first?" Faith suggested.

"The only ones we can trust to tell and keep it from spreading are Dot and Nhiari," Darcy said. "And they'll be busy cleaning up the town."

Sam's phone rang, startling them all. He withdrew it with a grimace. "Sorry, Ed. I should have called you."

Ed was the youngest Stokes brother.

Sam put it on speaker. "Everyone's fine. Power's out and their phones have died."

A loud sigh. "I've been trying to get hold of someone for hours," Ed exclaimed.

"We've been a little busy," Georgie said. "Is Tess with you?"

"Yeah, I've got you on speaker."

"No one else is around?" Brandon asked.

"No."

"We found the treasure," Lara shouted.

"What?"

"You heard her," Darcy said. "We're staring down at a chest of gold and jewels."

"Holy shit. Tess and I might be able to get on the next flight up."

"Don't you have work?" Brandon said.

"I can get leave to help family. There's damage from the storm, right?"

"Lots," Matt said. "You'd better bring your work boots." The men grinned at each other.

Ed wasn't a work boots sort of guy, but he'd help in a pinch.

Tess spoke. "There's a six o'clock flight in the morning."

"We'll pick you up," Amy said.

Sam hung up and looked at the others. "What now?"

"Now we hide the treasure," Brandon said. "At least until we get the chance to speak to Dot and Nhiari."

"We'll talk to them when we head back to town," Sam said.

Arthur studied the chest. "The trunk won't survive another trip with that much weight in it. It protested enough when we took it off the ute. We need to take some of the treasure out and put it in bags."

Amy left the room and came back with some backpacks. Georgie took photos of the treasure for reference and they spent some time transferring the riches to the bags, with Amy cataloguing it.

"This is beautiful," Penelope breathed, holding up an emerald necklace.

There really were some stunning pieces amongst the gold and silver. Gretchen had her turn at removing treasure and Jordan dug enthusiastically through the coins. He drew out a jewel encrusted dagger. "Cool!" Then he hissed as the blade cut him.

"Careful." Arthur took the dagger from him while Gretchen examined the cut. "We'd better disinfect this."

Amy went to the cupboard and drew out a first aid kit, and Gretchen tended to Jordan's cut. "I can't believe it was still sharp after all these years," Amy said.

Hopefully, none of the potential diseases would still be alive on the blade.

When they were done transferring the treasure to bags, Darcy said, "Lara, take Jordan into the lounge room. Neither of you need to know where we're hiding the treasure. It's safer that way."

Lara hesitated, then nodded. "This way, Jordan."

Jordan glanced at Gretchen, protest on his face.

"Darcy is right," Gretchen said. "Go with Lara."

With Faith standing guard to make sure the kids didn't sneak back, they carried the bags down to the cellar and afterwards rolled the old linoleum floor back over the door, hiding it completely. There was no hint the cellar was there at all.

Probably the safest place for now.

Faith went and got the children.

"I need to get back," Sam said. "The forecast is for more rough weather and I need to cancel tomorrow's tours."

Gretchen nodded, checking her emails. "School says they're reopening tomorrow. A couple of classrooms were damaged, but they'll work around it."

Jordan pouted. "Can't we stay here?"

"No, sweetheart." The idea of being so close to the treasure freaked her out a little. If Stonefish came looking for any reason, she didn't want to be here.

"I'll talk to Dot and Nhiari," Sam said.

"Do you want me to pick up Ed and Tess tomorrow?" Arthur asked. "I can bring them out so you can finish cleaning up here."

"That would be great," Amy said. "Do you know Ed?"

"He visited after I was discharged the first time." Arthur shifted uncomfortably. He probably hadn't been receptive to the visit.

They walked out to the car and said their goodbyes. It wasn't long before they were heading back to town, with Penelope in the front with Sam.

Jordan sat quietly next to Gretchen. "Are you all right?" she asked.

He shrugged, looking out the window, taking a bite of the sandwich Amy had sent him home with.

"It's pretty exciting, isn't it?"

Another shrug.

Gretchen sighed. "We couldn't have stayed there longer."

"It's not that. I'm just thinking," Jordan said.

"What about?"

"Stuff."

Right. She let him be and turned her thoughts towards what to do about Kurt. She needed to get rid of him for good.

Could the Lee they'd mentioned be any help? Perhaps he could get information which would lead to Kurt's arrest. But she had no idea where to find him and if he was dangerous, she didn't want to risk getting herself into more trouble.

The rivers across the road had lowered, and it wasn't difficult to get back into town. Most of the debris had been cleared from the roads, but there were still power lines down, and piles of branches and rubbish on the sides of the road. Tarps covered a lot of houses and there were signs pointing to the recreation centre if people needed food or shelter. Many of the streets were dark because power hadn't been restored, but the town was bouncing back. Gretchen felt a pinch of guilt for not helping here.

"I'll tell you what Dot and Nhiari say," Sam said as he pulled up in front of Gretchen's place.

"Thanks, mate," Arthur said.

Inside, Gretchen did a loop through the house to make sure they hadn't missed anything this morning, but it all seemed to be in good condition. Lucky. One street they'd driven down looked as if it had caught the brunt of the storm, with roofs missing and trees down all the way along it.

"Shower and then bed, Jordan," Gretchen said, gently nudging her sleepy-eyed son towards the bathroom. He went without complaint, and it wasn't long before she tucked him in and turned off the light. She returned to the kitchen, where Arthur had made them both a cup of tea and had chopped some cheese and fruit for dinner. Gretchen popped a piece of cheese into her mouth and savoured the taste. She settled on the couch next to Arthur and curled into him. "What a day."

He rubbed her arm. "I can't believe we found buried treasure."

She grinned. "I felt like a kid again."

"Me too."

She lifted her head and kissed him. "Good sleuthing, Sherlock."

He chuckled. "Thanks."

She closed her eyes, enjoying the way his laugh reverberated through her chest. "Will you spend the night in my bed?"

She felt his intake of breath. "You don't think Jordan will mind?"

"I doubt he'll be up before us, but no, I don't think he will."

"Then I'd love to."

She smiled and snuggled into his embrace.

Chapter 19

Arthur woke, a soft warmth by his side. Slowly his awareness returned. This wasn't his bed. Gretchen was curled into him, her arm stretched across his waist, hugging him in her sleep. He smiled, his heart expanding with more love. He felt great, wonderful even. The normal foggy eyes and clouded head he'd woken with since the accident were gone. He'd slept solidly the whole night, not dreaming at all. When had he last taken a pain pill? He'd been too distracted yesterday by his concerns at the Ridge to ask Sam for one. In fact, the lingering constant pain was all but gone.

Progress. Finally.

He grinned and checked the time. He needed to move in case Ed's flight was on schedule. Now, how to extract himself without waking Gretchen? Gently he shifted, lifting Gretchen's arm off him and sliding out from under it.

She grumbled and opened her eyes. She stared at him a second before she gave him a sleepy smile. "Good morning."

He kissed her forehead. "Sorry for waking you. I

wanted to check whether Ed's flight is on time."

She stretched and moved away. "I should get up."

Arthur placed a hand on her arm. "Stay in bed. You don't have work today. I'll bring you a cuppa and breakfast."

"You don't have to."

"But I want to." He bent to kiss her again. "Would Jordan like breakfast in bed as well?"

"Both he and I would love it."

"Then stay there. I won't be long." He attached his leg, grabbed his phone, and headed for the kitchen. After putting on the kettle, he did a round of the house to make sure it was all secure and then checked Ed's flight. He had just enough time to make breakfast before he needed to leave.

He made the porridge and found a tray in the cupboard for the bowl and mug. He walked into Gretchen's room to find she'd fallen back asleep. Arthur didn't want to wake her, but Jordan would need to get up for school soon. He placed the tray on her bedside table and then called, "Wake up, honey."

She smiled and opened her eyes. "Did I fall asleep?"

"Yeah. Your breakfast is ready. Sit up for me."

When she was seated, he handed her the tray. "Enjoy. I'll go wake Jordan."

Concern crossed her face. "Maybe I should do it."

"I've got this." He'd make sure not to startle the boy.

He headed into Jordan's room with a bowl of porridge and a mug of Milo. "Morning, Jordan."

The boy barely stirred as Arthur placed the breakfast on the bedside table and switched on the light. When that didn't work, he opened the blinds as well. "I've made you breakfast."

Maybe it was the words, or Jordan could smell the food, but he stirred and opened his eyes, frowning when he saw Arthur. "Sherlock?"

"Hey. Sit up. I've made you breakfast." He gestured to the bedside table and Jordan's eyes widened and he shuffled up.

"That's for me?"

"Yeah. Be careful you don't spill it." He passed the bowl over. "I've got to go to the airport. Finish your breakfast and then get ready for school. Your mum will drop you off today."

"Thanks, Sherlock. You're the best." Jordan shoved porridge into his mouth and grinned at him.

Arthur showered and hesitated before putting on shorts. No point hiding his fake leg. It was part of him now, and he was thankful he was alive. To think he'd almost missed out on meeting Gretchen and Jordan. He cringed. That would have been a tragedy. He headed back to Gretchen and outside a car horn beeped. Sam. "I'm off."

"Tell Ed I said hi."

Arthur kissed her. "I'll see you later."

He joined Sam in his car. "What did Dot and Nhiari say?"

Sam chuckled. "That it was a whole lot of trouble they didn't have time for," he said. "But they'd make some enquiries. A couple of their colleagues working down in Blackbridge had some issues last year that they needed federal help with. They might have contacts they can ask, so no one knows the questions are coming from up here."

"Dot trusts them?"

"She wouldn't have suggested it if she didn't."

Good. He'd been thinking about how he could force Kurt out into the open, get him to show his hand, but so far all of his ideas would put Jordan or Gretchen in danger.

Sam parked at the airport. A plane was coming into

landing, but already parked on the tarmac near the terminal was a huge military cargo plane. Arthur's muscles tightened at the reminder of his service, and he exhaled. All of that was in his past now. Retribution Bay was a far better place for him to be. This was his future.

They walked into the terminal and headed towards the gate. The cargo plane outside the building was being unloaded, and a few military personnel were inside talking to terminal staff.

A familiar figure caught his attention.

Arthur's footsteps slowed, and his entire posture straightened until he felt as if he had a pole running through him. It was impossible to stop the instinctual check of his appearance, but the sight of his leg and his casual attire made him nauseous. The one day when he'd been feeling his best, and he had to run into him. Just his luck.

Sam turned around. "You coming?"

Arthur said nothing, staring at the tall man he'd spent his life trying to impress, the man who'd made his life miserable. Sam followed his gaze and swore. "We can avoid him."

The urge was so strong, he took a couple of steps in the opposite direction before he stopped himself. "No. I've got things to say."

"The major won't give you any time of day," Sam said.

"Yeah, he will." The major spoke to the person who must be the town's delegate for the army. With him was a lieutenant colonel. He wouldn't dismiss his son in front of a senior officer.

But what did he want to say to his father?

Should he ask him why he'd been such a prick? Why Arthur had never been good enough for him? Did he care about the answer anymore?

His lips twitched as he realised the answer.

No, he didn't. He had friends who supported him, and a woman and her child whom he loved. He didn't need anything else.

The town's delegate walked away. Before Arthur figured out what he was going to say, he called, "Major!"

His father and the lieutenant colonel looked over. His father's nostrils flared in displeasure and Arthur smiled. He nodded to the other man. "Lieutenant Colonel."

"Arthur. I was sorry to hear about the incident." He nodded to Arthur's leg. "You seem to be getting around all right."

"Yes, thank you, sir. It was difficult at first."

"I'm disappointed you chose a medical discharge," the lieutenant colonel continued. "You were one of our best."

Surprise raised Arthur's eyebrows. He'd never considered himself that good. The major tried to speak, but Arthur spoke over him. "Actually, the major told me I would be a hindrance, and the only honourable thing to do was to walk away."

The man's lips pinched. "Did he? Well, you're welcome back any time."

"Thank you, sir. I'm really enjoying civilian life. I've reconnected with my sister, who I lost touch with after Father didn't see to her care, I've caught up with some mates—" he gestured to Sam who stood back. "And I've met an amazing woman who has a wonderful ten-year-old son."

His father's face was bright red and a vein in his temple pulsed.

"Sounds like you've fallen on your feet, so to speak," the lieutenant colonel said. "Congratulations."

Arthur nodded as the warmth of realisation filled

him. His life was better now, more fulfilling, more enjoyable than the army had ever been. "I wanted to thank my father for being an absolute asshole after my injury." He grinned and gave a half salute, which would irritate his father. "Because if he hadn't been, I wouldn't be the happiest I've been in my life." He walked away. Sam fell into step with him and let out a low belly laugh.

"Perfect! And his commanding officer heard it."

"I know." Arthur smiled. "Let's go find Ed and Tess."

He was done with the army.

Gretchen checked the time again. Still another few hours before school finished. She wanted to wait outside for Jordan, unable to get rid of the unease that had been tickling her skin all day. No, she'd seem like an over eager mother and Jordan would be upset.

But she could do with some exercise. If her walk took her past the school, she could check that everything was all right. The kids might still be on their lunch break. She grabbed her hat, keys and phone, and then exhaled, to calm her nerves.

Jordan was safe at school. The teachers would not allow him to leave with anyone they didn't know. But she couldn't quite settle today.

Maybe it was finding the treasure.

That much money was enough to make even the most sensible person do something crazy, and Kurt wasn't sensible. If word got out...

She'd reiterated to Jordan when she'd dropped him off this morning that he couldn't breathe a word about the treasure to anyone, not even Cody, and he promised he wouldn't say anything.

Her phone rang as she reached the end of her street. "Hello?"

"Gretchen, it's Myra Simpson from the school."

Dread lodged in her stomach. "Is Jordan all right?"

"He's not with you? Jordan and Cody didn't come back to class after lunch."

She froze. No, that couldn't be right. "Where are they?" Panic laced her tone.

"We're not sure. My colleague called Cody's mother, but she hasn't seen them either."

Gretchen started running down the road towards the school, her mind whirling. "Is Lara Stokes there?"

"Yes. She's upset and all the children are spouting some nonsense about buried treasure."

Shit. "Let me speak to her."

"She's in the classroom."

"Then get her," Gretchen growled. "Now! Every second counts."

Jordan's teacher huffed, but it didn't take long before Lara was on the line.

"Lara, it's Gretchen. What happened?"

"Jordan brought one of the coins to school," Lara exclaimed. "Natasha stole it and showed everyone. Then at lunch, this man came and Jordan and Cody left with him. I told Miss Simpson, but she didn't believe me."

Gretchen fought back the nausea and stopped running. "What did the man look like?"

"Short, scary and with lots of tattoos."

Kurt. "What kind of car was he driving?" She sucked in air, to get her breath back.

"A black four-wheel drive."

"Thanks Lara. You stay inside with your class until Faith picks you up, all right? Don't go anywhere alone."

"Is Jordan going to be OK?"

"Yeah, we'll find him. Call your dad and tell him what happened." A black four-wheel drive turned onto the street in front of her. "I think the man who took

Jordan is coming towards me now. Pass me back to your teacher."

Miss Simpson spoke. "Gretchen, Lara's distraught. She has an active imagination."

How dare she ignore Lara! "Call the police. Tell them the following number plate." She read it out as Kurt pulled up in front of her. "Do it now." She stared down the barrel of a handgun and hung up. "Where're Jordan and Cody?"

"Safe, for now. Get in." He flicked the gun, gesturing her around to the passenger side.

The tinting was too dark to see into the car. Slowly she walked around. Getting into his car was stupid, but Jordan was missing, and Kurt knew where he was. This was the only way to get to him. She opened the door, glancing into the empty back seat. "I want to see my son."

"And I wanted you to tell me everything you discovered about the Stokes, but you didn't."

She pressed her lips together. How much did he know? Someone at school had to be telling him what the kids were saying. Her mouth dropped open. Was it Miss Simpson? Had she ignored Lara because Stonefish had told her to? If so, she wouldn't have called the police. Gretchen might be on her own. "And I told you, I didn't know what you knew." She buckled her seatbelt. "So why don't you ask me?"

Kurt drove at the speed limit through the town, only speeding up when he reached the limits. "Where's the treasure?"

"What treasure?"

Kurt slammed his hand on the steering wheel. "The treasure you and Jordan and the Stokes dug up yesterday. Jordan told me about it, but he didn't know where it was taken."

Thank God they'd made the children go into the

other room. She needed to stall. "Why do you think I know?"

"Because you were there. If you don't tell me, you'll never see Jordan again." His tone carried no emotion.

Fear settled deep within her gut. "You never cared for him, did you?"

"Children are weak. They're a liability, as you're now discovering."

She didn't argue. No point. He would never see it any other way. He'd never bring a child breakfast in bed or teach them things. Not like Arthur.

"Where's the treasure, Gretchen?"

She couldn't rely on the police having been informed, but Lara would get a message to her father. Of that Gretchen was certain. If Darcy knew what had happened, there was time for them to prepare. "It's at the Ridge."

Kurt laughed. "The Ridge is a quarter of a million acres. Can you be a little more specific?"

"Not until I know Jordan is alive. I want to speak to him."

He slammed on the brakes and the seatbelt cut into Gretchen's chest. She grunted at the pain.

"I don't have time to play these games." A tiny flick of fear flashed in his eyes before it was replaced by loathing.

If Kurt was scared, that meant Stonefish was terrifying. She clenched her teeth to stop the hysterical demands to see her son from pouring from her mouth. Staying calm was the only way to come out on top. "Do you know where Jordan is?"

"Of course."

"Then I want proof of life."

"There's no reception where he is."

So not in town. "Then how will you tell them to bring him back?" she demanded.

Kurt smirked. "The person holding him will tire of him.

"And then what?"

He shrugged. "We'll see."

"No." She shook her head as the terror tried to take control. "You will not harm my son. I won't help you until I know he and Cody are alive and safe." She reached for the door handle and the locks clicked into place.

Kurt pressed his gun against her temple. "You are expendable. One of the Stokes will tell me if you don't."

Gretchen's hand shook as she stared into his unblinking eyes. He meant it. He would shoot her without hesitation. Every muscle in her body tightened.

"Where's the treasure?"

She had no choice. He had all the control. She exhaled. "Near the farmhouse." She prayed Lara had called Darcy. Arthur and Sam would be there, but so would Ed and Tess and Amy.

"I said details." He pressed the gun harder to her head.

"And you said I was expendable. If I tell you everything now, you're likely to shoot me and shove me out of the car. I'll take you to it when we get to the farmhouse." She held her breath.

He grunted, withdrew the gun, placed it on the arm rest on his right-hand side and sped down the road.

The clock on the dash said only fifteen minutes had passed since she'd left her house. It was an hour's drive out to the Ridge, if Kurt followed the speed limit.

Hopefully enough time for the Stokes to find out he was coming. They would call the police.

They could help her stop him.

Chapter 20

"That looks incredible."

Arthur finished the final brush stroke and looked up at Ed's comment. "There're a few spots where I couldn't get the dents out." He washed his brush and examined the Ridge sign for any spots he'd missed.

Ed shook his head. "Charlie would love the dents, and Mum would love that you've used her paints to fix it."

Arthur allowed the praise to sink in. "Thanks." It had been easier than he'd expected to make amends with Ed. He and Tess had come out to the Ridge where they'd spent the morning in the cellar with Amy, Brandon, Matt and Darcy, looking at the treasure and debating what their next steps should be, while he'd fixed Charlie's sign. Faith and Lara were in town, and Georgie had gone to work.

"Let's have some lunch," Amy said as she walked in, her gaze going straight to the sign. "Oh," she breathed. "That looks just like new."

Darcy and Matt both nodded. "I can't wait to rehang it," Darcy said.

Brandon placed sandwich fillings on the table.

"Good job, Sherlock."

Arthur smiled and leaned the sign against the wall so it could dry, and then made himself a sandwich. He gazed around the table at the people who had become part of his life. Friendship and family, two things he'd been missing without realising it. The only thing that would make it more perfect was if Gretchen and Jordan were here.

Darcy's phone rang and he answered. After a beat, he said, "Lara, slow down. I can't understand what you're saying."

Everyone stopped talking. Lara was supposed to be at school.

Darcy flashed Arthur a glance full of concern. Something was wrong with Jordan. Arthur stood and pulled out his phone.

"A tattooed man took Jordan and Cody from school," Darcy repeated. "Wait, when did you speak to Gretchen?"

Arthur was already dialling Gretchen's number. It went straight to voice mail. She should be in town. The only reason she wasn't out at the Ridge was she didn't want to leave Jordan in town on his own.

"She saw the black four-wheel drive that took Jordan?" Darcy asked. "Have the police been called?"

Brandon dialled a number on his phone.

"OK, Pumpkin. It's all right. We'll find Jordan and Cody and Gretchen. I'll call Faith and get her to pick you up. Don't leave the school until she comes, all right? And don't go anywhere alone with your teacher." Another pause. "Yeah, she might be like Jay. Love you." He hung up.

"What happened?" Arthur barked.

"A short, tattooed man came up to Jordan at lunch and said he'd hurt Gretchen if Jordan didn't go with him," Darcy explained. "Cody stood up for Jordan and they both left. Lara ran to tell her teacher, but Miss Simpson wouldn't believe her. When the boys didn't come back to class, the teacher called Gretchen. Gretchen asked to speak with Lara, and Lara told her everything. But then Gretchen said the car that took the boys was coming towards her."

Kurt had Jordan and Gretchen. Arthur clenched his hands. If he hurt them, Arthur would kill him.

"I'll call Faith," Amy said.

Brandon looked up. "Dot says it wasn't reported."

"There's more. Jordan took a coin to school and Natasha stole it, showing it to everyone. Stonefish know we found treasure."

"They're coming here," Arthur stated. Gretchen would do anything to save Jordan.

Sam nodded, getting to his feet. "How much time do we have?"

"No more than an hour." Was Jordan with Gretchen, or had they taken him as collateral?

"Let's get to work," Brandon said.

Matt was on his phone. "Georgie, where are you?" Relief swept across his face. "Keep an eye out for a black four-wheel drive, or a car where it's not supposed to be. Jordan and Cody have been kidnapped. We think Gretchen is on her way here now, but we don't know if the boys are with her."

Sam brushed by Arthur. "Stonefish took Lara as leverage to get what they wanted. They might do the same with the boys."

Which meant they could be anywhere with anyone. Steely determination filled him as his mind switched from civilian to soldier. Next to him, Sam and Brandon were taking stock of their resources.

"Amy, you and Tess take a radio and go to the windmill gate," Brandon ordered. "Radio us as soon as they drive past." Amy nodded and Brandon continued,

"Ed, you take the beach track in case they come from that direction."

Getting the civilians out of the way. Smart.

"If they're after the treasure, they'll come in here," Arthur said. Nowhere to hide in the kitchen, but he could hide behind the laundry door. They'd want one person outside for cover and two inside for hand to hand. The wooden floorboards creaked in places, which wouldn't help a stealthy approach. "We need to disable his vehicle."

Brandon nodded. "Darce, you and Matt are outside with the rifle. If the vehicle is left unattended, you disable it."

The men nodded, and Darcy and Matt headed towards the shed.

Brandon kissed Amy. "We'll be careful."

She clung to him for a second then gestured to Tess. "Let's go."

They all grabbed radios as they left the house, leaving Arthur with Brandon and Sam. Brandon opened a cupboard and passed out military grade ear coms.

Arthur placed one in his ear. "Where did you get these?"

Sam spoke. "We've stocked up." He turned to Brandon. "Guns?"

"I'll get them."

Arthur analysed the room. They would come in via the kitchen door, as it was the only one always left unlocked. Kurt may have a weapon, but not necessarily. Gretchen would go with him because of the threat to Jordan. And that was part of the problem. Without knowing where Jordan was, it was difficult to plan. He prayed Jordan was with them.

No one was going to hurt his family. He would get them back alive.

Brandon returned with two hand guns and a knife.

Time to go to work.

***

The absence of the Ridge sign seemed foreboding as Kurt drove past. What if no one was here? Her grip on the hand rest made her fingers ache, and she relaxed her hold. They'd passed only a few cars on the way out to the Ridge, and now as they bumped over the gravel track to the farmhouse there was no one in sight. She scanned the campgrounds, the shearers' quarters, and the shed, but aside from the pet sheep and the horses grazing in the yard, nothing moved. As they rounded the farmhouse, the yard was empty. No utes, not even Sam's car, which should be there if they had picked up Ed.

She swallowed hard. So much for Lara contacting Darcy. Darcy was probably out on the Ridge working with Matt and Brandon, fixing more fences after the storm. It was possible Dot had contacted them with information which had caused them to move the treasure into town. She might be on her own.

"Where is everyone?" Kurt demanded as he pulled to a stop.

Gretchen swallowed and went for nonchalance, forcing herself to shrug. "The storm did a lot of damage. They're probably out fixing it."

"Everyone?"

"Lara is at school, and Georgie and Faith will be at work."

"What about your cripple? He headed out of town with Sam."

"They were coming here to help, so Brandon's probably set them to work doing something. I haven't heard from Arthur since he left this morning."

Kurt grunted. "You fucked him yet?"

Gretchen didn't answer.

Kurt placed the gun to her temple. "Answer me."

Her skin flushed cold and her hand trembled. "Why do you even care?"

"Because then I know how much he'll do for you. He wouldn't get a lot of love the way he is."

Kurt had no clue. He was so focused on some old-fashioned idea of strength and power that he didn't see how much strength Arthur had. He underestimated him, which would be his downfall.

When she continued to stare at him, Kurt swore and said, "Where's the treasure?"

"Where's Jordan?"

"He's with a friend."

"Who and where?" She got out of the car, clenching her hands to stop the shake. Only a few metres to the farmhouse. She could see through the fly screen door. Could she get up the steps and inside before Kurt shot her?

"Don't even think it." Kurt kept the gun trained on her as he got out. She flinched as the door slammed.

She raised her voice in case anyone was within hearing distance. "Who has Jordan, and where is he?"

"He's with a bloke called Lee," Kurt said. "He's a mean mother-fucker who doesn't like to be kept waiting, and he knows the ranges inside and out. You won't find him unless he wants to be found."

Lee. A sliver of hope slid through Gretchen's veins. Georgie thought he wasn't as bad as he seemed. Surely, he wouldn't hurt children.

Kurt walked around the car, gun still directed at Gretchen. "The treasure, Gretchen."

"It's hidden inside."

He pressed the gun into her back. "Let's go."

She climbed the steps and entered the cool kitchen. Empty. No mugs on the table, nothing cooking in the oven, nothing to show anyone had recently been there.

She was on her own.

Gretchen closed her eyes and exhaled, bracing herself.

She would save herself.

***

The fear in Gretchen's voice pulled at Arthur. He fought every instinct to rush out there and kill Kurt. That wasn't the military way. Shut off the emotions. Stick to the plan.

Maybe that was why Brandon had given him the knife and not a gun. So he wouldn't do something stupid.

"Kurt's got a gun pressed into Gretchen's back." Sam's voice came through Arthur's ear piece. "No one else seems to be in the car. Lee has Jordan and Cody."

He tucked that piece of information away. If Georgie knew where Lee was, they could get them back. They were safe, for now.

"They're coming into the farmhouse."

A creak followed Sam's words as the steps announced their arrival.

Arthur gripped the knife and kept his eyes on the door to the laundry. He would attack when they came this way.

"No more games. I want the location of the treasure." Kurt sounded frustrated and a little fearful.

"I'll show you. You won't find it on your own." The determination in Gretchen's voice scared Arthur. What was she planning? Didn't she realise they were here, ready to help?

"Where is it, Gretchen?"

Steps moved closer. She was bringing him into the laundry. Arthur readied himself.

"It's in here." Gretchen stepped through the doorway and spun, reaching for the door.

Arthur exploded into action as Kurt barged into the room. He grabbed Kurt's hand, thrusting it down and towards the door as a shot exploded, piercing the wooden door, splinters flying everywhere. Gretchen shrieked, but Arthur's full focus was on the threat.

He slammed the gun and hand against what remained of the door and Kurt grunted, letting go of the weapon. Arthur followed up with an elbow to Kurt's face. Behind Kurt, Sam and Brandon raced into the room, guns raised.

A sickening crunch as his elbow met Kurt's nose and blood spurted everywhere.

Then a tearing pain below his knee as Kurt kicked his prosthesis, and it ripped from his leg. Arthur clung to the door frame, his balance gone.

Fuck.

"Arthur, here." Gretchen thrust his prosthetic leg at him, and he grabbed it and swung, hitting Kurt square across the head.

Kurt slumped to the ground and Sam and Brandon covered him.

Arthur regained his balance, panting. Gretchen was curled on the floor, holding her side, her fingers red.

Blood.

Horror filled him and he lowered himself to the ground, shuffling over to her. "Are you hurt?"

She hissed as he touched her side. "Wood splinter caught me."

"Medic!"

Brandon was instantly by his side, first aid kit with him. Arthur moved Gretchen's hands so he could get a better look. The splinter was still embedded in her, a good three centimetres long. "We need to get you to the hospital."

She shook her head. "It's not deep. We need to find Jordan and Cody."

"I'll patch you," Brandon said, cutting off Arthur's argument.

The fly screen door slammed and Darcy called, "Dot and Nhiari are here."

Good. They had to keep moving. Arthur attached his leg as Brandon withdrew the splinter and applied pressure to the wound.

"What the hell is going on?" A short woman with black hair and a commanding presence strode into the room, her blue uniform identifying her as an officer, the three bars on her shoulders denoting her as sergeant. Behind her stood an indigenous woman in uniform, with two bars denoting her as a senior constable. Dot and Nhiari.

Arthur got to his feet. "Kurt kidnapped Jordan, Cody and Gretchen."

Kurt held a hand to his head and wiped the blood from his nose with the bottom of his shirt while Sam trained his gun on him.

"His gun is in the laundry."

Dot moved towards Arthur, and he got out of the way so she could enter the small room. She gasped when she saw Gretchen. "Were you shot?"

"Ricochet," Brandon answered. "She'll be fine. Gun's over there."

Dot took gloves out of her pocket and put them on before picking up the gun. "Do you have a licence for this?" she asked Kurt.

"What do you think?"

Dot placed the gun in an evidence bag while Nhiari got out her handcuffs. "You're under arrest for kidnapping and assault with a deadly weapon." She read him his rights, as Arthur pulled Gretchen to her feet and held her close, needing to know she was really all right.

She squeezed him and then pushed him away. "We

need to find Jordan."

"We will." Kurt shouldn't know they had contact with Lee. He pulled her away from Kurt and towards Matt. He lowered his voice. "Have you called Georgie?"

He nodded. "She's heading to the ranges now. We should meet her."

Yeah, he wouldn't want her to be alone with a killer.

"What?" Dot asked, her voice flat.

Arthur waited until Nhiari left the house with Kurt in tow. "Kurt said Lee had Jordan and Cody. Georgie is trying to find them."

Dot's eyes narrowed. "How does she know where he is?"

Matt spoke. "Apparently, she sees him from time to time at work." He nodded at Dot's growl. "I'm not pleased either. We didn't know until recently."

Nhiari returned. "We need to document this place."

"We also need to find those boys," Dot said.

"We'll do it," Gretchen said.

Dot shook her head. "Nhiari, you go with them. They think Lee has the boys."

Nhiari sucked in a breath, her face hardening. Definitely some history there.

Dot continued her orders. "I'll stay here. Brandon, you're with me. Sam, you and Arthur go with Nhiari."

Brandon seemed as surprised as Arthur felt. "You want us to work with you?"

"What choice do I have?" Dot snapped. "You'll do it anyway, and the rest of my team are busy in town with the clean up."

"Yes, ma'am." Brandon saluted.

The sound of tyres on the gravel outside. Darcy called, "Ed, Amy and Tess are back."

Which meant they had a four-wheel drive. "Let's go," Arthur said.

***

Gretchen's wound throbbed, but it was nothing compared to the fear squeezing her insides at the thought of Jordan and Cody alone with a Stonefish representative. Matt was directing Sam to the base of the ranges where they would begin their search.

Nhiari was silent in the passenger seat, but Gretchen knew her well enough to know she was seething. Nhiari had gone out with Lee before they'd discovered who he worked for. This had to be difficult for her.

Arthur slipped his hand into hers. "They'll be all right."

Gretchen nodded. She had to believe it. Georgie was convinced Lee was a good person. He wouldn't hurt the boys. But damn it, she wanted Jordan in her arms. "Can't you drive any faster?"

Sam chuckled. "Not with a police officer in the car."

Nhiari grunted. "When we get there, I go in first. You wait until I give the all-clear."

Arthur shifted next to Gretchen, but it was Matt who spoke. "Not going to happen, *gunyjan*. None of us are letting you in there without backup."

"I'm in charge here," Nhiari said. "You'll do as I say."

"With all due respect," Sam said. "That's not in our nature. We're a team and we protect and support the team."

Arthur nodded.

He was like a different man, determined, focused, strong. If anyone could get Jordan back safely, it was him. Some of Gretchen's terror faded.

Nhiari growled. "I'm going to throw the lot of you in gaol when we get back."

"You do what you need to," Arthur replied. "Just like we will."

It was an interminable journey. Matt directed Sam off the main road and along a dirt track towards the ranges. Sam pulled up next to an abandoned Parks and Wildlife four-wheel drive.

Matt sprang out of the car. "Georgie!" His call echoed off the ranges. Matt swore. "I told her to stay in the car until we got here."

Had Lee taken her?

Arthur slapped Matt's back as he got out. "You just lost us the element of surprise."

"He would have heard the car and seen the dust a mile away."

Nhiari ignored them all and moved towards the range. The red rock was covered in shrubs as it stretched high above them, but a dark hole broke up the rock. A cave. Gretchen followed, with Arthur right behind her.

Nhiari pulled out her gun and Arthur shifted in front of Gretchen, knife in hand. "Stay behind me," he murmured.

Behind them, Sam and Matt had caught up, and Sam had his gun out, moving behind some shrubs to come at the cave from the other side.

"Where are they, Lee?" Georgie's voice echoed out of the cave.

"I told you, I don't know."

Gretchen froze. He didn't have them? Then where were they?

Nhiari held up three fingers. Sam and Arthur both looked at her as she lowered one finger at a time, and on zero, they stormed into the cave. "Hands on your head, Lee."

Gretchen was right behind them, and she blinked to adjust to the dim lighting. Georgie shrieked, as Matt charged towards her and dragged her out of the way. A slim Asian man slowly raised his hands.

Sam and Nhiari kept their guns trained on Lee as Arthur strode forward. "Where are Jordan and Cody?"

Lee's gaze tracked everyone, acknowledging them. It lingered on Nhiari as he said, "They escaped."

"What?"

Gretchen hadn't realised she'd spoken until Lee looked directly at her. "Your son and his friend escaped their bonds." He shook his head. "I don't know how."

The area was deserted. They could easily get lost, and without water, they'd be in real trouble. "Why didn't you take better care of them?" She scanned the cave. Where would they have gone?

"What happened?" Arthur moved closer, his voice soft but demanding answers.

"I had the boys cable-tied in here," he said. "They were safe, but I didn't know if anyone from Stonefish was coming to get them, so I had to keep them tied." He directed the last comment to Gretchen. "I heard someone approach, so I went outside to investigate. It was Georgie. I was gone five, maybe ten minutes."

"I taught the boys how to get out of cable ties," Arthur said.

Thankfully. The boys had escaped the enemy. "How long ago did you leave?" she asked Lee.

"It's been fifteen minutes."

She went to the mouth of the cave. "Jordan! Cody! Come out."

"Where were they tied?" Arthur asked.

Lee motioned to the back of the cave, which had a tunnel running off it. Matt and Arthur examined the ground, Arthur shining his phone torch to get a better look.

"Everyone stay where you are," Matt said. He moved over to the tunnel, shone his light down that way and then shifted towards the entrance. He glanced at Arthur. "Did you teach them to backtrack?"

Arthur nodded.

"Good job. There are footprints leading into the tunnel and ones leaving the cave."

"They'll have left the cave," Arthur stated.

"Impossible. I would have seen them leave," Lee said.

"We don't have time to argue," Nhiari stated. "We need to find those boys before it gets dark." She turned to Lee. "You know these tunnels?"

He nodded.

She walked over and handcuffed him. "You and I will search the tunnels. The rest of you search outside. We'll meet back here in an hour. If we don't find them by then, I'll call in search and rescue."

"I'll call Parks and Wildlife now. Get my colleagues to look for them," Georgie said.

They couldn't have got far.

Arthur joined Gretchen at the entrance. "The footprints go that way."

She followed him, happy for him to lead as he tracked the faint prints on the dusty red soil. "Jordan! Cody!" Her voice echoed, but there was no reply.

The ranges threw a deep shadow across the ground as the sun already sank towards the ocean on the other side.

Matt and Georgie climbed the slope of the range to get a better view over the plain and Sam moved parallel to them about ten metres away.

"Jordan!" Gretchen yelled again. "It's Mum. Come out."

"The boys were running," Arthur said. "Their stride has increased. They must have moved slowly until they were out of eye shot and then run." He sounded proud.

She would be too, after they were both safe with her. "Cody!" She raised her hands to her mouth. "Coo-ee."

Nothing.

Where were they?

Arthur moved faster and Gretchen had to almost jog to keep up. "Will they hide somewhere?"

"Probably not. They know no one will look for them here. They'll keep moving. Is Jordan familiar with this area? Is there a walking trail or anything tourists might use?"

"There's a road up to the top of the ranges," Gretchen said. "It's a couple of kilometres from here."

"They'll keep heading that way," Arthur said.

Gretchen wiped the sweat from her brow. They didn't have any water with them, and neither did the boys. If they ran for too long, they might get dehydrated or heat stroke. "Jordan!"

They kept moving, the silence broken by calls of the boys' names.

After half an hour Gretchen was out of breath and fear was clawing her control. "Where are they?" she cried.

Arthur turned, gathered her into his arms. "We'll find them."

"I'll head back to meet Nhiari," Sam called. "You keep going."

They would call in more searchers.

Arthur rubbed her back. "Jordan's a smart kid. We'll find him. He'll stick to the shade and he knows home is this way."

"They're ten," Gretchen said. "They shouldn't be out here alone."

"No, they shouldn't be. We'll find them, honey. I promise." He kissed her forehead and in those simple words, she believed him.

She nodded and stepped back. "Jordan!"

Arthur raised his hands to his mouth. "Jordan!"

A faint sound. Maybe a call. Her heart leapt. "Jordan!"

"Mum!"

She ran towards the sound. "Jordan!"

"Over here."

She shoved past branches and leapt over small shrubs as she ran towards her son's voice. The branches scraped her arms, but she ignored the pain as she entered a clearing and found Jordan on his feet, Cody next to him seated on the ground. She swept Jordan into her arms, clinging to him. "You're safe."

Jordan hugged her back but squirmed in her arms. "Cody's hurt."

The words tempered her elation. She let go of Jordan and looked at Cody. "What happened?"

"I twisted my ankle. I told Jordan to keep going, but he wouldn't leave me."

Arthur moved into the clearing and knelt by Cody, examining his ankle. Sam was right behind him.

Gretchen checked Jordan. "You're not hurt?"

He shook his head. "Dad didn't hurt us, but he said he'd hurt you if I didn't tell him about the treasure. I told him everything."

"That's OK. Dot arrested your dad. He can't hurt either of us again."

Sam pulled a first aid kit from his backpack and handed a compression bandage to Arthur. "What about the man you escaped from?"

"He said he wouldn't hurt us, but we didn't believe him," Cody said. "We ran as soon as we could."

Jordan nodded. "We got out of those ties just like you showed us, Sherlock."

Arthur finished the bandage and smiled. "You were both brilliant."

Jordan sagged against Gretchen, obviously tired from the adventure. At a call above them, she glanced up and waved to Georgie and Matt who were at some distance up the slopes. Georgie gestured they were heading back and Gretchen gave her a thumbs up.

"Let's get you back," Gretchen said.

"How about piggybacks?" Arthur suggested. "Cody can't walk on that foot and you both look exhausted."

"That would be awesome," Jordan said.

Arthur lifted Jordan onto his back as if he weighed nothing, and Cody climbed on Sam's back.

"Ready, Watson?" Arthur asked.

Jordan beamed. "Ready."

Gretchen pressed her hands to her chest as love filled her. Her baby was safe.

She followed them back to the cave.

Chapter 21

Jordan was safe. The weight of him against Arthur's back comforted him. He'd had to push memories of other rescue missions out of his head on their way to the ranges. Some kidnappers had no qualms about torturing children. He'd been surprised at how easygoing Lee had been. How his concern for the missing boys seemed genuine. But what would he have done if the boys hadn't escaped and it had been Stonefish and not them who had arrived?

Jordan had become heavier and heavier as they walked until Gretchen whispered, "He's fallen asleep."

Arthur ignored the fierce pain from his prosthesis rubbing. There was no way he was waking the boy up to walk. Jordan's hands clasped around his neck and the warmth of him on Arthur's back filled Arthur with purpose and joy, but he was relieved when the cave came into sight.

Cody wanted another look inside, but Gretchen gestured for Arthur to take Jordan to the car. Together they placed him onto the backseat and he barely stirred.

Gretchen's eyes welled with tears, and he hugged her. "It's all right. He's safe now."

"Thank you."

"There's nothing to thank me for."

"Yes, there is." She pulled away. "You taught my son how to protect himself. He freed himself because of you. He wasn't in danger for long."

Arthur smiled. "He wanted to learn." He shifted back and winced as his prosthesis rubbed.

"Your leg. Does it hurt?"

He hesitated and then nodded. "It's a bit raw."

She opened the front door and pressed him to sit. "Let me have a look."

She took off his prosthesis, her hands gentle, but firm. She hissed when she saw the red, inflamed rash. "You should have said something."

"There was nothing you could do. I had to walk back, and I wasn't stopping until I found Jordan."

She cupped his cheek. "I love you."

He smiled. "And I love you."

Sam strode over, still carrying Cody, but his expression was dark. "We've got a problem."

Arthur reached for his leg. "What is it?"

"Lee's taken Nhiari." He placed Cody on the ground and opened the passenger side door so he could get into the car.

Arthur frowned. "Nhiari had him handcuffed." He'd recognised a trained operative in Lee, but hadn't thought him a threat.

Sam nodded. "He left a note in the cave."

Georgie and Matt joined them, Matt's face a thundercloud. "He's taken my sister," Matt growled. "I'm going in after her."

"You can't," Georgie said. "Lee's had months living in those caves. He knows how to avoid you. He says he just needs a little more time."

"This is bullshit," Matt said. "I'm not leaving her behind."

"He saved our lives, Matt," Georgie said. "He says she'll be safe."

"Why take her then?"

"Because she'd go after him," Georgie replied. "She's been trying to find him for months. Now that she knows where he is, she'd keep at him."

Arthur glanced at Sam. "Thoughts?"

"I don't like it, but if he's trying to stop Stonefish, we need him to do what he needs to do."

Matt swore. "She's my sister. I'm not abandoning her."

"She's extremely competent," Sam countered. "She's likely to free herself and arrest Lee before we get back to town."

"Those tunnels are a maze," Georgie added. "No one's mapped them completely. Without the right gear, we'd get lost."

"You're not coming with me."

Georgie raised her eyebrows. "You think I'd let you go in there alone?"

Matt swore again.

Thunder rumbled, and Arthur glanced up. Dark rain clouds were blowing in.

"It's about to rain," Gretchen said. "The tunnels won't be safe, and I need to get Cody and Jordan home."

Matt looked back towards the ranges. "I'm coming back."

Arthur clapped him on his shoulder. "We'll all help look for her."

Matt relaxed a little. "Thanks, mate."

As soon as they got phone reception, Gretchen called Holly and told her they'd found Cody. Arthur heard her tears from where he sat in front of Gretchen. She organised to meet Holly at the hospital so a doctor could examine Cody's ankle.

While they were there, the doctor checked over Jordan and prescribed some cream for Arthur's rash. It was dark before Sam dropped them all at Gretchen's house.

"I'll call you tomorrow," Sam said as he drove off.

While Gretchen placed the parcel of fish and chips on the table and added some condiments, Arthur called Amy to update her.

"Dot took Kurt to the Carnarvon gaol," Amy said. "She's organising a search for Nhiari in the morning if the weather is clear."

Arthur hated the thought of Nhiari with Lee. It didn't matter if Georgie believed he was on their side, Nhiari was being kept against her will. "What about Miss Simpson?" At the least she was complicit in ignoring the situation.

"They can't find her. Dot rang her team to go and question her and she wasn't at the school or home."

Sounded guilty to him. "We'll keep an eye out for her."

"Yeah. Take care."

Arthur hung up and Gretchen pressed him into a chair. "You need to rest. Take off your leg."

Jordan nodded. "You helped me, now it's time for me to help you." He got some glasses and the cold water from the fridge and poured Arthur a glass.

Arthur squeezed Jordan's arm before he walked away. Such warmth filled him. "I love you."

Jordan smiled and then threw himself in Arthur's arms. "I love you too. I wasn't really scared today, because I knew you'd come for me."

The absolute faith on his face staggered Arthur. He squeezed Jordan, blinking back tears. This child was incredible.

"I didn't tell Dad though." Jordan grinned. "He thought you were useless, but we proved him wrong."

"We did," Arthur agreed.

"You were both amazing." Gretchen joined their hug.

Arthur held on to them, savouring the moment.

"Are you all right?" Gretchen asked.

"I don't want to let go," Arthur admitted.

Jordan hopped onto his lap. "We're not going anywhere, are we, Mum?"

"I'm not planning to," Gretchen said.

Jordan's eyes widened, and he glanced between Arthur and Gretchen. "What's up?" Arthur asked.

"I had a brilliant idea." He hesitated. "I just gotta talk to Mum, but we'll be right back." He jumped off Arthur's lap and tugged his mother into the lounge room. She crouched down so he could whisper in her ear. The image burned into Arthur's mind. The two people he loved most in this world, planning something wonderful.

Gretchen grinned. "Do you want to ask him?"

Jordan seemed a little uncertain but nodded. He slipped his hand into Gretchen's and they walked back to Arthur.

Arthur smiled. "What was your brilliant idea?"

Jordan glanced at Gretchen.

"It really is a brilliant idea," she said.

Jordan glanced at the ground. "You might not like it."

Arthur raised Jordan's chin. "I'd like to hear what it is."

"Well, here's the thing… you said you didn't want to let go…" He gestured to himself and Gretchen. "If you want… you could… you know… become part of our family. Move in with us. You know… if you want."

Arthur's jaw dropped. He glanced at Gretchen. "You agree?"

She smiled, a little nervously. "Yeah. Do you want to

move in permanently?"

Giddiness rose so fast in him and he laughed. "There's nothing I'd like more." He lifted Jordan onto his lap. "There's so much we can do together." Jordan buried his head into Arthur's neck. Arthur pulled Gretchen onto his other knee. "All of us." He kissed her.

For the first time in his life, he didn't feel adrift. He felt anchored, right where he needed to be.

Thank you for reading!

I know this book ends with a bit of a cliffhanger in regards to Senior Constable Nhiari Roe's situation. I hope you'll forgive me, especially when I tell you her book isn't the next one. The timeline of Dot's and Nhiari's stories run concurrently, and Dot's story needs to come first (Wrecked in Retribution Bay will be out at the end of 2023). In the meantime, I have written a bonus scene so you get a peek into what happened to Nhiari. You can access it by signing up for my reader group where you'll not only get this bonus story, but also bonus scenes from Return to Retribution Bay, Beached in Retribution Bay and a copy of Lilian's journal.

https://www.claireboston.com/reader-group/

If you're already a member, look for the link at the bottom of the monthly newsletter to get your copy.

Acknowledgements

I was a little nervous writing a hero with a disability, because I really wanted to make sure I got it right. I spent time reading people's stories and watching videos on YouTube about recovery, different prosthesis, PTSD and a whole bunch of topics.

I want to acknowledge that healing both physically and mentally can take a long time and I have shortened that period for the sake of the story timeline.

As always I want to thank my team, Ann Harth, Teena Raffa-Mulligan, Michelle Diener and Mayhem Cover Creations for their feedback and work in making this book come together.

Wrecked in Retribution Bay

Aussie Heroes: Retribution Bay
Coming 2023